FACELESS GALAXY

ALSO BY AUSTON HABERSHAW

If Wishes Were Retail

Saga of the Redeemed
The Oldest Trick
No Good Deed
Dead But Once
The Far Far Better Thing

FACELESS GALAXY

AUSTON HABERSHAW

Published by JABberwocky Literary Agency, Inc.

Previously published stories:
Adaptation and Predation. Escape Pod, #513. December 2015.
Applied Linguistics. Analog Science Fiction and Fact, Vol 139. January 2019.
Proof of Concept. Analog Science Fiction and Fact, Vol 142. May 2022.
Punctuated Equilibrium. Analog Science Fiction and Fact, Vol 142. July 2022.
Planned Obsolescence. Galaxy's Edge, #62. May 2023.
Tool Consciousness. Analog Science Fiction and Fact, Vol 143. November 2023.
Brood Parasitism. Analog Science Fiction and Fact, Vol 144. March 2024.

Cover art by Dirk Berger

ISBN 978-1-625677-39-6 (ebook)
ISBN 978-1-625677-69-3 (paperback)

JABberwocky Literary Agency, Inc.
49 W. 45th Street, Suite #5N
New York, NY 10036
http://awfulagent.com
ebooks@awfulagent.com

CONTENTS

These stories are dedicated to everyone who moves unseen through the world

Part 1:
On the Origins of Interstellar Life

The central lesson here is this: civilization, technology, history, sociology, economics—all of these things are simply a part of nature. We are not beyond the grasp of the fundamental building blocks of the universe. We are not outside of this great, unknowable pageant. We are no more than flocks of birds, schools of fish, a forest in a valley. To us, our existence seems permanent and utterly essential to the basic meaning of the galaxy, hence our history becomes the central narrative of the universe at large. After all, what would be the point of existence without us?

If humility is the first casualty of technological progress, take heart—the universe is a good teacher. We will all learn it again.

—excerpt from *Meditations on Physical Reality* by Rantothorianak, Scholarly Elder of the Consortium for Universal Wisdom and Knowledge

Adaptation and Predation

Everyone thrives in someone else's version of hell. For the Quinix, this meant sheer canyon walls a hundred kilometers deep, every surface coated with a thick layer of red-orange vegetation and bioluminescent fungus. The arachnids liked to string cables in complex patterns from wall to canyon wall and built nests where the cables crossed. For them, each oblong, womblike nest was no doubt cozy and safe. For me and every other off-worlder on Sadura, you were made constantly aware of the fact that, with just the right (or wrong) application of balance, you would plummet to a death so far below you that you'd have plenty of time to think about it on the way down.

I'd seen more than a few fall—Dryth tourists to little fluffly Lhassa pups, all screaming their way down into the abyss. In the dim, humid depths of the Saduran canyons, the bodies were hard to find.

For that reason, among others, I came here to kill people for money. I make a good living.

Tonight, I had a fat contract on a big Lorca—an apex predator, both because of his fangs and his wealth. As a scavenger, living on the bottom of the food chain my entire life, the irony was delicious. Here I was, a lowly Tohrroid—a slop, a gobbler, a *smack*—paid a small fortune to do in some big shot whose trash my ancestors have been eating for ages. Sooner or later, the bottom feeders always get their due, don't they?

Either that, or I was going to wind up dead.

I knew the Lorca liked to dine at the Zaltarrie, and I knew he'd be there tonight. I'd spent the last few weeks shadowing one of the waitstaff—a Lhassa mare with the fetching chestnut mane, a full quartet of teats, and the long graceful neck that fit with Lhassa standards of beauty. I had practiced forming her face in a mirror—the big golden-brown eyes with the long, thick lashes were the hardest—and now I had it down. I could even copy a couple of her facial expressions; augmented by my standard repertoire of Lhassa body language and behavioral techniques, I doubted anybody would be able to tell us apart unless they knew her well.

The Zaltarrie hung like a fat egg-sac in the center of one of the deeper canyons, webbed to the walls by at least five hundred diamond-hard cables, some of which were thick enough to run gondolas from the artificial cave systems that honeycombed the walls and were home to the less authentic Saduran resort locales. The Zaltarrie, though, was all about local flavor and a kind of edgy, exotic energy that appealed to the young, the bold, and the hopelessly cool.

I came in through the staff entrance already "wearing" my uniform—a black, form-fitting bodysuit with a wrist console tying me into the club's central hospitality net. The Quinix manager at the back door gave me an eight-eyed glare, his palps twitching, which I took to indicate curiosity. Most staff changed once they were here, I guessed, but I'd simply shaped my outer membrane to mimic the look of the clothes without bothering. It was a necessity; while I understand how elbows and ball-in-socket joints work in theory, mimicking the biomechanics of it all while stuffing your "arm" in a bodysuit sleeve is something else entirely. At any rate, I brushed past his fuzzy, leggy body and headed to the floor.

The music hit my whole body at once. It was a sultry, lilting

Dryth ballad sung by a particularly attractive Lhassa mare dressed in a kind of micro-thin smart-gown that barely qualified as a garment. She was backed up by a small clutch of Voosk with the matching plumage to indicate they were part of the same flock. They had no instruments; with Vooskan vocal cords, they didn't need them. The song shook me to my core, and I mean that literally. I see, I hear, I smell, and I feel with the same organ—my external membranes, my skin. The volumeon that Lhassa crooner was such to make me wish I had a garment to hide behind. It made me sag in the door for a minute while I acclimated myself to the ambient sound. Between the thick pipe smoke and the freely flowing narcotics, nobody noticed.

The Great Races can't appreciate the things they have. Take the Zaltarrie, for instance. Lush carpets, thick as a bed of centuries-old moss. The scent of finely spiced food. Each chair and cushion hand-stitched by arachnid feet from synthetic fabrics so smooth and soft, they barely existed but as a sensation of cool breath on the backside of so many clothed bipeds. The music, too, and the pipe smoke and the low murmur of polite conversation in a half-dozen languages—all of this world of sensation, and it had to be funneled through a tight array of tiny sensory organs clustered at one end of some clunky organism's static body. I could feel, taste, see, and hear it all at once and wear the experience as a garment, yet I was surrounded by organisms who sat in little fortresses of their own mind, carefully sifting through a couple streams of sensory information as suspiciously and greedily as customs agents looking for a bribe. It almost made me pity them, moments like this.

Don't worry—the feeling passed. Screw those people.

I glided across the floor, sweeping the faces clustered around the tables for my "date" for the evening—Tagrod the Balthest, the Lorca shipping mogul. He was easy to spot; Lorca always are. He would have topped three meters standing, had he been standing. Instead, the great businessman lay across a mammoth divan probably custom-designed for his use, his four lower limbs tucked beneath his lithe, muscular lower body. His torso was wrapped in Quinixi silk, which was black as charcoal, and broad as the gondola that probably took him here. His fore-limbs were folded across his chest, and I noted his talons were untrimmed—a mark of wealth. If all went well, I'd see him dead inside two hours. If not, I'd probably get a first-hand look at his digestive tract.

Lorca of such stature as Tagrod are never alone. He had a half dozen retainers—two Dryth bodyguards in armorgel suits, a snail-like Thraad with a control rig and a few servo-drones floating around, and a trio of overweight Lhassa mares chained by the neck and marked on the forehead with Tagrod's personal sigil. These last were feed-slaves. Tagrod kept to the old ways, where the predator/prey relationship between his species and the Lhassa was still observed. Just judging from the expressions on a few Lhassa faces elsewhere in the room, there were even odds I wasn't the only person there planning to kill the big Lorca. I was, however, the only person sauntering toward his table with a packet of metabolic poison stashed in a vacuole hidden in my "abdomen" and a multipistol likewise concealed within my "ribcage."

"Hey, my filly!" An intoxicated Lhassa bull leaned out of a booth and pinched my backside. "You carrying, sweets?"

I tossed my long neck so my mane flipped away from him—Lhassa body language that indicated I wasn't interested in cou-pling with him—and kept moving. The bull followed me with his eyes until it was clear I was heading toward Tagrod's table. Then he mouthed something cruel about me to his friends and turned away. Any mare who was going to speak with a Lorca was clearly beneath him, anyway. Suited me.

The ballad was wrapping up just as I reached the corner where the big Lorca was splayed out. There were hoots of adulation in languages made with as many different sets of alien vocal cords, noise bladders, or what-have-you as there were tables. Tagrod clapped his taloned hands a couple times and roared, smiling. I got a good look at his three interlocking rows of needle-sharp teeth. I found myself hoping I'd estimated the dosage on the poison correctly—a half-dead Lorca could still do some pretty serious damage to an entirely-alive me.

One of the Dryth guards stopped me before I'd gotten within arm's reach of Tagrod's table. Like a typical Dryth, he was a compact and functional biped, knots of bumpy muscle in all the right places, and a face as smooth and streamlined as the prow of an airship. "We've already ordered," the Dryth announced.

"I understand, sir. We've got a few specials, though, and the manager was concerned that your master hadn't heard them before making his selection."

The Dryth wasn't buying it. His eyes—blue-white and sharp as ice picks—searched my face for some sign of deception. My deadpan, though, is unbeatable—it isn't even really a face, after all.

Tagrod's voice was a deep, resonant purr. "Othrick, please— the lady wishes to speak with me. Let her through."

I had to keep my external membranes from shuddering in relief. Killing a Lorca is a lot like fishing: it's all about the bait you use. Tonight, the bait was my assumed shape, and I'd just gotten a nibble.

One of the Thraad's servo-drones pulled a chair out for me. The Dryth patted me down for weapons without so much as an "excuse me." Since my weapons were in vacuoles hidden inside my body, he didn't find anything. I just needed to keep from being scanned for the time being.

Behind me, the Lhassa singer started into another number, this one in a language I didn't recognize. Reflexively, I fiddled with the translator box I'd hidden inside my "head" until I got the words right. It was a Lhassa dirge from a subculture I wasn't aware of. The Voosk did their best impression of a trio of sultry woodwinds, striking a jazzy backdrop to what was essentially a song about a mare's children all dying in a fire. Leave it to the Lhassa to make something like that sound sexy.

Tagrod gave the Thraad a significant glance, and the slimy bookkeeper twiddled a few tentacles. One of the servo-drones chirped an acknowledgement, and the song dimmed behind a dampening field. The big Lorca gave me an exploratory sniff from his perch. Even with two-thirds of his body lying down, I was only barely at his eye level. At this distance, I could easily see how his species could devour a full-grown Lhassa in one sitting—his great jaws could probably fit around my shoulders even before they unhinged to swallow me. There was a second—just the barest second—where I felt a sense of terror at his presence and wanted to run. I had to remind myself that, between the two of us, I was the dangerous one here. Predatory species or not, he wasn't a trained killer; he was a business-man—a three-meter-tall, five-hundred-kilo, carnivorous busi-nessman.

For some reason, I didn't feel much better.

"You don't usually work this shift," Tagrod observed.

I made a conscious effort to blink. "You noticed?"

Tagrod smiled but didn't show me his teeth. "My dear, every Lorca can't help but notice the Lhassa around them. An old instinct, you understand—don't be frightened."

I made my eyes flick toward the feed-slaves, who were absently stuffing their faces with sautéed crimson slugs. They hadn't even given me so much as a glance since I'd sat down.

Tagrod picked up on the gesture and nodded. "All my slaves

are voluntary. Their families are handsomely paid. I'm sorry if they make you uncomfortable."

I shook my head. "No. No, it's all right."

Tagrod purred at a low, powerful volume that made my body shiver. "So pleasant to meet a Lhassa who understands. So few of your kind can rise above their instincts. Our two species are interdependent. Your people have provided the numbers and done all the great labor. We Lorca have provided the vision. Like all good predators, we drove our prey to greatness."

It was an old tale—the famous refrain of the oppressor: *"But where would you be without me?"* I know more about this than even the Lhassa do. Intelligent blobs of omnivorous, asexual goo do not advance well in a society full of so-called higher-order beings. My cousins eat trash in waste dumps and everybody thinks they've done us a favor. I was hardly even spoken to by one of the Great Races, even though I once worked in a restaurant like this one, surrounded by people. I was paid in table scraps.

"Are you all right?" Tagrod asked.

I realized I had been neglecting my facial expressions. I went back to work, batting my long eyelashes and smoothing my mane with one hand. "Sorry. I was just…just remembering something."

The Dryth guard who had patted me down returned from some kind of errand—probably talking to the manager, probably about me. He leaned over and whispered in Tagrod's ear. I turned my head away, making it look like I was watching the stage, but I focused most of my attention on the Dryth's lips. I didn't catch it all, but I caught the gist.

"Othrick tells me that you aren't even on the schedule today, Tal." Tagrod reached down and speared a slug with a single talon. He popped it in his mouth, again giving me a chance to see those impressive teeth. "Is this true?"

I curled my neck in the Lhassa gesture of embarrassment. "Yes."

"Then what are you doing here?" Othrick asked, his hand resting on the ornately carved butt of his multipistol.

"Forgive Othrick," Tagrod said, grinning. "He always suspects that a Lhassa is planning to kill me. We're friends, though—aren't we?"

I shrugged. "I suppose."

The big Lorca nodded. "Good, good. I'm glad." He leaned forward, sniffing me with his broad nostrils. "You smell strangely."

"I wear perfume."

Tagrod grunted. "I don't think that's it."

I stood ready to pop the multipistol out of my chest and drill the giant merchant at the slightest sign of the Dryth going for their weapons or of those big talons reaching out for me. Had I underestimated the Lorcan olfactory abilities, or maybe Tagrod had had them boosted somehow? It didn't matter. I made my face look confused; I decided to reel him in a little early: "I'm sick."

"I see." Tagrod hummed. "Is it serious?"

I mimicked embarrassment as best I could. I leaned close but not too close—no free Lhassa gets too close to a Lorca willingly—and stage-whispered. "I had an accident. A couple organs were ruined real bad. I got some germline-engineered replacements, but..."

"But they're losing integrity, aren't they?" Tagrod shook his mammoth head and clicked his muscular tongue. "A cheap clinic, poor standards. Probably promised you the stars, didn't they?"

I hung my head. "Yeah...pretty much."

A single talon caught me by the chin, but so gently that it was barely a caress. Soft pressure made me raise my head and meet the grand, yellow eyes of the Lhassa's ancient predator. "Which organs, pretty Tal?"

"My kidney, a liver, part of my heart…" I tried to whip up some tears, but I've never had the knack—no really effective valves for that kind of thing in my external membranes. I settled, instead, for a shuddering sigh.

Tagrod frowned at this for a moment, then rolled his massive shoulders in a Lorcan shrug. "That sounds like quite an accident."

"There are a lot of accidents on Sadura," I shot back, putting a little steel into my voice. I was letting the big fish play with the line now, giving him some slack to drag out. If he thought the catch was too easy or if he smelled a trap, my hook wouldn't set.

Tagrod hummed. "Quite true."

Everybody at the table was watching me. Othrick and the other Dryth were ready for action, probably worried I had a sliverblade secreted in my marsupium or something. The Thraad had both his eyestalks trained on me, his tentacles quivering in academic interest at my behavior. Even the feed-slaves had finished their feasting and were eyeing me with expressions that were probably unreadable even for other Lhassa, let alone me. I wondered what that was about—was I competition of some kind? Did they hope Tagrod would devour me before them?

"Tell me, Tal, why did you come to see me?" Tagrod asked. He folded his arms.

Carefully, carefully… "I was interested in speaking with you. You don't seem as cruel as… as…"

"As you've heard Lorca to be?" Tagrod laughed sharply. "Charming, simply charming. This truly is the planet of the adventurous, isn't it?"

I bowed my head in acceptance of his praise. It never hurt to stoke the ego of an apex predator.

Tagrod smiled at me and told me things I already knew. "My

slaves have dined, and I regret I am about to depart. I have appreciated your company, little Tal."

"I'm leaving too," I said.

I could see the thoughts clicking into place in the Lorca's head. The words he said next were the words I had been hoping to hear all night. "Would you care to accompany me? It is so rare I am able to converse with a free Lhassa. I would hear tales of the homeworld."

I did my best to look cautious. "I don't know." I made a show of glancing back at the other Lhassa scattered around the floor at the Zaltarrie. I knew that many of them had been shooting me and Tagrod dirty looks ever since I came over here, but this was the first time I allowed myself to act as if I knew.

Tagrod snorted. "Don't mind them. Small minds and small hearts—vestiges of a bygone era. You've outgrown them, Tal." He held out his hand, talons and all, for me to take. "Shall we?"

I have a lot of textural control over my external membranes, but simulating skin that felt perfectly to the touch could be difficult. I focused as much of my concentration as I could spare on making my hand feel right and gently laid my palm on his. My little Lhassa-size hand seemed like a dry leaf atop the large, flat boulder of the Lorca's palm. Had I bones, I might have been worried about him crushing me. As it stood, he merely placed his other hand atop mine and held it there for a moment. He smiled, still keeping his teeth hidden. In his great yellow eyes I saw something like affection. Maybe he thought of me as a pet; maybe his overtures of companionship were sincere. I doubted it. "I'll go with you," I said.

Tagrod stood, his massive bulk shifting the delicate balance of the entire club as it was suspended between its thousand Quinixi spindles. The Zaltarrie swayed slightly, as though moved by a gentle breeze. At the great Lorca's stirring, a host of Quinix servants seemed to appear from nowhere. The arachnids shifted tables and shooed patrons from his path with a flurry of hairy-legged activity so he could move to the service entrance—the only door large enough to easily admit him. Othrick preceded his master out the door while the other Dryth kept his unblinking eyes fixed on me. I fell in with the Thraad, who evidently wasn't the chatty type; he slid along on his single muscular foot with barely even a flick of an eyestalk in my direction. As we left, our little parade drew the baleful glares of more than a few Lhassa. I knew they considered me—well, considered *Tal*—a traitor, but that fact made no impact on me. How easily they judged how others sought to survive, the self-righteous prigs. Every creature had to find its niche—how did they know this wouldn't be Tal's? Who were they to deny her it?

This train of thought was academic, though—I wasn't Tal in the first place, and I was about to do something most of the Lhassa in that room would approve of, anyway. I focused on the task at hand. Slowly, I pushed the multipistol near the surface of my body and held it between my Lhassa breasts. It was a sleek model and only made the slightest bulge beneath my "clothing." We would see how long it would take the Dryth to notice it.

Outside, we found ourselves standing on an aluminum terrace that jutted out of the side of the Zaltarrie. Just over our heads were wrist-thick bundles of Quinixi cabling that protruded from the spherical bulk of the club at regular intervals. Large bins of garbage were lined up on either side of the door. In one bin I could hear the thumping and squelching of one of my own species, feeding on the scraps tossed out for vermin like itself.

Like me.

As we stood there, waiting for Tagrod's air-yacht to arrive, the scavenging Tohrroid poked a pseudopod above the edge of the trash bin to get a look at us. It colored itself bright green to attract attention and warbled something in a loose approximation of Dryth Basic. "Food? Food? Please?" It reached out to us, forming a crude four-finger hand.

The feed-slaves recoiled from its touch. The Dryth behind me stepped forward to slap away its tendril. "Get back in the trash, smack!" The Tohrroid withdrew its tendril immediately and went back to trying to digest whatever semi-organic refuse it had come upon. The Dryth wiped his hand on his sleeve. "Ugh. I think it slimed on me."

Tagrod laughed in rich, musical tones. He reached into his robe and withdrew a small confection of some kind. He threw it in the trash bin and gave me a wink. "The Dryth never have understood charity, have they, Tal?"

I hugged myself, as though cold. "The smacks have always creeped me out, too. I think everybody should look like…like something. Like what they are."

"Ah," said Tagrod, "but that would remove all the excitement in life, wouldn't it?"

That statement bothered me. I managed to suppress a shudder—he didn't know anything. He was a sham—his charity, his gentility, his humor—all a big lie designed to lure in prey. Just like me. Just like everybody.

We all looked up as the yacht appeared with the heavy thrum of AG boosters. It swung as close as it could without brushing the spindles and extended an umbilical for us to travel up. The yacht had an open-deck plan, kitted out like a pleasure cruiser but with a former military frame. I could see where the guns had once been mounted in the prow, and I wondered what the ship's core AI thought of its new role in life, assuming they'd left the AI intact when it was repurposed.

Once on board, we rose about three hundred meters at a slow climb, the yacht pivoting itself gently to avoid all the spindles and cables that crisscrossed every open space. The Thraad disappeared belowdecks along with the Dryth and Tagrod himself. That left the feed-slaves and me, as well as a couple of the servo-drones. One of them brought me a drink unbidden; I wasn't so foolish as to drink it.

"He'll have you first, you know," one of the slaves said. It was the first time she had spoken since I'd laid eyes on her. She was fat, probably middle-aged, but with larger breasts and darker eyes than "Tal." Her mane was well kept and silver in color, which I knew to be a genetic rarity in the Lhassa genome.

I gave her a blank stare. "I don't know what you're talking about."

"Please." She rolled her eyes. "I know what you're up to. His stable's full. If you think you're buying yourself a few more years of life by offering yourself to him, you're wrong. He'll have you inside a week."

"Conza!" One of the other feed-slaves—younger, prettier—flicked her tail and gave the older slave a withering glance. "Leave her alone!"

I tossed my mane at Conza. "Well, I don't plan on being eaten."

"As if it's up to you!" She snorted. "I know his tastes as well as anybody. I've been his slave for almost a full cycle."

I laughed. "You must not taste very good." I looked at the other two slaves. They were both watching our exchange carefully, but neither reacted to my little quip. The one who had spoken up for me hugged herself, though not against any external chill—the canyons of Sadura were hot as jungles and just as humid.

"Shut your mouth about things you know nothing about," Conza snarled.

I smiled. "Same to you."

The two Dryth returned to the deck. Othrick had a hand scanner, while the other one had his hand on his pistol. Behind them, strutting along on his rear four legs with all the cockiness of a bird doing a mating dance, was Tagrod the Balthest. He had shed his clothing and now moved toward me slowly, his eyes shining. "Just a formality, Tal. I'm afraid Othrick insisted."

It took Othrick less than a second to find the multipistol. Dryth faces are poorly suited to little self-satisfied grins, but there was a tightness in his eyes and nostrils that indicated some degree of vindication. He seized the pistol and held it up for his Lorca master. The other Dryth drew his weapon and leveled it at me. "An assassin, sir," Othrick announced. "As I suspected."

Tagrod frowned at the tiny weapon. He shook his head. "Ah, Tal, I thought you were different." Tagrod shook his great head.

Othrick tossed my pistol over the side and then grabbed me by the collar. It's easy sometimes to forget how much muscle is crammed into a Dryth's compact frame until they lay a hand on you. Othrick dragged me over to the edge of the yacht and probably would have pitched me over with little trouble, had Tagrod not stopped him. "I want to know why."

I smiled. "The usual reasons."

Tagrod grinned but showed his teeth this time. They glittered in the dim light of Sadura's bioluminescent fungi. "The Lorca are no different than the Lhassa, Tal. We both feed on one another and on those around us, as does everything. The Lhassa have never understood this, which is why they consume whole planets with the ravenous appetites of their many young. We Lorca—we *true* Lorca—eat you to thin the herd, which benefits all."

"Except the meals." I tested Othrick's grip by struggling a little, but he held me with geological firmness. Without bones, I had no way of leveraging an escape without abandoning my form entirely.

Tagrod waved Othrick away from the rail. "You care so deeply for my slaves, but so do I. This may be difficult for you to understand, but I love them. When, at last, I consume them, it will not be a barbaric act. It will be the course of nature—the way of the world. There is beauty in it."

"Keep telling yourself that." I wished right then I could have spat at him, but I'm not much good at it. All that nonsense about the beauty of nature made me ill. I wanted to grab him by his fat head and make him watch the little kids falling off the cliffs of Sadura. I wanted him to smell the dumpsters I'd slept in, slowly eking out nutrients from the festering remains of long-dead vermin. Screw him and his natural order. The civilized species of the galaxy had conquered it for a reason.

I let this show on my face. Tagrod watched me with the intensity a predator can only muster for prey. "I see you disagree. Come. Let me show you."

Othrick muscled me close to the big Lorca. I pushed my face into a sneer. "Careful—I might still disagree with you once this is over."

The Lorca's middle limbs reached out and seized me by the legs and waist as easily as if I were a candlestick. "Understand, pretty Tal, that it is you who have made this come about. I wish…" He lost the words and shook his head.

"Just do it already. I'm getting tired of talking to you."

Tagrod sighed. "I do this out of honor, not pleasure."

His giant, gaping mouth snapped down over my head faster than I thought possible. The pressure was incredible—were I the real Tal, my skull would have been crushed and my spine snapped in an instant. As it was, I compressed in his mouth like a half-full balloon. I felt the dozens of needle-sharp teeth pierce my outer membranes, each puncture burning with intense pain and weight. I let myself flow around his jaws and pulled myself up and into his mouth as quickly as I could, abandoning my Lhassa form with all the speed and alacrity of deeply ingrained muscle memory. The great Lorca immediately knew

something was wrong. His forelimbs clawed at my amorphous body, but most of me was in his mouth, filling his jaws and throat like a tumor. With a simple internal jerk, I expelled the metabolic poison down his gullet—the poison that the pistol had diverted his guards away from finding.

Tagrod threw himself on his side, still clawing at his own face, but by now the poison was hitting his system. After the fires of adrenaline cooled, his motions became sluggish, erratic, uncoordinated. The Dryth were on top of their master, trying to pry me out. When they were close enough, I let some of myself stretch into a pseudopod that pulled Othrick's pistol from his holster. My aim has never been good, but at that range, it didn't need to be. I set the pistol to shoot slivers and unloaded a burst into Othrick's forehead and another into the other one's face. They dropped like the eighty-kilo sacks of meat they were.

When it was all over, I flowed out of Tagrod's throat and formed myself into Tal again. I saw the big Lorca's eyes were still open, one eyelid twitching sporadically. I gasped for air and did my best to seal the dozens of little puncture wounds that leaked from my body. Everything hurt. "Shit, that took a long time."

"You monster!" Conza darted to her master's side. "What have you done? You've doomed us! You've doomed our families!" Her eyes were glassy with tears. "He was generous to me! My children...what will they do?"

I didn't bother trying to shrug—I was too tired. "I dunno—get jobs?" I checked Othrick's pistol. Like all Dryth weapons, it was high-quality but needlessly ornate. I weighed the advantages of keeping it with the advantages of pawning it.

"Of course you wouldn't care, you miserable smack!" Conza spat at me. "What does a pointless, disgusting trash-eating blob know about honor and decorum and...and decency?"

"I gotta admit, not a lot." I pointed the multipistol at her,

considered shooting her. Before I could make up her mind, she screamed and darted belowdecks. I could hear her yowling as it shuddered up through the deckplates.

The other two said nothing, still clinging to one another, keeping their distance. "Which one of you is Yvret?"

The youngest one raised her hand. I nodded. "Your uncle Jainar sends his regards and his love."

A tear welled in the mare's eye. "He…he hired you?"

I shrugged. "Guess I was cheaper than the cost to buy you back from the Lorca." I produced a data rod in my hand. "Here is the Q-link ID at which you can reach your uncle. Contact him using the skennite link on this yacht."

She stood there, staring at me. "Now?"

"I don't get paid until you do, so do it now, yes."

Yvret vanished. This left me alone with the third feed-slave—the one who had stood up for me a few minutes earlier. I had seen, though, how she looked at my cousin in the trash bin; she looked at me no differently now. I was some horrible abomination, no matter how I'd saved her. "He treated us well. He was generous to our families," she said at last. "Conza hadn't lied about that. I…I think he actually cared for us."

I spun my Lhassa neck around in an impossible circle, just to creep her out. It worked—she backed away a pace. "I really don't care. He could have been the long-lost love of your life, saving your pups and atmospherically reconditioning a moon just for all the orphans of Lorcan appetite, and I still would have killed him. I don't owe you miserable bipeds anything. If the Thraad belowdecks spots me a fiver, I'll put holes in you, too."

She blinked at that. "We're not all bad."

"You are," I snarled. "But that's beside the point. I'm just making a living, and killing people beats the hell out of eating garbage."

"That can't be the only reason."

I laughed in her face. When Yvret got back on deck, I used the skennite link to confirm the trade credits had been transferred to my account, and then ordered the ship to dock at the nearest side cavern. I left without saying goodbye or giving anybody any advice—not my problem. I slunk off into the shadows, reverted to a faceless blob that nobody would give a second glance, and oozed toward home.

I thought about what the third slave had said, but only much later. I was taking the form of a Dryth diplomat, House Ghiasi colors braided into my uniform, at a private table at the Zaltarrie. There was food—better food than I'd eaten in ages—piled high on warm plates, a Quinixi server hovering over my left shoulder, his palps quivering at the prospect of the tip I'd promised him. I was comfortable, respected, left alone.

I held out a plate of algae noodles. "This food is terrible."

The Quinixi bobbed and swizzled something in its language that translated as *"I'm terribly sorry, sir! I shall take it away!"*

I deposited the plate in the arachnid's fuzzy limbs. "I want you to throw it in the dumpster. Out the service entrance—to the left."

"Sir?"

"Just do it."

The server left. I wondered if the Tohrroid would be there or not; I wondered if it mattered one way or the other.

How many reasons does a creature need to do what it does, anyway? I made my body shrug, just for practice. I ate well.

Applied Linguistics

I first learned to speak in prison. Things are fuzzy before that, honestly. Before I learned how to speak, I couldn't really learn how to remember. Nothing to attach the images to—no filing system, if you know what I mean.

My early life is hard to describe. I remember the environment, sure—the smell of stale air, the dim glow of radioactive isotopes buried in the tunnel walls, the wild swings in temperature, the ever-present shouts and echoes of alien voices, never very far away. I remember the taste of their physical waste, piled in isolated corners, still wet and warm from the heat of their bodies. The sensation of it being taken in through my membranes and stored in a vacuole, solid and heavy inside me, so that I could digest it at my leisure while the heat of the reaction warmed my blob-like body.

But what was I thinking all this time? How did I *feel* about my world? That I can't explain; every word I hang on the experience bears with it the weight of learning the word itself. Was I afraid? I must have been—if caught by the prisoners, they would kill me. I have memories of the deflated bodies of my cousins hanging from lines, drying over a fire. A lot of the prisoners used them as clothing, as cushions, or, in a pinch, as a source of food (assuming their digestive systems could process us). I was hunted every moment of my life.

But I can't say I was afraid. Not exactly. Since I'm still alive,

I must have known the consequences of being caught—that *implies* fear—but I don't remember the sensation as I know it now. I possessed the instinct but not the knowledge to understand that instinct. Without the knowledge, the instinct passes without leaving an impression. It's just a thing that happened to you once, and then it's gone. This was, so far as I can tell, how I lived.

In a certain sense, the prison was an ideal habitat for my species. We Tohrroids are scavengers and opportunists, and whatever process led to our existence—evolution, bioengineering, or whatever—has made us ideal for that purpose. We have no bones, no obvious sensory organs, no rigid form. We can ooze through spaces only a couple of centimeters wide; we can change the color and texture of our outer membranes to mimic our surroundings; we can eat pretty near anything, even a lot of inorganics. Our outer membranes also serve as one giant visual, auditory, and olfactory sensor, letting us hear and see and smell omnidirectionally. This made it hard for the prisoners to get the drop on us, even assuming somebody managed to spot us in the first place. Thinking about it now, we (or some ancestor of mine) were probably placed there intentionally. We were a kind of custodial crew.

The prison was bored into the icy rock of some nameless moon—a series of corkscrew tubes, about three meters across, spiraling down and branching out so that the tunnel network was about two kilometers down and maybe five kilometers across. Between these main arteries was a tangled network of capillaries—little narrow tunnels, some wide enough for the average prisoner to walk or crawl through, some smaller. I don't know if these little passages were intentionally dug or were some side effect of the organism or organisms who bored the tunnels in the first place, but they served many purposes—air vents, sleeping nooks, isolated corners in which to stash the occasional dead body. The thinner ones served as the hiding spaces for me and my kind—a place to escape to, a place to drag a particularly juicy morsel to digest in peace.

There were no guards in the prison. No walls. The moon's frigid surface environment kept us belowground; the vast expanse of the Marshal that enveloped the moon kept others out. It—the Marshal—was warden, wall, and guard altogether. A void-dwelling macroorganism in the form of a vast, rust-brown cloud. A ship-eater. That was the price for imprisoning someone there: a ship sent drifting, the prisoners aboard locked in their cells. The Marshal and its various sub-organisms would fish the prisoners out and drop them to the surface in quasi-organic pods. The ship was then broken down, its materials repurposed to support the vastness of the Marshal.

You could hear the pods hit the surface—dull thumps that caused dust to shake loose from the ceiling. You could never be sure what was in them, but chances were it was food. Sometimes it was other things—garments, simple tools—but usually it was food and water. Even if it was new prisoners, that *also* could be construed as food and water. It depended on who got there first.

I learned to listen for when the pods dropped and the frenzy that set off. Every gang in the prison raced to the surface, armed with rocks, bone knives, and simple clubs. They scrabbled and bled as they tore apart the hard, chitinous outer shells of the pods, still smoking from the descent through the thin atmosphere. Then, as the prisoners limped back, in either triumph or defeat, I would wait in the shadows, looking for stragglers—the dead, the wounded, or even the weak. Given enough time with a dead body, my species can even digest bones.

This must have been how I met him, though I confess the memory is as much a fiction constructed from likelihoods as a true event. There I was, exposed, glomming over a puddle

of blood or perhaps a hunk of flesh hacked off by some razor-sharp knife, when the alien approached me.

He was bipedal and stick-thin, with long limbs and a long neck. Two legs, two long arms with bony-fingered hands, two shorter arms with delicate fingers. His face was round, with deep eyes of brown and a set of white whiskers above a small mouth. He probably said something, but to me then it would have sounded like any other bleating syllables from any number of other creatures consigned to that place.

But he did not attack. This I know for certain because he never did. He probably sat on his haunches, his long arms spread for balance, his short arms smoothing his whiskers, and watched me. I may have recoiled at first, gone still and mirrored the tunnel wall behind me, but eventually I continued eating.

I saw him several times after that. We Tohrroids were a curiosity to him—a being without definite shape. He could not tell us apart, of course—we even have trouble doing that among ourselves, assuming we bother to try—but *I* noticed *him*. In this way, he and I began our relationship.

Well, perhaps "relationship" is a stretch. He started feeding me. For all I know, he fed a half dozen of my cousins *and* me and it is by sheerest chance I'm the one here talking to you, but that was how it started. That I *do* remember. Because how could one forget this: he didn't feed me his waste. He didn't feed me carrion, or castoffs, or the rinds of stale food. He fed me from his own rations.

I remember—the first real, true memory I can attach to—being utterly, wildly perplexed by this. Why would this be done? Why would you take food from your own mouth and feed it to another? I had never seen nor conceived of such an act before the alien did it for me. I would be lying to say I was filled with gratitude—this behavior was perverse to me. Unspeakably strange.

Perhaps that's why I kept coming back; perhaps that's why none of my cousins did.

If you have never had the misfortune to eat Marshal-constructed food, the nearest thing I can compare the rations to are fat seedpods full of pale, spongy material which tastes like just about nothing at all but is dense with nutrients. With each shipment, the winning faction for control of the dropped supplies would parcel out the rations to their followers and vassals. The curious, four-armed alien was of no particular faction—an unenviable position—and so he performed work for what food he received, which was precious little. Nevertheless, he seemed to save at least a third of those rations for me. Compared to my standard fare, they were delicious.

Mine is not a social species. We are asexual; there is very little reason to speak to one another, even supposing we had a language to do it with. I guess there is a kind of unspoken agreement not to eat each other, but even that is prone to violation. To the extent that we communicate at all, it is through touch—you slide up against one of your cousins and vibrate through your membranes—but the kind of information exchanged is very basic: there is danger, there is food, et cetera. It's hard to say how this differs from merely reading the body language of another species—a kind of communication, certainly, but an involuntary one. A limited one.

For that reason, I don't really know how long it took me to realize the alien that was feeding me was also trying to speak to me. I heard the sounds, of course—my hearing is quite keen—but what were they to me? Lots of things make sounds—pod impacts, cave-ins, the sounds of beings breathing, eating, sleeping. Sound does not always mean communication.

But the sounds were there and they were constant. Being consummate mimics, we Tohrroids can copy sounds, too, though it takes a lot of practice to get them just right. Eventually, I

began to repeat back the phrases the alien spoke to me. Then, gradually, over a period of time I cannot guess at, I started to understand him. I thought of it as a game at first—when he made a particular sound, I would see what patterns of sound in response would make him react. It was fun.

In the times that I was away from him, which was often, I would hear the sounds again, sometimes many times, from the mouths of the other prisoners whom I spied upon. They were of a dozen different species and cultures, but Dryth Basic was the common language, and it was Dryth Basic that I was being taught. I began to make connections—that object was known as a "rock"; to injure someone was to cause "hurt"; to cease to live meant to "die." Puzzling out these connections became, I suppose, my primary activity. I found I could understand the movements of the prisoners and their intentions more clearly, which in turn made me a better scavenger than my cousins. I ate well. I grew.

When I was twice the size of my cousins, I voiced my first question. "What are you?"

My voice was a pitch-perfect imitation of the alien's own. He smiled at the question, showing a line of blunt teeth. "I am a Verian."

I filed the word away—"Verian." I puzzled over something for a moment, and then asked, "Where are your others?"

"What others?"

I had trouble explaining this, as I had very little frame of reference. I came up with "Other Verian?"

The Verian closed his mouth and rubbed his face for a moment. Then, quietly, he said, "No. There are no others."

"Here?"

"Nowhere." He threw up all four hands. "I am the last, you see? Alone."

This seemed to explain a lot to me, at the time. I saw being alone as an advantageous position—no competition for food. No wonder he could afford to share.

Our meetings went like this for some time. The Verian lived in a larger offshoot of one of the main tunnels at the outskirts of the prison. It was cold in his tunnel, his only heat from a distant isotope buried in the floor below, which also bathed the chamber in a pale green glow. The Verian had few possessions—possessions of any kind were hard to come by in the prison—but what he did have was a small stone-working awl or chisel made from some kind of crystal. He was constantly tinkering with the thing—chipping away here and there on the wall, making shapes and then figures and then murals.

"What is that?" I asked one day. I'd learned to point, and so I did with five different pseudopods, trying to indicate the whole three-meter breadth of the figures he had carved into the stone wall.

"It is a carving." He answered, blowing some dust away from some piece of detail work he was picking at.

I thought this over. "An image."

He nodded. "It is my home."

I pointed around to the tunnel. "This is your home."

"No." He pointed to the carving—an image of great pyramids with flat tops rising from some flat, endless terrain. Of tall, three-legged creatures, striding across the land. "This is my home."

"An image."

He threw up his four hands. "You are right. It is not my home. It is an image. A place long gone." He shook his head and laid it down on his shoulders with his long neck. He said nothing for a time after that. Eventually, I grew bored and left.

Grief was a foreign concept to me; I could not see it or connect with it. I only knew that if I spoke of his home, of his species, he grew quiet and stopped answering my questions.

I stopped asking. I focused my questions on our shared environment, as that seemed more immediately useful and did not drive the Verian into his silent moods. When he sank into these, often gazing at his murals, I would leave. Sometimes, I would not return for long time.

Once, I came back to find the Verian battered and bloody, his eye swollen shut and many of his fingers broken at strange angles. He lay on his back, panting, moaning. He saw me. Reached out with a bruised short arm. "Help me…"

My first instinct was to eat him. He was weak and, though skinny, there was enough meat on him to keep me fed for a long, long time—probably even enough to make me large enough to split and produce another Tohrroid. I quickly oozed over his warm legs and thought about how best to begin—dissolve the meat off his toes first? Or perhaps burn through just below the knee and have the whole lower leg to digest at leisure? That plan would take some minutes, though, and who knew if his attacker would return?

"Help," the Verian moaned again, his long neck lolling over to one side to look at me.

It occurred to me that by my eating him, he would no longer share his food. The revelation came as a surprise—a kind of cause and effect I had never considered. I withdrew from his legs. "How?"

"Help me up," he said.

I slipped underneath him and pushed him partially upright. Holding on to the wall with his only uninjured arm, he pulled himself into a sitting position. He then reached around behind him and there, in a crevice formed by the muscles that flanked his spine, he pulled out the little rock-carving tool. "They wanted this," he said.

"Why?" Since I had begun to understand their language, I had often wondered about this—about this ceaseless struggle for tools and possessions among the prisoners. The Verian, in halting speech, sought to explain it for me as he straightened out his fingers.

This was when I first learned I was in a prison. Everyone here had been brought against their will. The Verian explained, with geologic patience, the nature of the world to me for the first time. Of the wars that raged once every twelve sidereal years, of the invincible Dryth Solons and the Houses they led, of the Lhassa Cartels and their devious contracts, of the Thraad Consortiums and their traitorous gifts, and of the Marshals— the void-dwelling macroorganisms that enforced the peace. I listened closely, savoring each word.

The world around me took on a new shape. I was able to identify the different factions in wholly new ways. The Dryth were dominant in our section of the prison—blunt-faced bipeds, square-shouldered and solidly built, their smooth bodies a patchwork of colors and patterns (clan and house symbols, I later learned—a popular use for their semi-chameleonic skin). The Dryth gang that held sway over the Verian was one known as the Green Band. All food and all protection (or lack thereof) stemmed from their indulgence.

The Green Band ruled over a smattering of Lesser Races— species who failed to develop FTL technology before they were discovered and annexed to the Union of Stars. The Verian was one of these, his planet claimed as colony by some Dryth House. The Verians had not liked this—evidently, his species tried to assassinate a Dryth Solon and came very close. In response, that Solon ravaged their planet and killed nearly all of them. The only ones spared were Verians like the one I knew— collaborators granted, as reward, a lifetime in this prison. He was the last. The faces of his lost friends stared at me from his cavern walls.

With the Verian injured, I knew it would not be long before

somebody—either his attacker or another—decided to come back and finish the job. He may not have had much, but his bones were long and light and strong. They would make good tools in and of themselves. I stood to lose the steady supply of rations I had come to rely on. In a sense, I guess you could say that I had become domesticated.

But how could I protect him? The instinctual, low cunning of my scavenger existence told me it would be best to distract attention from the Verian. Hide his weakness by showing his predators even weaker prey.

So I began my career as a murderer.

The first was a soldier of the Green Band—those whom I suspected had carried out the attack, in any case. He was resting in a crevice, taking an inventory of his many knives. He was a mass of muscle and thick bones—there was little I could do to fight him head-on. But I didn't have to.

I slid up the wall beside him, centimeter by centimeter, careful to keep my outer membranes perfectly camouflaged, until I hung above him. Then I dropped. I wrapped the balance of my mass around his head and clung there. He could not stab me unless he intended to stab himself, and so he dropped his knives and clawed at my body. I let him, allowing ropey tendrils to split off wherever he seized me, neutering all his strength until, at last, he smothered within me, his screams muffled to near-silence. I left his bone jewelry, his flesh-leather cloak, and all but one of his knives. I ate his eyes, as they were juicy and easy to pluck out quickly.

Just beyond the soldier's crevice, I hid and watched, slowly digesting his eyeballs in little sacs within my body. His body was discovered in a matter of minutes. Soon, a great many hulking, brutish Dryth gathered to fight over the fallen soldier's treasures. Blood was spilled. When it was over, there were two more dead bodies left in the hall, looted and nude.

Their killers left the bodies for me and my cousins to deal with. They would return later to scare us off before we ate the bones, which they would then fashion into weapons and jewelry and other valuables.

My strategy worked, it seemed. I took note of the faces and voices of those other brutes, and once the furor surrounding the murder had subsided, I tracked down another and killed again. It was easy work—surprisingly so. I came to wonder why I hadn't thought of it before. The scavenger had become the predator. The weak could become the strong.

I presented my findings to the Verian, during his period of recovery. He listened to my halting report, gathering the meaning of what I said. He bowed his head. "This you should not have done."

I couldn't believe it. My membranes quivered with indignation. "Why?"

"You have not learned the lesson of my people." He looked at his murals. They had expanded during his convalescence—new faces, new landscapes, things and places I could scarcely identify. "Violence leads to more violence. There are always consequences."

"Yes." That seemed obvious. Hadn't I explained that already?

"Violence is a beast untamed—you might seize it by its hind parts, might whip it towards your enemies, but one day, the beast will come for you."

I took some time puzzling out the metaphor. I asked him to explain what a beast was again. At last, I formulated my response: "The beast comes for you anyway."

The Verian laid his head atop his shoulders and closed his eyes. Grief again. I went away, but not before I took some of his rations. I noted, with some interest, that he had very little left. He had not been out of his little sanctuary for some time, it seemed.

After I had killed my sixth Dryth foot soldier, my prey became wary. They had realized at last that the mysterious killer took care only to attack those who went alone. Word from the captain of the Green Band was to only travel in pairs. I had become bold but not that bold.

My plan to protect the Verian would no longer work.

But of course, the question was whether or not I needed the Verian at all any longer. My murder spree meant I had eaten very well—I had even reproduced, splitting off a hunk of myself in a deep crack, adding to the Tohrroid population in the prison but sending with it some portion of the knowledge I had gained. Even with that loss, I knew to ask this: what could the Verian, with his sad murals and his dwindling rations, provide me with? What responsibility did I have to him now?

The Dryth overall are an intensely individualist culture, and so too does their language emphasize the autonomy and sanctity of individual will. This language was now my language. The words I learned, first from the Verian and then from the Dryth I stalked, had built within me a sense of self that had not originally existed. This might sound strange—even in my primitive state, was I not ultimately concerned with self above all other things? Yes, true, but there is a difference between self-preservation and individual will. An animal shies away from a fire; a person seeks to conquer the flames. I was more than what I had been—survival was not my sole concern. The language had taught me such things as "wealth" and "comfort" and "freedom." I developed a craving for things beyond food and safety.

It was around then that word came down from the surface—a ship. Someone had been given permission to land. I overheard the gossip from a dozen different mouths. A Thraad research vessel, looking to employ laborers for a dangerous mission. The prisoners, of course, were no fools—the Thraad would only bribe the Marshal for this privilege if no free beings would be willing to sign on. The mission was a likely death sentence.

But no more so than the prison already was.

I went to tell the Verian. "Escape," I said. "We escape!"

The Verian looked at me for a long while. "No," he said at last. "No."

I hadn't made my meaning clear. It was frustrating. I gave it another attempt, more carefully: "Help me escape."

He cocked his head. "How?"

I slithered up his back and stretched myself to be as thin as possible. I covered his whole body and looked very much like a thick cloak of flesh-leather. "See?" I said.

"I understand. You would use me to stow away. Very clever." He looked at his murals. "But no. I will not."

"Escape!" I repeated, suddenly angry. I pushed off his back, knocking him onto the ground. "Now! Listen!"

The Verian didn't get up. He lay on his face, four arms splayed. "You don't understand. There is nowhere else for me to go. Out there"—he pointed up, past the Marshal—"there is nothing but more Dryth and more Lhassa and more Thraad. And more violence."

I couldn't understand—more violent than *here?* And what was so bad about that, anyway? I was pretty good at surviving violence, I felt. The Verian was weak—he'd just given up. There were always ones like this in the prison. Most wandered off into the frozen wasteland of the moon's surface and were never seen again. Others, like the Verian, sat in some likely crack and sulked until they died.

I was angry with him then. "You will die!"

He nodded. "Everyone dies."

"Do not die here!" I shouted.

"I do as I wish," the Verian countered, rolling up onto his feet and cradling his head.

I turned my body a bright, angry color so as to explain my disgust. Why would he be willing to die in this rotten, stinking cave? Who knew what lay beyond the Marshal? Who knew what he and I could become? I yelled and cajoled and pleaded with him to help me. He said nothing, lost in one of his gloomy trances. I gave up.

Why should *I* be punished here, in this place, when I had done no wrong? Why should *I* live in fear? Why should this world be inflicted upon me? What else was out there that I had been denied?

I went to the surface.

The Thraad, of course, do nothing in a hurry. Their ship—a quadrangle of fat metal spheres surrounding a bulbous main fuselage—squatted on a clear patch of bare ground about half a klick from the prison entrance. Thus far, no Thraad had emerged from inside. A mob of a few hundred prisoners had formed around its landing struts, hooting and hollering.

The surface was bitterly cold—I felt myself freezing no more than a few meters from the entrance—I'd never survive the trip across the cratered expanse of open ground to the ship. Angry, I slipped back into the warmth of the caves. There were others of my cousins there, too—lurking in the dark, waiting for whatever spoils would be left after this ended.

I needed some kind of insulation that my body, with its semi-permeable membranes, could not afford me. What was more, I realized that a cloak would not be enough. No Thraad would pick a Tohrroid as a laborer. I would be passed over, abandoned forever. The thought was abhorrent. I couldn't stay in that place. I'd outgrown it. I was *better* than it.

With great effort, I formed my body into that of a biped. It was easy to mimic the shape and look of a Dryth. Moving as one, though, was sloppy, disjointed, and incredibly difficult. I was fatigued after only twenty steps or so—holding my whole body aloft on two thin pseudopods and then managing the rhythm of it all sent my membranes quivering. I tripped and "fell," though it is more accurate to say I flopped into my natural form, hitting the floor with an audible, wet smack. I cursed in the words the Dryth language had supplied me for that purpose. I needed some kind of support—a framework to assist me. And I needed warmth to sustain me outside.

I searched for some hours for something that met my requirements but found nothing. All the bipeds were outside and the prison had fallen strangely silent. The Tohrroids emerged from their hiding places, glutting themselves on unguarded supplies. I passed them by, disdainful. It was not food that drove me any longer.

Finally, I returned to the Verian's cave. I knew at last what I had to do.

He was waiting for me, his arms splayed outwards, his legs crossed beneath him. His large eyes watched me carefully. He knew. "Doing this will not save you. Someday you will choke on your regrets."

The bone knife slid from its hiding place inside my body. I meant to strike quickly, but I hesitated. The Verian looked at the blade but did not draw back. His nodded slowly and turned to look at his murals.

In a flash of anger, I slashed his throat. I watched him crumple to the floor, saw the strange light of life go out of his eyes.

His murals gazed out at me, spattered with his orange blood. I looked at them—the half-remembered images of a world long dead and a people now extinct. Piles of bones ground beneath the feet of the Dryth Houses. I trembled again.

But hadn't he already been doomed? He sought no escape—he was to remain there forever. In the end, what did it matter if I had killed him? To my scavenger instincts, this made sense. To my new sense of identity, it was also abhorrent. I could not then understand the conflict that churned my insides; grief was too new.

The Verian's body was still warm. I slid over it and began to eat. I was not as deeply thinking a creature then as I am now. I felt disgust—at myself, perhaps, but also at the Verian. I was convinced that his weakness had led him to this pass. But so had my strength. I could not puzzle out what it all meant. The murals on the walls—those three-legged creatures, those wide plains, the gaze of unknown faces, long dead—seemed to echo with the Verian's voice. *There are always consequences*, they seemed to say.

The Verian people had sought to murder a powerful Dryth once—a Solon, no less, the god-beings that ruled Dryth society—and they had paid for it with the erasure of their species. Their last member had taught me their conqueror's language, and by that I had changed. I had been cursed to finish what the Dryth started, and also cursed to forever regret it. But it is too late now to change things. I do not even think that I would, had I the chance. The world is like that sometimes. We all must bear our choices.

The Verian's skeleton, while not as robust as a Dryth's, made assuming a bipedal shape far, far easier. I used the bones as a framework and took the form of a Dryth laborer. The Verian's warm flesh, held in vacuoles within my body, warmed me as my digestive fluids dissolved them. With new purpose, I strode to the surface, practicing my gait as I went. I knew I looked strange, but no one would expect any less of a half-naked Dryth surviving on some barren prison world.

I joined the throngs of expectant prisoners, raising my "arms" to plead with the Thraad overseer that selected volunteers from a hovering platform above the mob. I shivered, near-frozen despite my precautions, but I took some strange solace that the bones of my friend were holding me aloft. When I reached out for mercy, he reached out with me.

By sheer chance, I was selected and escorted aboard. It happened quickly, without drama or any sense of ceremony. One moment I was a prisoner, the next I was not. There was a message here as well—the world could change quickly. The adaptable would survive.

I watched the airlock rumble shut, closing out the cries and curses of those left behind—the damned. And then we lifted off.

I found a grav couch, as instructed, and peered out the viewport as we rose up. It was the most I had ever seen of the moon—a flat, sunless landscape, choked by the Marshal's cloud. As I looked to the horizon, I saw something—a pyramid, broad and smooth, its top cut flat. There were others, too. The higher we climbed, the more I saw. Hundreds of them, spread out across the landscape in orderly patterns. Landmarks in a vast, flat plain.

I had seen them before—the Verian's murals. This, then, was his planet all along. The one the Dryth had killed, now just another barren rock for the Great Races to dump their trash. The pyramids were a warning from the past. A portent of the world of which I was now part.

I turned my false head away and pretended I could not see.

Proof of Concept

There are times I wish I had a brain—just one organ surrounded by layers of bone or flesh that kept everything straight. You put your chit in one pocket and then you *watch that pocket*, right? It's the whole reason helmets exist.

Instead, my mind is spread out more or less evenly *throughout* my body. Little nodules of thinking tissue, linked together by a million strands—a net of nerves that grows with me. I mean, sure, this has its advantages—I don't have to worry about getting shot in the head and dying instantly. Instead, what happens is somebody shoots a hole in me and I lose a chunk of my memory. Which is how I wound up squeezed into this air vent, leaking from a gunshot wound, and having almost no idea how I got there or why.

I mean, I knew I'd been shot. I even knew what I'd been shot *with*—a buzzgun. They're a Thraad invention; a kind of weaponized insect hive that shoots genetically engineered bugs armed with a variety of nasty toxins. I'd been hit by at least six of the vicious little things, each tearing an eyeball-sized hole in me and dissolving a lot of the tissue underneath with whatever toxins they had stored in them. The bugs were dead now—I was slowly digesting their hard little bodies in vacuoles inside my blob-like body—but the damage was done. I was oozing the watery fluid that made up most of my mass through the wounds, try as I might to squeeze them shut with my muscular outer membranes. I'm not a doctor—I had a strange feeling a doctor for my species didn't even *exist*—so I had no idea how long this would take to heal.

I ran back my memory as far as it would go, trying to find the gap. I remembered being hurt—the pain was really intense, like I was on fire from the inside out—and I remember having to abandon a bipedal form I had adopted. I do that sometimes, to blend in—constrict my outer membranes to simulate the forms of others, usually bipeds. It was physically very taxing—I don't have a good frame of reference to what it would feel like to a biped, but I'm guessing it would be like having to contract every muscle in their body and hold it *just so* for long periods of time. I vaguely remembered only being able to do this for short periods—seconds, maybe a minute—but I'd built my endurance a lot by now. I'd practiced and practiced. My outer membranes, which used to be weak and thin, were now thick and muscular. If it weren't for that punishing physical training, I probably would have leaked to death by now—those same membranes were the things holding my fluids inside.

I probably had to abandon the biped form when I was shot, because I couldn't handle the injury and the stress of the upright form at the same time. Then I remember fleeing—into a gutter or something, which led to a vent, which led to a series of other vents, each smaller than the last. I remembered that I knew where I was going at the time. The memories had burned away somewhere during the journey. Now I only knew that I was where I had intended to go. I don't know why I intended to come here or even where "here" was.

Before being shot were a lot of gaps. Me among a lot of other aliens—a tough crowd, by the looks of them. Right—convicts. I was among prisoners who were...doing something. I don't exactly remember. The details were fuzzy—as I healed, hopefully more of the memory pathways would reconnect and I could make sense of it all. There was an image of a Thraad—squat, snail-like, and massive—showing me a table full of esoteric weapons. A lot of poison needles and sliverblades, a few small pistols, some tiny, lightweight grenades. "Go ahead," the Thraad said, gesturing with its chin-tentacles, its eyestalks trained on me. "Take your pick."

Well, whatever I picked, I didn't have it anymore. For all I knew, that was a full cycle ago.

Voices echoed up the vent shaft. *Trouble.*

"…gotta be somewhere around here," a voice said in Dryth Basic. Which is a language, I guess. A language I speak. It occurred to me that, as of a few seconds ago, I didn't actually know that last part. Maybe my memory was coming back. Who knows? Sure wasn't going to hang around to find out. If there was one thing I knew—I *know*—it's that holding still is a great way to hide but not a great way to solve your problems.

Another voice echoed up from beneath me. "Well, it ain't here, is it? And if we don't find it, we're slagged, understand? Completely *slagged!*"

I zeroed in on where the noise was coming from—a grating; I oozed closer to it and extended one little tendril through to let me take a look around and carefully modulated the color to perfectly match that of the steel around me.

The room was some kind of storage area—racks for securing stuff lined the walls, sealed compartments made up the floor. Only two walls were relatively clear: the one with the door and the one with the ventilation duct I was currently clogging. In this room were two bipeds armed with compact plasma throwers. I didn't know the design exactly, but they looked like weapons of Lhassa manufacture, which meant they were lightweight, powerful, and completely unreliable in adverse conditions. And I also had no idea how I knew *that*, either.

The two bipeds were a Dryth and a Lhassa. They were both wearing basic pressure-foam coveralls with a Thraad glyph etched into the shoulder. I couldn't read it with only a tendril sticking out of the grate—I'd need to expose more of my membranes to resolve that much detail. In any case, wherever I was and whatever I was doing seemed to involve at least three distinct alien species. Were these the convicts? Hard to say.

The Dryth was relatively short and broad, with the compact musculature and smooth, thick hide common to her species. Also, there was a thick bulge at the base of her neck, just above the shoulders. From my mysterious repository of knowledge, I knew that this was a fatty sac that could store lots of water—handy for surviving on their almost-waterless homeworld—but that most Dryth had it surgically removed at birth, as it was a sign of affluence to not have one. That made this female a poor, probably unhoused Dryth, and a poor, unhoused Dryth with a plasma thrower was bad news.

The Lhassa was a male—a "bull"—who was taller than his Dryth companion but with long, slender limbs and the sleek frame famous to *his* species. He had a long neck, a flowing mane, and a pair of horns that probably drove the mares wild. He had trimmed his copious rust-brown body hair into elaborate patterns that probably did stupid nonsense like brag of his sexual prowess and list off the other bulls he'd bested in single combat. While the Dryth was probably stronger than him, he was probably faster and had better reach and was also more aggressive. If there was anything worse than an unhoused Dryth with a plasma thrower, it was a Lhassa bull without a mare to keep him in line.

And these two were already mad at each other.

The Dryth was opening compartments in the floor, one after another, and yanking out the storage containers held inside. She kicked at the latches until they popped open and proved themselves to be full of stuff like uniforms or Lhassa ration bars or battery packs; this made her roar with frustration and then she'd start the process all over again. The room was rapidly getting filled with random piles of junk.

The Lhassa, meanwhile, kept his weapon trained out the door to the room, which was propped open by a steel bar. He was acting like he was expecting someone to poke their head into the corridor beyond, and when that happened, he was going to open up with his plasma thrower and reduce that someone to a puddle of bubbling goo. Given how jumpy he was, he didn't seem that confident it would stop whatever it was he thought was coming. "Did you *find* it yet?"

"I'm looking, I'm *looking!*" the Dryth replied, and kicked open another container. This one was full of socks.

Okay, so, I didn't know if the reason I'd been shot and the fact that these people were clearly worried about *being* shot was related, but for the time being, I was going to assume it was. Since I was still alive and not an ashen stain on some deck-plate somewhere, these weren't the people who shot me, which meant that it was possible that they and I had a mutual enemy to overcome. The fact that we were all headed here—to this storage bay—was even more evidence of that. I wasn't about to ask them about it, though—that Lhassa was too twitchy with that thrower. But I did need more information.

While they kept conducting their search, I began to ooze through the grate and stick to the ceiling. My injuries I kept inside the vent for the time being—squeezing *them* through that little opening would hurt an incredible amount, and there was just about no way I could prevent some of my internal juices from squirting out, and the last thing I needed was for these two idiots to look up just then.

Once there was more of me "in" the room, so to speak, I could make out the patches on their shoulders better. I read the glyph, remembering now that I also could read Thraad glyphs. It said "Consortium for the Furtherance of Genetic Knowledge." I knew sort of who they were, too—in a general sense, Thraad Consortiums were the only real organizing entities in Thraad society, each of which was dedicated to a specific scientific, political, or economic goal of some kind; this Consortium had the nickname "the Gene-Seekers." As far as I knew, I had nothing to do with them, though the fact that I was shot by a Thraad weapon and could remember being offered a weapon by some Thraad meant I was probably wrong.

I produced one of the dead buzzgun insect projectiles and spat it through the door and down the hall when the Lhassa wasn't keeping his eyes where they should be. It made a little *tick tick tick* sound as it bounced off the hard steel plating on the walls and floor.

Their reaction wasn't exactly what I wanted. The Lhassa bull turned around and fired his thrower *from the hip*, like a psychopath, and a sun-bright little ball of superheated gas shot down the corridor, hit something, and started a plasma fire immediately. Both the Dryth and the Lhassa looked shocked at this. I don't know what they expected would happen, honestly—that's how plasma throwers *work*, right?

Anyway, this created the diversion I needed to squeeze the rest of me out of the vent, squirting juices everywhere, and drop down to the pile of junk behind them. I formed my outer membrane to exactly mimic piles of socks and extra boots and battery packs and stuff, which only took me about a second. It hurt like you wouldn't believe—good thing my instinctual response to pain isn't to make noise.

With the plasma fire starting to suck oxygen from the room (and probably whatever safety systems to prevent that about to kick in), the two aliens turned back to the unopened compartments. They were frantic. "Hurry!" said the Dryth. "Help me look!"

I, also, needed an escape plan before this whole section of the ship was locked down and vented into space to kill the fire. I didn't have a lot to work with, so I made a play: I pitched my voice to sound just about exactly like the Lhassa's and said, "What's it even look like?" to the Dryth.

The Dryth snarled at her partner. "It's a metallic cylinder, you idiot—biohazard markings, handle at one end. Were you even paying attention?"

Lucky for me, the Lhassa was not paying particularlygood attention just then either. "What? What are you talking about?"

Okay—cylinder, metallic, biohazard marking, a handle at one end. I figured I could handle that. While the idiots rummaged around in more storage units, I sucked myself into a cylindrical shape, gave myself a nice metallic sheen, and produced the Thraad glyph for biohazardous waste on one side. The handle was the easiest part—a loop of matte black, textured to be ideal for a Thraad chin-tentacle. I let myself fall over and roll, almost hitting the Lhassa.

"Hey!" he said, looking up. "There it is!"

The Dryth stopped rummaging through a box of spare plastic piping. "What? Where did you find that?"

"Who cares? Let's get outta here!"

To punctuate his point, an alarm klaxon sounded and a croaking voice in the Thraad tongue began to repeat some kind of warning. I could read Thraad but not speak it, apparently, but you didn't really need to know the lingo to know what was about to go down.

The Dryth knew too. "Move it!"

The Lhassa bull grabbed me by my "handle" and lifted me with both hands as he started to run. "Shit! This thing is *heavy!*"

"Just don't drop it!" the Dryth yelled over her shoulder. She was taking point, plasma thrower pointed straight ahead, as though firing those things indoors hadn't caused enough trouble already.

The corridor outside was choked with an acrid, metallic stench and was maybe fifteen degrees hotter than in the storage room. Since I was maintaining a glossy sheen, I couldn't see that well through most of my body, but the part of me that was a handle got a glimpse of a hexagonal corridor that was partly melting, partly on fire, and filling with black smoke. The two seemed to know where they were going, though, since they made a quick right turn and began to sprint. The Lhassa, unable to control my weight with one hand, picked me up and hugged me like a pup so he could sprint toward a quickly closing blast door. This made me squirt a little fluid from my wounds, which hit him in the leg. I felt him react—tense right up—but he was too busy running to investigate.

The Dryth made it to the door first and stood in the closing gap. "Throw me the bioweapon!"

I knew how this was going to go before the Lhassa did, and it didn't occur to him until it was too late and I'd already been tossed underhand. The Dryth caught me with one hand and with her other hand pointed her plasma thrower at the Lhassa and pulled the trigger. There was a sharp flash, a whoosh of heat, and a choked scream. Then, no Lhassa.

The Dryth squeezed through the closing blast door, chuckling to herself. "Idiot."

I began to reevaluate this person as a potential ally.

The corridor we were in now had a much better view than where we had been before. It was long and broad—long enough that I could see how it curved gently upward. This view was supplemented by long windows on either side that revealed the full vista of space. Or, at least, I guessed as much—I couldn't really afford to drop the glossy sheen on my disguise to get a good look. What I could see was that we were definitely on a ship—a big one. My memory at present didn't have a lot on ships—"they fly through space" was about the extent of it. It looked to be a couple kilometers long—a huge central cylinder that hovered above us from which branched a variety of ring-shaped structures, in one of which we were probably standing right now.

I was pretty heavy, so the Dryth set me down for a second after the blast doors closed and tinkered around with some wafer-thin gizmo grafted to the back of her hand—some sort of interface. "Skennite," she said, "where is the Elder Council now?"

Skennite…skennite… I knew that term. For the thousandth time I cursed the burning wounds in me that had blown out whatever pieces of my memory I needed just then. I clenched myself together a bit, taking care not to make my cylindrical appearance ripple too much, and I thought as hard as I could.

A synthesized voice came through the link. *"The Elder Council is on the command deck, Hystra."*

"How many of the others are still alive?"

"I cannot accurately answer that question as asked, Hystra."

Hystra groaned and cut the connection with a sharp jab of her thumb. "Stupid crystals."

Right—skennite was some kind of hyperintelligent mineral. A big ship like this would probably need a skennite core to help run all its systems. How exactly it was possible to talk with it, I didn't know, but I knew that you could if you got a link like the one attached to the Hystra the Dryth's hand. I made a note to watch for an opportunity to snatch it, preferably when she wasn't toting around a plasma thrower.

Hystra picked me up and started running. This was extremely uncomfortable, since now I had to maintain my shape while being swung back and forth at the end of her stupid arm *and* I was still nursing gunshot wounds from a series of weaponized insects. I spent most of my effort in keeping the "handle" part of me rigid, hoping she wouldn't be looking down at me while she ran. Bits of my internal fluids spattered out; I felt like I was going to tear apart. I seriously doubt I looked very cylindrical most of the time, but Hystra was focused on where she was going, not the supposedly "inert" object in her hand.

We must have travelled a full kilometer or something before she got to where she was going: the big doors to a transport tube through which some kind of maglev platform would likely take us up to the central core of the ship. When she set me down, it was all I could do to prevent from collapsing into a blob.

I also didn't *clank*. You know, like metal is supposed to do on a metallic deck.

Hystra noticed. She picked me up again and then set me down again, and if I was *able* make myself hard enough to make a clanking noise, I would have, believe me. Gut-shot shapeshifting blobs have their limits.

She crouched down over me and put a finger in a little spot of my sticky internal fluids that had dripped onto the deck. "What the…"

My cover was about to be blown, but the good news was she had set down the plasma thrower to inspect me, which put it just about in my reach if I ditched my disguise and dove for it. Not that I wanted to shoot it—using a plasma thrower at close range was a good way to wind up really, really dead—but having the plasma thrower seemed a better idea than *not* having it.

I was saved by a gentle tone announcing the arrival of the maglev platform. The doors slid open smoothly, noiselessly, and Hystra looked up.

The platform was not empty. Five short, colorfully feathered avian aliens, each with a slender laser pistol clutched in their weird little wing/claw things, fanned out around Hystra with

Hystra shrugged. "Never liked that Housed bastard. Like I said, Tagga is dead—got caught in his own plasma fire hysterically trying to shoot it. Mishad, the other Lhassa, had her throat cut in a sealed room, if you'll believe it. I heard her die."

With each and every relation of a fellow crewmember's death, I got a fleeting image of what they were talking about. A Dryth with geometrical skin patterns indicating a House loyalty, silently screaming as he clawed at the porthole of an evacuated airlock; a huge Lorca, its fore-talons raised, its arms wide, roaring as it dove down a shaft in my direction, falling past me, me reaching out...

A svelte Lhassa mare, tears staining her cheeks, as I came up behind her, knife in pseudopod...

Wait.

Wait a minute.

"We accept your accord. Who knows how much time we have left?" The Voosk said.

Hystra picked me up by the handle and took me onto the maglev platform. When she set me down, I was extremely pleased that the floor in here was padded.

The doors closed and the platform hummed to life, propelling us upward from the ring structure toward the central core of the ship. The acceleration was gentle, but I was deeply uncomfortable, and not just from my wounds or the exertion of holding my shape. I—myself—was the monster all these people were paranoid about. The monster they would shoot on sight, if they ever knew it was in their midst.

But *was* I a monster?

What was I, anyway? I knew a lot about how my body worked, a lot about my limitations, but what was *my* species? I searched for a word. I found one, I think, but not of my own memory, but a voice—a Thraad voice—saying "It's a Tohrroid."

But what was a slagging *Tohrroid*?

I tried to think of a reason I would want to kill anyone. I felt distrust for these creatures. I knew, almost instinctually, that they weren't my friends. But that didn't mean a murder spree. And yet, there was the image of that Thraad in my memory, gesturing to the table full of weapons: *Go ahead*, it had said, *take your pick*.

"Hystra," the Voosk said. "Where will you go?"

The Dryth looked out through the transparent dome of the ship, out toward the numberless stars. "Home. I'll go back and start over again. Not make as many mistakes."

"Do you think they're telling us the truth?" the Voosk asked. "About the reward?"

Hystra grimaced as she fiddled with the settings on her plasma thrower. "When have they told us the truth about anything?"

The gravity increased as we approached the central trunk of the giant ship. I felt as though my whole body was fraying like an old rope—the fatigue of holding the cylindrical shape—but I couldn't drop the form. Not yet. The risk of the Voosk spotting me was too high, and then I was as good as dead.

We were moving along the side of the trunk now, heading for the tip—the command deck. Soon, one way or another, my ruse was about to be revealed.

I rummaged through the fatty grab bag that was my mind; I scoured every fleshy pocket, every airy vacuole of my being to understand what was going on. I stumbled upon a memory—me in the form of a biped, sitting on the floor in front of a low table, with a hovering drone pouring drinks. Across from me was Hystra. She raised the glass and poured a little on the ground. "To freedom."

Another Dryth at the table did the same. It was the one with the geometric patterns on his face. The one I'd later blow out the airlock.

In the memory, I raised my cup and did the same as them. Because at that point, they thought I was a Dryth.

They all had.

When we arrived, Hystra picked me up with both hands, her plasma thrower slung over her back, and it was all I could do to keep from trembling from exertion in her grasp. I left a little sticky puddle behind me as I left the ground.

The Voosk pointed. "What's that?"

Hysta shrugged. "Dunno. This thing is leaking. The Council said it wouldn't hurt us, though. C'mon."

The command deck was a spherical room, with the lift depositing us on the bottom and starlight pouring in from windows in the distant, domed ceiling. The air was murky and humid, filled with the swampy smells the Thraad prefer. Around us, ramps wound upward to a shelf-like catwalk that ran around the equator of the sphere. Here, nestled into little alcoves and surrounded by holographic displays, were a bunch of snail-like Thraad technicians, their eyestalks looking in two directions at once and their chin-tentacles delicately manipulating data and plugging in numbers for the skennite core to crunch for them.

Apart from these were four "command" Thraad, identified as such by the particular gloss and sheen of their shells and the fact that they weren't recessed into some little alcove but instead were looking down at us or, alternately, looking up at the huge three-dimensional holo-display that showed a series of colorful parabolas and blinking lights that I took to indicate where the ship was relative to other moving bodies in space. Sometimes, they were looking at both. Their eyestalks were always moving.

The Elder Council.

One of them I recognized—it was wearing a red shell. *Go ahead*, it said in my memory, *take your pick*.

All of them looked down at us as we entered. "Cooperation," one of them in a gold shell said to the others. "Unexpected."

"No, inevitable," came the retort from a blue-shelled snail. "Predictable."

"Quickly!" the red-shelled snail said, cruising along on its slimy foot to the top of one of the ramps. "Bring me the bioweapon!"

Hystra didn't move a muscle. "First you give us the codes to a transport off this death-ship, *then* we think about handing it over."

"Belligerent." Gold-shell curled its chin-tentacles.

Blue-shell didn't like that. "Resourceful! Have we given them any reason to trust us? Have they any reason to trust anyone?"

Red-shell wasn't interested in whatever academic argument they were having. "Give. Me. The. Weapon!"

Hystra slung the plasma thrower off her back and pointed it right at me. This was pretty uncomfortable for a couple reasons, one of which was that now everyone was looking directly at me. I did my best to look inert, even though I felt like I was going to pop like a blister from the strain.

"See?" said Blue-shell to Gold-shell. "Resourceful."

"Slag you both!" Hystra snarled. "Now pay up!"

"Don't you see? That *thing* is still on the loose! It could be on its way here right now! Give me the biotoxin so I can release it into the air supply and kill it!"

The Voosk, which had been paying close attention to all of this, swiveled and pointed their laser pistols at Hystra. "You heard them," said one member, and then another chimed in with "Hand it over, Dryth."

Hystra spat on the floor. "Fucking birds—we had a *deal*!"

"Opportunistic," Gold-shell observed. "To be expected."

Blue-shell bobbed its eyestalks in agreement. "Ruthlessness is a knife with no hilt."

That phrase jogged another memory, or maybe more connections were being restored. I remembered sitting on this very dark, going by nothing but touch. It was slow going, because I couldn't expand and contract the way I normally do. And the buzzgun wounds were still there—sealed over now by quick-healing membranous flesh but still a fat, painful series of holes dug into me.

But wait—I didn't have any *new* buzzgun wounds. The Thraad had filled the area all around me with the little toxic suckers, and not a single one had struck me. It wasn't dumb luck—buzzgun targeting is very precise. If they wanted me dead, I would have been. I recalled that my comparatively bizarre body chemistry rendered me far more resistant to the toxin than other species, but even still, a few dozen of the things would have done the trick, even if just from the holes they'd make. I'd leak to death.

They'd killed Hystra and the Voosk but not me.

So, they wanted me alive.

While I pondered this and tried not to move, I inspected the hunk of whatever I'd nabbed in the chaos. It was a hand—Hystra's hand. With the skennite link still attached.

I felt no remorse. Hystra would have killed me and felt nothing. She was a prisoner from a prison world, like the rest of them—violent, selfish, focused only on her own survival. Like me. Like all of us.

"Skennite," I said into the link, "Define 'Tohrroid.'"

The skennite's musical voice came back over the link a moment later. *"A Tohrroid is an amorphous, asexual alien species capable of complex mimicry in the visual, auditory, and tactile sensory areas. They are also omnivores capable of breaking down almost all organic materials and many inorganic compounds for nourishment. For this reason, they are commonly kept in tanks aboard starships and in other closed systems to dispose of organic waste and excrete water and carbon-dioxide, which in turn can be used to keep algal cultures in atmospheric processors active."*

Kept? We were *kept*? "Skennite, are Tohrroids enslaved?"

"The common definition of enslavement does not apply to Tohrroids, as Tohrroids do not demonstrate the kind of complex consciousness necessary to have what Thraad philosophers call 'directed agency.'"

"Are you saying we aren't *intelligent* enough to make choices?"

The skennite paused for a moment. *"Who is speaking? I do not recognize your voice."*

"I'm a Tohrroid!"

"You are? Interesting."

I cut the link.

That's what I was? *That?* A garbage disposal? A thing held inside a "closed system" to eat other species' shit and fart out plant food? And…and…what—I *proved them wrong* and now they wanted…what? These were the Gene-Seekers we were talking about. Biological pioneers. Genetic explorers.

That's it.

They'd come down to a prison planet, scraped up a biological sample to play with, and hit paydirt: me. A Tohrroid that bucked the curve. A genetic outlier? No, not that. We reproduced asexually; we were genetically nearly identical. These slagging Thraad scum-suckers had stumbled upon a new intelligent species that nobody had bothered talking to—one found in every single starship in the galaxy—and now I was their pet science project.

This? This whole thing was a game. A hunt. A test of my ruthlessness against all the other little test subjects they'd fished off the prison world. It made me wonder if there was a control group.

It disturbed me that I even knew what a control group was. How long had I been on this ship? How long had the Thraad been playing with me?

I felt a hot breeze come up the vent behind me—the fire-safety the kind of seamless teamwork you got when you were a collective intelligence. They blinked their black little eyes and tilted their heads side to side and back and forth while they chirped and beeped and hooted at each other in their crazy-complicated language. A Voosk flock, and a hostile one, at that. How many slagging aliens were *on* this stupid barge, anyway? And were any of them friendly?

One of them spoke to Hystra in Dryth Basic. "Don't try it."

Hystra slowly backed away from her plasma thrower. Not that it would have done her any good, anyway—even if she killed two of the little creeps, the other three would cut her apart.

"Where is Tagga?" another Voosk, though essentially the *same* Voosk, asked her.

"Dead," she said, her hands still up. I presumed she meant the Lhassa.

"How?" the Voosk asked.

"It got him, how else?"

It? By *it* did she mean her deteriorated sense of fair play? I guessed not.

"Did you see it?" the Voosk asked.

Hystra laughed. "That's the whole problem, isn't it—*nobody* sees it."

"It got two of our number," the Voosk replied. Their incessant peeping underwent a momentary pause—a moment of silence, I guess, for their departed members.

Hystra and I were wondering the same thing. "How?" she asked. I had admiration for anything that could get a drop on a Voosk flock—the little birds were pretty much always looking everywhere at once, and they were in literal constant communication with each other. If you wanted to get one and not deal with all of them, you had to disrupt their hearing somehow.

"It tampered with an alarm klaxon—the noise and the flashing lights made it difficult to coordinate," the Voosk said. Two of its number raised their pistols and trained them on Hystra. "But we survived. And we will continue to survive."

I was getting a better picture now: some kind of monster was on the loose. It was picking off the crew, and the crew, predictably, was losing its shit. I had to be a part of that Gene-Seeker crew—made sense, really, given how much I knew about other alien species and whatnot. I guess I could have revealed myself but, again, everybody was pointing guns at each other and now was obviously not the time for surprises.

One of the Voosk hopped forward and grabbed me by my handle. It tried to lift, but it didn't have a fifth of the raw strength that Hystra had—the thing could barely budge me. Another hopped forward to assist—this time they did lift me up, but only a couple centimeters and the strain was evident on their lightweight frames.

Hystra was smiling. "You'll never get it to the command deck. Not without a hand cart and all birds on deck."

"We could find one," the Voosk countered. "If we kill you, we don't even need to cover our backs."

"I propose a truce," Hystra said. "I carry it, you guard me, and we all go up to the command deck together."

"We share the reward, then? With you?" A couple of the Voosk cackled at a ridiculous volume. It was funny to them, or an insult, or both. The Voosk language is so informationally dense that it is literally impossible to translate without machine help.

Wait a minute—a reward? For what?

"We're the only two left, right?" Hystra said.

The birds exchanged a series of rapid glances and beeps, and then one of them said, "The last time we saw the Lorca, it was charging down an engineering shaft with a belt full of grenades, and the whole shaft went up afterwards. The other Dryth was sucked out an airlock."

seals had been lifted, which meant the plasma fire had been snuffed. I could have gone back and confronted them. But that would have been holding still. As I had since the start, I pressed forward. There was something *else* I wanted to confront.

If what the skennite had told me was true, then all the gutters, all the tubes, and all the vents and sewers of this ship all went one place:

Home. Or a version of it, anyway.

It was a huge, spherical chamber—the mirror image of the command deck—at the center of which was a massive centrifuge. A hemispherical bucket, twenty meters across, was being spun around at a steady speed along the edges of the sphere, moving in a pattern that meant it would eventually scour every surface of the sphere, which was peppered with secure doors and finely grated vents—input and output. In the bucket, held essentially in place by the centrifugal force, was a fat, rippling mass of my cousins.

I sat on the maintenance platform at the center of the huge room, watching the bucket spin and watching the flat, almost-colorless membranes of the captive Tohrroids suck up little morsels of garbage that were gathered up by the movement of the bucket, and then watched them burble and belch out the helpful gasses that kept the ship operating. I sat there a long time.

The green-shelled Thraad from the Elder Council slid serenely to the top of the access ramp. It was unarmed. "You could join them, you know. Go back."

I had no weapons; I was injured beyond the capacity for violent action. Even still, I made myself larger and spread out pseudopods in a show of defiance. "Stay away from me!"

"We don't bother shielding this room much from radiation." Green-shell said, unimpressed. "You Tohrroids can absorb an awful lot of radiation without any significant damage, or, at least, damage to anything we have traditionally cared about. It's the current operating theory that this radiation inhibits your ability to form memories and conduct higher-level thought."

I drew back from the Thraad as it slid down to the observation platform. One of its eyestalks followed the bucket as it swung around the room, while the other remained fixed on me. "If you went back," it said, "eventually, the radiation would break down the connections you've built up. You'd forget all about this. All about me. You'd forget everything you ever learned. Or, at least, that is the current theory."

"I bet you'd love to test it."

"Your existence offers tantalizing opportunities for study, I must admit." Green-shell said. "We had initially worked under the assumption that you were simply a talented mimic—a creature without true agency. We had hoped you could be trained."

"Sorry if I ruined your little experiment."

That got both of its eyes to focus on me. "*Ruined?* In what way? You are proof of concept. We have learned so much from you, it will take cycles for us to fully explore the implications."

"You could free all of us," I said, pointing toward my cousins in their centrifugal prison. "*Teach* all of us!"

"And then what becomes of the atmospheric-processing and waste-disposal systems on this ship? On *all* ships?" The Thraad's chin-tentacles waggled in a gesture I knew to mean refusal. "Think of all the damage you have done. The command deck had to be abandoned. Our repair drones inform us it will take hours to restore full functionality. No, I am inclined to agree with the council—you are too dangerous to duplicate."

I flexed my membranes, laser-scarred and stiff with burns. I had enough strength for one rush—I could charge it, maybe bowl it over. Thraad were nothing if not steady on their single foot, though. It would be like trying to tackle a giant suction cup. I wanted to scream at it, but what came out was really more of a croak. "But all of this was *your idea!* I didn't even slagging *know* what was going on! I didn't want to kill anyone!"

The Thraad's chin-tentacles curled up—the expression was smug. "It was all an experiment to see what you'd do, to see what the rest of them would do—there never was any bio-weapon. The killing was a decision you made on your own, I believe. Just as you are planning to kill me, working under the assumption that I am unarmed."

I didn't like the sound of that. I still had too many blind spots from the laser burns—I couldn't take in my full surroundings the way I usually did. Was there a drone somewhere I couldn't see? Some sort of nasty toxic slime it was coated in? A projectile weapon concealed in its shell?

But that wasn't Green-shell's point, was it? I'd kill it if I got the chance. I'd kill all of them. Because they deserved it.

That's what made me dangerous—that I knew all about them.

I retracted into a ball. "What happens now?"

The Thraad's shell ejected a small, crystalline cylinder. It reached back with its chin-tentacles, keeping one eye on me the entire time, and yanked it free. "There is a courier pod leaving this ship in ten minutes. Skennite has plotted a slipdrive course that will take it to the nearest inhabited planet. This"—it threw me the cylinder—"is the access key. You will be aboard when it leaves. Or else."

I could scarcely believe what I was seeing. "You're...letting me go?"

"Are you offering to stay?" The Thraad pointed at the whirling mass of my cousins, mindlessly eating and excreting, forever. "As I said, you could always go back."

I reached out and scooped up the key. "No."

Green-shell backed away up the ramp. "Good. Skennite will direct you."

When it was gone, I took one last look at the Tohrroids—a

numberless mass of potential, just like me. But none of them would ever escape. Even I couldn't free them. The Thraad was wrong—there *was* no going back. Whatever force led me here, it was still pushing me forward.

I didn't know where I belonged. Maybe nowhere. But it wasn't here. I had to keep what I had learned. I had to survive. And to do that, I had to keep moving.

Part 2:
Discourse on the Social Contract of Distant Suns

In this sense, we do not live in a civilization as we understand it at all. We are all part of a food cycle of sorts, with the macro-organisms known as Marshals as the apex predators. We have a "society" insofar as we have carved an evolutionary niche in the galactic fabric. We persist because the Tenets of the Law provide us with a kind of adaptation that other cultures—those we term the "Lesser" races of the galaxy—lack. They will perish for it, eventually. We continue to thrive.

The Union of Stars is harsh, often callous, frequently arbitrary, and rarely just. But it is stable, self-propagating, and dynamic. In an amoral universe, the continuance of these latter three traits is vastly more important than the banishment of the preceding four. As microscopic individuals living in a vast, unknowable galaxy, this is hard for us to accept. But the galaxy does not care if we accept it or not. It simply is.

—excerpt from *Meditations on Physical Reality*
by Rantothorianak, Scholarly Elder of the Consortium for
Universal Wisdom and Knowledge

Punctuated Equilibrium

The murders were almost nightly events in the garden of Amoth of House Vanyi. It was why I had stayed so long, after all—not the thick beds of colorful flowers, not the gracefully arching trees and the dappled sunlight filtered through the polarized skylights, but the dead bodies. When the murder was over, Amoth would have his retainers roll the corpses into the lily pond, and there I would eat them. It was not an exciting life, but I ate well, and nobody asked too many questions about the dead.

I had disguised myself as a particularly large lily plant—a sprawling thing, with big white blossoms and wide flat leaves spread about me like the tentacles of an aquatic predator. I was not the only such plant in the pond—there were four or five others. It had been a challenging form to mimic, but by this point in my life, I had a lot of practice doing difficult disguises. My outer membranes stretched and thinned themselves, their chameleonic pigments matching the greens and whites and pinks perfectly, until I looked for all the world like another big, floating flower—innocuous and beautiful. I did not smell like a lily, nor would I feel like one—the plants were colder than I was and held their shape more easily. But, so long as I kept a vacuole full of air inside me, allowing me to float like a boat, I could cruise around the pond at leisure and nobody even bothered looking at me.

I, however, saw everything.

We Tohrroids are not even considered sentient by the Great Races of the galaxy, but of course we *are*. It was just that nobody bothered to ask. If they thought about us at all, it was with revulsion. Before, I had been unaware of this—my memory was spotty, but I recalled being confused most of the time at my treatment, and very keenly recalled my disgust when I understood the truth. I was vermin to people like Amoth Vanyi and his goons.

And yet *he* was the one killing people.

Not that I objected to killing people, mind you, but I struggled to understand a world view that held eating trash to be a dirtier occupation. I mean, really?

Granted, there was a sort of ritual to Amoth's whole murderous habit. The victim would present themselves on the dirt path beneath the manicured asdo trees in the garden—willingly, it seemed. They were usually armed with some kind of weapon—knives, swords, guns—and Amoth would have the same.

There would be someone they called a "witness"—a strange, hybrid creature. It looked like a Dryth: bipedal, symmetrical, two arms, two legs, etc—just like Amoth and many of his victims—but it also had various…growths. Mutations, perhaps? They were large and crusty and of a clearly different organic provenance than any Dryth-borne disease or condition. The growths had lidless eyes and jawless mouths and other things—parasitic growths.

Anyway, this "witness" would explain to both parties why they were there and what was expected. The reason was always some variation on the same theme: House Vanyi was accused of taking something from the victim, which made the victim angry enough to challenge House Vanyi to a duel, and the duel ended with Amoth—the House's designated champion—killing them and dumping them in the pond. Dryth bodies are not very buoyant—they would sink quickly, and I would feast on their corpses for days.

There was more to all of it than that—even then, I suspected—but this is what I saw happen. House Vanyi, it seemed, took a lot of things from a lot of people, and those stupid enough to complain about it came to this beautiful garden and Amoth murdered them.

I, myself, had no complaints about this arrangement.

When I'd first arrived on this world—a dusty moon in orbit around an angry orange gas giant—I'd tried to mimic a Dryth form to fit in. It didn't work, or at least not for long periods of time. Holding a bipedal shape exhausted my muscular outer membranes, and I could only do it for so long. My natural form was an amorphous blob—I was more comfortable looking like a rock or a pile of dirt. But, as the first Tohrroid I knew of to escape the sinks and gutters my people were banished to, I wanted to be more than just an object. I wanted to be part of this new, broader world. I didn't want to eat shit in a sewer for the rest of my life, however long that was.

There were a lot of problems in achieving this simple goal. Though the Dryth's technology was so advanced that they had exceeded the notion of scarcity, those who benefited from this arrangement were all members of one or another Dryth House. These were powerful social entities with their own distinct subcultures and settlements and so on and joining them involved things like detailed genetics tests that I, an alien species and a reviled one besides, obviously could not pass.

The rest of Dryth society—the "Unhoused"—were expected to labor for their resources in various ways. Many of them were artists, some were shopkeepers and merchants and chefs and waiters and things. I tried many of these jobs, but none of them worked. There was always something I did wrong or floor, salty with the taste of the slime the Thraad excreted to allow them to glide around. These same four Thraad stood up on their catwalk and stared down. In judgement? I couldn't tell. I only remember the Blue-shell saying its bit about ruthlessness and then the Red-shell saying, *"We know what you are."*

Which meant they knew. They knew all about me. It was all coming together now—a ship full of convicts, sprung from prison. Me, a stowaway from said prison—an impostor. I had been discovered, maybe. Maybe that explained the buzzgun wound. Maybe, because I'd gotten away, the Thraad had offered freedom to the pet criminal that hunted me down.

But they'd underestimated me. They all had. I somehow knew, deep in my protoplasm, that they *always* had.

"Give me the toxin now!" Red-shell yelled.

The fourth Thraad—the one who hadn't spoken yet, the one in a green shell, spoke up. "She can't."

"She can if we kill her," the Voosk said, raising all its weapons.

"You misunderstand," Green-shell said. "She can't, because she doesn't have it."

Everyone looked confused for a moment except for the Green-shell...

...and me.

Hystra laughed. "What do you mean, I haven't got it? It's right slagging *here*, you stupid snail!"

I let myself explode out of my constrained shape and snatched the plasma thrower from Hystra's surprised hands. Even in the high gravity, it felt good to let my membranes relax for a second. I scuttled back and away from the Voosk and the Dryth and the red-shelled Thraad at the top of the ramp. "Stay back!" I said in a voice that came naturally to me—my own, I guess?

A lot of things happened at once.

The Voosk shot at me—thin ribbons of violet light traced back and forth across my membranes, causing them to sizzle and blister. The pain was intense, the injuries blinding—I couldn't see anywhere in the 180-degree arc where the Voosk and Hystra and the red Thraad were. I pulled the trigger on the plasma thrower over and over without really caring where I aimed—each shot a blazing ball of death, able to combust steel itself. Alarms sounded, flashes of heat—hotter, even, than the laser burns I'd sustained—washed over me.

The air hummed with a thousand buzzing projectiles—projectiles that banked and whirled and sought targets independently. Someone was firing a buzzgun. I heard Hystra scream and the Voosk screech in terror. I kept backing away, backing away, looking for a way out—for anything. I still couldn't see. The thrower stopped shooting—system crash, maybe—so I threw it in the general direction of the chaos I'd caused, but the lasers had stopped. I flailed around for an escape, for anything. I found a charred lump of flesh and snagged it by reflex, sucking it inside myself.

A pseudopod found something else—a little drainage gutter, probably for when the Thraad flushed the chamber to wash away their motile slime. It was small enough. I wriggled through and down a drainage tunnel, leaving the fire and the alarms behind. No sooner had I escaped than a little hatch slammed closed behind me—the fire-control measures kicking in. Plasma fires were no joke.

And here I was, back in a pipe again. Another dark little crevice to hide in, just like a monster should. The stinging pain in my outer membranes was almost too much for me. If I were a biped, I might have passed out, but I recalled that my species—the Tohrroids—don't lose consciousness. All we can do is rest.

I slid through the narrow little pipe a couple dozen more meters, though it was hard to judge distance perfectly in the some aspect of the work that outed me as non-Dryth. It turned out that the only thing worse than being a Tohrroid was being something that looked like a Dryth but *wasn't*. I'd never had so many apparently docile people try to kill me before.

So, after a while I found this place for myself—a lily plant in a beautiful House Vanyi garden. Not *quite* a member of society at large, but certainly a long way from the gutter. For the first time in my memory, I was enjoying life. I had food and safety. I was left in peace. And every couple days, there was a show.

Then came the intruder.

It was late, or at least that was the term applied to the period during which the moon was so far behind the gas giant it orbited that the world was draped in its shadow. The sky, depthless and black, loomed above the vast trapezoidal skylights that formed the garden's ceiling. It was this way that the assassin came— cutting her way through the glass with a laser and then coasting down to the garden path on a rope she affixed to the ceiling with a suction cup.

She made not a whisper as she came; I might never have seen her were it not for the fact that I look in all directions at once. I saw the flash of the laser, if only for a split second. I watched her land on the dirt path, placing her feet carefully in the footsteps of others. On her face was a thick, opaque visor—some sort of sensor array, perhaps compensating for the darkness, perhaps outlining the footsteps of other visitors in the dirt for her.

My first assumption was that she was a thief, but other than plants, there was nothing here to steal. The gardens did not grant unrestricted access to the rest of the Vanyi compound—a fact I knew well from my time here. She had broken into a courtyard, not a sensitive or valuable area.

When she got to the arched garden bridge, she slipped off the side and into the water below. During this time, I had been floating slowly along to as to keep her in sight, but it never dawned on me she'd enter the pond. Could she be after me? My instinct was to scrunch up and sink beneath the waves, but I had spent a long time taming my instincts. I remained a lily, but a watchful one.

The stranger waded under the bridge and removed a thick disk from her satchel, which she affixed to the underside. I saw her enter some kind of code into the device, saw it blink once—an affirmation, perhaps—and then she pulled herself back up on the bridge, again walked carefully along the path back to her rope, and climbed up. Once through the skylights, she gathered up her rope, returned the part of the glass she had cut away and, using some tool of hers, fused the glass together again, so that it was once more an unbroken pane.

Of course I had to see what she had left behind.

I had knowledge of explosives—some Thraad scientists had caught me at one point and tried making me into a trained killer—so I knew what I was looking at was a bomb. What kind, I did not know, but the target was obvious: Amoth. The killer wanted him dead but was not so large a fool as to face him here, as so many had before. I admired her at once.

I also took the explosive from its perch and shuttled it away to the far end of the garden where, should it explode, it would at most disrupt the root structures of a gnarled old saigath tree down that end. Maybe it would blow up a gardening drone, and just as well—the creepy little things were always spraying noxious chemicals on me and trying to snip off pseudopods of mine that I suppose they thought had gotten too long.

The next day, I watched and waited to see what would happen. Amoth had a challenger. This victim was a skinny Dryth juvenile with an enormous handgun. His skin was a riot of color and shape—an indication of his Unhoused status, an expression of his individuality. Amoth, by comparison, was like a statue, his skin a pale ivory shade with chevrons of violet and lavender along his cheeks and temples, which were the colors of his House. In his colossal hands, his massive pistol looked rather more proportional.

They faced each other on the garden path. Between them stood the witness; it was laying out the particulars. "The challenger, Yrikkan, charges that House Vanyi has defrauded his biological father of funds he earned for mercenary work in the Cybrali Belt. The House of Vanyi denies this charge and chooses Amoth as their champion. The contest is to be fought with plasma throwers, to the death."

Neither Amoth nor Yrikkan had anything to say to one another. No arguments, no rebuttals, not even any taunts. This was always the way it went. I gathered that the challenge was supposed to settle that kind of thing. I wondered how they could continue on in this way, knowing that the right or wrong of the accusation had no bearing on the outcome. Then again, I had no real experience in settling disagreements, so I figured I wasn't one to pass judgement on their system. At minimum, a plasma thrower had no biases.

The witness ordered them to pace off a distance of fifteen meters between them—another thing they had agreed upon beforehand. I watched Amoth walk until he was standing more or less exactly in the center of the garden bridge, right above where the bomb had been. It all clicked—this had been a setup. Yrikkan had hired the assassin to plant a bomb at Amoth's feet. Only it wasn't there!

"Fire!" the witness shouted.

Amoth raised his weapon and took aim. Yrikkan pointed vaguely in Amoth's direction and pulled the trigger. The gun did not fire, but at the same time, the corner of the garden in which I had planted the bomb lit up in a white-hot blossom of plasma fire. Alarms sounded. Amoth's seconds rushed to the plant with some kind of tool designed to douse plasma fire.

Yrikkan's eyes bugged out. He stared at the tree, well away from where he had actually aimed (which would have been a wild miss, anyway).

Amoth, meanwhile, took his time, lined up his shot, and then Yrikkan was nothing but hot ash and a smoldering pair of shoes. A disappointment for me, personally—there would be no feast tonight.

I was also worried my interference would be noticed or that somebody would figure out that there had been a bomb. If they did, I couldn't tell—I overheard one of Amoth's goons say that Yrikkan must have used some kind of high-velocity plasma thrower, perhaps of Thraad design. Amoth chuckled at this and retired to his midday meal. The excitement was over.

A few nights later, the assassin came again.

She arrived the same as before, but this time was more cautious. She dangled on the rope for a time, surveying her surroundings with whatever sensor suite was contained behind that visor. I let myself drift behind some of the real lily plants, hoping that they could provide some cover from whatever she was scanning for. Her attention did seem to pause on me but only for a second or two. Then she was down again, as before, stepping lightly on the path and then sliding into the water. She examined where she had placed the bomb and then looked around again. Having spent a long time reading bipedal body language, I could tell she was confused.

She climbed out of the water and pulled a series of little discs from her satchel, each of which she placed along the path. I heard a faint whirring sound as the things burrowed into the packed soil. The assassin then used a brush to conceal where they were with careful strokes, like an artist completing a painting. Then up the rope again.

The first time I had interfered, it had seemed a trivial act. I lived here in this garden, I ate what Amoth unknowingly provided me with—why should I let someone blow it up when I could so easily prevent it?

These devices, though, were more sophisticated. I didn't even know if they were bombs. I couldn't even say with any accuracy where they had all been planted. The effort to remove them would be substantial, and I am, in the end, a pretty lazy creature.

But if Amoth died, what would become of this garden and my safety and my unlimited supply of food? I had lived many places before this, as I said, and all of them had been terrible. Even those I could only remember as vague impressions, the primary thing I remembered was fear. I had no desire to leave.

But how to save him? Revealing myself would be equivalent to Amoth being killed, so far as the regularity of my meals was concerned. No one wanted a filthy Tohrroid—a blob, a gobbler, a *smack*—living in their pristine, tranquil murder-garden. No, just telling somebody was out.

But perhaps I could spoil the surprise somehow.

I floated over to the edge of the pond and, keeping careful watch for any late-night visitors, I formed myself into a rough simulation of a square of neatly trimmed lawn and oozed onto shore. It felt good having most of me bunched together rather than all strung out for a change. I'd almost forgotten the sensation.

When I reached the path, I formed one pseudopod into the shape of a Dryth foot in a boot. The tread was an imprecise copy, but I figured that if the assassin had been so determined not to leave a tread of any kind, then leaving several mysterious treads in the center of the path would raise alarms. I stomped about, alternating left and right foot-shapes in what I hoped was a convincing pattern and then, my makeshift warning done, retreated to my pond and resumed my lily shape, floating aimlessly with the other plants.

The next morning, the gardening drones came out for their

morning rounds and paused over the curious footprints, their little machine brains puzzling over this new input. Then they sounded an alarm.

The alarm was a sharp, pulsing tone—deeply, deeply unpleasant. I allowed myself to sink somewhat beneath the surface of the water, to cushion my blob-like physiology from the vibrations. That portion of me that remained above the water had difficulty maintaining its shape and form, because my outer membranes kept trembling with the force of the sound. The skylights above were covered by metal shutters. House Vanyi dragoons, dressed in bone-white armor, multipistols drawn, stalked into the garden from all directions, their own visors scanning in much the same way the assassin had. Again, they paused when their gaze passed over me but never for very long.

When the place was secure—no intruders that they had detected (not counting the "weirdly warm flower over there"), they turned off the alarm and removed the shutters. I felt the garden around me sort of *relax* when the sunlight poured down and the noise stopped. Having spent so much time with plants, it seemed I was beginning to understand their moods, such as they were. Interesting.

I wondered briefly if my belief in plants' nonsentience was the same as the Great Races' belief in my own. I wasn't afforded very much time to wonder.

The dragoons, using their sensors, discovered the little discs. One even dug them up and promptly collapsed when a little cloud of some kind of toxin spurted into the air. Blood leaked from her mouth and she appeared to die in seconds.

Not explosives, then—poison mines. Again, I was impressed.

There was a whole inquest. An investigation. When the mines had been isolated and safely detonated, Amoth came to inspect the scene, a white cape clinging his shoulders, his chest bare. He looked down at the dead dragoon, who had her helmet removed and was lying by the edge of the water, her white armor stained with blood. "These were meant for me," he stated. Not a question. It was arrogant but not incorrect.

With one foot, he pushed the dead dragoon into the pond in the same way he disposed of his murder victims. She was nothing to him. I don't think I expected anything different, but I was surprised that no one there—none of the six other dragoons and the pair of advisors and the team of gardeners batted even a single long Dryth eyelash at one of their own being dumped in a pond like so much fish food.

I cannot claim that I am the most empathetic of beings— my species is not social, and so caring for others was a concept I was still grappling with—but even I understood the casual monstrousness of that act. For some time now, I had assumed the Dryth were dominant as a species because they *did* work together and care for each other. The dragoons worked as a team to secure this compound, the gardeners and their drones worked as a team to maintain the garden, it only followed that their leader would hold these team members in some esteem. It seemed I was wrong. I'd missed something crucial about them that I didn't understand.

The murders likewise began to take on a new light with this revelation. I had assumed that Amoth was killing those who transgressed against the social order—I saw him as a kind of gardener for social cohesion. Those he killed were like branches being pruned—they had to die for the good of the whole. Even I understood how that could be advantageous. But I realized that his casual cruelty toward those who literally saved his life meant it couldn't be true.

I waited in keen anticipation for the assassin to return. I had to wait a long time.

Her method of entry had been discovered. The skylights were equipped with more sophisticated alarm systems and patrolled, now, by an armed drone at all hours. A dragoon was also posted in the garden at all times except for duels. They walked along the winding paths, their eyes alert, their weapons holstered. The guards shifted every few hours, in a pattern I couldn't detect, assuming there even was one. It was an effort to throw off would-be infiltrators—they wouldn't know when the guards would change, wouldn't know when a guard would be at the end of the shift and tired.

It seemed a lot to secure a garden, but Amoth Vanyi was worried for his safety.

Amoth's murders continued as scheduled—a few times a week, some kind of crime involved, a witness present, and then a battle to the death. Amoth was invincible with blade and gun: huge and powerful, his muscles likely enhanced through retroviral genetic therapy, no ordinary Dryth or Lhassa or Thraad could hope to best him. This some seemed to know, but there was something about that ritual—the witness, the pronouncement of the accusation, and the consequences—that hypnotized them into obedience. All of them wanted to believe they could kill him if they just tried something different. None of them were right.

As I ate them, drawing up bits of their flesh inside myself to be dissolved by my digestive fluids, I ruminated upon their fate. I wondered what world this was where Amoth was immune to consequence. Not unlike other worlds, I decided. Everywhere I had gone, the powerful could do as they pleased and the rest were compelled into obedience or destruction. It was the way of the galaxy, perhaps. It was certainly the universal fate of my species.

One day, the dragoon guard on duty brought a handheld scanner on her rounds. She produced it as soon as her counterpart had left her and spent some time wandering the garden, bombarding things with whatever weird little beams or particles or whatever fed her machine information.

Then she came to me. Like all the others who had scanned

me in the past, she had to note that my body temperature was too high. Unlike the others, though, she took interest. She folded the scanner up and came close to me. I could see her eyes through the glare of her visor; they were a shade of green so light, they were nearly white. She spoke to me, her voice confident: "You're pretty clever for a Tohrroid, aren't you?"

It seemed safest to play dumb, so I did. I didn't move, didn't ripple, didn't even change color. It was a bluff, maybe. A guess.

"I'm guessing it was you who screwed up my traps the last two times, am I right?"

It was her! The assassin! I held my breath.

She wasn't deterred. "Look, I don't know if you understand what I'm saying, but if you're smart enough to detach a plasma bomb and smart enough to reveal my poison mines, that makes you a threat. My professional reputation has taken a hit already, smack, and either you and I are gonna hash out a deal, or I'm just gonna pull my pistol and see if you can eat bullets. You've got five seconds."

I considered attacking, but I was unarmed and she was in armor and had a large pistol at her hip that her fingers were hovering just above. I can be fast but not that fast. Instead, I elected diplomacy. "Please don't shoot—I mean you no harm."

She gasped when I spoke and backed up a full pace. "You... you *actually* talk!"

"Why shouldn't I talk?" I said. "*You* talk."

"Of course *I* do, but..." The assassin caught herself and looked over her shoulder, scanning the garden, making sure we were still alone. "What's the big idea, messing up my plans? Interfering with an assassination is a bad idea, smack—the Code would let me kill you as an accessory, you know."

"What's the Code?" I asked. "And don't call me 'smack.'" I knew the term—a derogatory name for my species. I didn't care for it.

"Well, what *should* I call you?" She chuckled at this—the novelty of speaking with a Tohrroid, I suppose. "Do you even have a name?"

I did not have a name. Up until that moment, I hadn't really seen it as a problem. When I impersonated bipeds, I didn't bother with a name. It was always "How much for this bright-fruit?" and "Can I have a medium kedjedge, hot?"—nobody cared if I had a name, just if I had something to barter with or maybe a couple credit chits knocking around. My relationship with the Great Races was transactional only. My identity—my very existence—was a closely held secret.

And yet here I was, conversing with one. "Why are you trying to kill Amoth Vanyi?"

The assassin shrugged. "Lots of reasons, but the first is that it's my job. I'll get paid when he dies—a lot of money, too. And you're making it harder for me to collect."

I felt I had a reasonable counterpoint to that. "If he dies, no more people will be killed in this garden, and I'll have less to eat."

The assassin held very still when I said that. I wasn't sure how to interpret it. "Do you think Amoth knows you're here?"

"He doesn't." I said. "If he did, he wouldn't allow me to stay. You Dryth dislike us. You think we're dirty."

"You are a blob monster living in a lake and feasting on dead bodies. Can you blame him?"

"If I didn't eat them, the other plants would. Or the fish. What difference does it make to you, who eats the dead?"

The assassin thought about this. "Fair enough—but what difference does it make who kills them? Wouldn't Amoth make a pretty good meal, himself?"

I wanted to point out that she was imagining an impossible scenario—they wouldn't just roll his body in the lake. There would be some sort of ritual or ceremony involved. House

Vanyi loved its rituals and ceremonies. I didn't say anything, though. I just floated there, a talking water lily, and waited to see where this was all going.

"I'm asking if you would be willing to help me," the assassin said. "I work better with a partner, and I lost mine a few weeks back, thanks to you."

"I will not help you kill my primary source of protein."

"Then maybe I should just kill *you*," she said.

I was worried perhaps for a second, but she made no move to pull her weapon. She was bluffing. "If you kill me, you would need to explain why you brought a scanner into the garden."

"It's pretty reasonable to bring a scanner to a place where an assassin has been caught planting mines."

That answer was rehearsed, not honest. A lifetime of watching and eavesdropping on Dryth didn't lie. "It's not the question you are worried about—it's about *being questioned*. They would realize you weren't supposed to be here. You would be found out."

Those pale green eyes hardened behind the visor. "You think over what I said, smack. We'll meet again."

I didn't say anything in response. She left.

I hoped we would meet again.

I saw her often after that. Whatever ruse she had used to infiltrate the Vanyi dragoons had been effective enough to permit her to stay or to come and go as she pleased. She made no further attempts on Amoth's life that I knew of, but she was never in his presence. Her shifts seemed to end just before he arrived for another duel or began immediately after one had taken place. In all other respects, things continued as they had.

And yet everything was entirely different.

My bafflement at the ritualized murders committed by Amoth upon his challengers had acquired a different…flavor. I had a distaste for the ritual that brought them to this garden of death. I began to wonder at my part in it.

I also wondered how the assassin fit in. I wondered at this "Code" she alluded to—another ritual but maybe a fairer one? So much was unclear and, unlike before, my curiosity was no longer satiated by feasting and floating.

For the first time in a long time, I felt confined.

One day, Amoth came to the garden with two of his attendants—not armed dragoons but assistants in robes carrying his effects. One of them had a weapon—a large harpoon with some kind of power source connected. It looked painful.

This was a peculiar visit because there was no challenger present for him to slaughter. No witness, either—just him, his two lackeys, and that giant harpoon. He stopped at the edge of the pond and took up the weapon, testing its weight, amping up the power. The air crackled around it.

Then he threw it directly at me. I was quicker than that, of course—I darted away, letting my lily shape go so that the blade wouldn't skewer me through the middle. I realized too late I had blown my cover. Also, the electrified head of the harpoon still struck the water right beside me. Pain and heat blossomed throughout my body, eliminating control over my membranes. I flailed and flattened; the air bubble I had kept trapped inside me released. I expected to drown.

But the harpoon, attached to a cable, slid past me and hooked my body, dragging me in like a limp balloon. I was brought up on the shore by Amoth's flunkies and tossed before him. My outer membranes rippled unevenly as they tried to regain control; my inner membranes did the same, trying to reestablish my breathing. I probably looked like I was gasping, desperate, pathetic.

"Fascinating," Amoth said in his rolling bass, squatting in front of me. "I never thought it possible."

One of the flunkies drew a hand-sized flamethrower. "Shall I kill it, sir?"

Amoth raised one hand. "No. Not yet. I want to know what she said to it."

"But, sir," said the other attendant, "Tohrroids can't talk!"

Amoth smiled, his nickel-capped teeth gleaming from between his bone-white lips. "This one is full of surprises, I expect." He glanced at his attendants, and they knew that glance, since they cleared out right away, taking the dragoon on guard with them. They left Amoth with the harpoon, though.

By this time, my breathing was back under control and my outer membranes were not twitching so badly. I could manage speech, if I wanted to. Complex shapes? Not so much.

"Well, smack—can you talk?"

I wished I remembered more profanity in Dryth Basic, because now seemed like a good time for it. Instead, I just asked, "What do you want?"

Amoth's eyes—lavender and settled inside pronounced bone-structure—widened as much as his engineered skeleton would allow. "You've saved my life twice now. I owe you a debt."

"Then leave me alone," I said. It was a futile request—I knew it right away. I was revealed. Nothing would go back to the way it was. What had been mine only a few days past was now irrevocably lost.

"Surely there is more you want from life than floating in my gardens. Ask, and it will be yours."

I did not have ambitions, but I did have questions. "Why did you send your stooges away?"

"Stoo—" Amoth laughed, a booming sound I had typically only heard after he had killed someone.

"Tell me."

"It seems to me that knowing a Tohrroid that can think and talk is a secret worth keeping," Amoth said, a caginess returning to his eyes—the wary eyes of a Dryth who had killed hundreds with his own hands.

Just like that, I saw how the rest of the conversation would go. I remembered the Thraad scientists in my past, training me like their pet. I remembered how they wanted to use me, just like Amoth would want to use me—a Tohrroid who could speak, who could understand, who could *obey*. The perfect infiltrator, the perfect spy. The perfect tool.

What he would offer me next would be things that bipeds wanted—glory, wealth, status, and so on. It might be a lie or it might not—it didn't matter. He didn't understand that I had been content. Content in this pastoral garden, peaceful save for his violent intrusions, and satiated by their aftermath. The assassin had ruined that for me forever.

I did have more questions, though: "Why do the people come to challenge you, knowing they will die? How do you compel them to do it?"

"That is a very interesting question, coming from a smack," Amoth said. He considered it for a moment and, I guess, decided to humor me. "There are only two means of changing society to fit your aims—from without, where you destroy the society with weapons and build a new one, or from within, where you use the systems created by the society to alter itself. The challenge—a foundational precept of the Union of Stars and the Holy Law—is the system that exists that allows for change."

"But it doesn't work!" I bunched my now-recovered membranes together, making myself less a two-dimensional puddle of flesh and more a three-dimensional blob. I cycled through a variety of colors and patterns, testing my readiness.

If Amoth saw this as threatening, he gave no sign. "It works very well, my friend. Dominated people require the illusion of hope. Despair merely breeds destruction. This"—he gestured to the garden—"is my service to them. One day, they believe someone will kill me, and their suit will carry. I realize this is difficult for some faceless blob to understand, but your comprehension isn't necessary for what comes next."

"You're right about that." I lunged at his face.

Amoth was used to fighting people who had fixed shapes, fixed limbs. He knew many, many ways to wrestle or pummel or break his opponents with his bare hands. But I had no bones to break, no limbs for him to trap or twist. I wrapped around his head and torso, muffling his cries for help, plugging up his mouth and nostrils. He struggled with me—he struck me and seized handfuls of me and twisted and yanked and pulled, but I was a being who had been a water lily, with all those spindly tendrils and long stems. His arms were not long enough to stretch me beyond my tolerances. He could not twist me farther than I could twist myself. And for all his engineered physique, for all his lifetime of training, he had never been engineered or trained out of a need to breathe. The more he struggled, the faster the end came.

Above us, the armed drone quietly watched the skylights for an assassin that never came.

When Amoth was dead, I rolled his corpse into the pond and watched him sink into the murky water, there to join the bones of all the others he had put there. Much as I wanted to, I could not join them, because they knew about me now. There was no going back.

With great pains, I formed my body into the shape of Amoth himself. I left the garden as the Champion of House Vanyi. No one questioned me—his attendants bowed at my approach, the dragoons saluted me out of respect. I was shown to a sumptuous chamber that overlooked the arid desolation of the moon's surface: the rocks a pale green color, the sand a deep brown, and the buildings somewhere in between. The place—the room, the *view*—was so palpably not my own that it was uncomfortable to occupy. Like everywhere, now that the garden was lost to me.

I could not stay here long. I would make a mistake, be exposed, wind up dead. My world, for a short time so stable, had returned to me looking for gutters to ooze into. I hated it. I hated it like nothing I had ever hated before. And I knew who to blame.

The doors to "my" apartments opened and another Vanyi lickspittle glided in, wearing robes of white. "You are issued a challenge, sir. From one of our own dragoons, it seems. She alleges you killed a friend of hers outside the bounds of a formal challenge. She demands satisfaction."

"What is her name?" I asked, my imitation of Amoth's voice pitch-perfect. I made a show of lounging in a deep, soft chair—casual, calm, as Amoth always had been.

"Ada," he said, and added, "she requests knives."

I made my imitated face grin. "I will meet her in the usual spot. Set it up."

If there was something about my orders that didn't sit right with the underling—some way I misspoke—he did not let it show. He pressed a hand to his chest, bowed, and left.

I knew it was the assassin who had challenged me. She had set some trap for Amoth, as before, that was now ready to be spring. It was just as well that she had challenged me—or Amoth, as she believed. She deserved what was coming to her. She would come expecting a Dryth and would face a large, angry Tohrroid. She had no idea what I was capable of. None of these fools knew what those Thraad scientists had taught me. They should have left me alone in my pond, at peace.

It was only a few hours before I was told that she was waiting for me. An attendant held up a lacquered case of some kind of dark wood. She opened it and inside was a knife—a fine resin blade, sharp enough to whittle steel and light as a whisper. I held it in my Dryth hand and it just…fit. A quasi-biological hilt, conditioned to match the wielder's grip. My knowledge of weapons was not exhaustive, but something like this cost a vast sum. I sheathed it and we went to meet my destiny in the garden.

The assassin was not in a dragoon's armor any longer. She wore a form-fitting suit of black gel-weave. She had abandoned her affected Vanyi skin pigmentation—the whites and violets and lavenders were gone, replaced with a striated pattern of jagged black lines across a base of rust brown. Her eyes—that pale green—leapt from her face in contrast. She had a blade at her hip and no other weapons, or so Amoth's attendants told me.

She stood, tense and ready, on the same garden path I had watched her drop to a week before. I stood on the bridge, making my simulated eyes look at her. She lifted her chin to meet my gaze and smiled. She was plotting something.

I returned the smile—I, also, was plotting something.

The witness stood between us, his mutated face gazing into the middle distance while the foreign eyes of his symbiotes looked me and the assassin up and down. I had a moment of worry—what could those eyes see? "Wait for me in the compound," I said to my underlings. "Leave us alone."

"But..." one of them started to protest, but another gave him a stern look, and they all left. It was just me, the assassin, and the witness.

The witness spoke to me. "You are not Amoth of House Vanyi. You are not Dryth at all."

The assassin gasped. "What?"

I was irritated my instincts had been correct. I drew the expensive knife. "What happens now? Do you raise an alarm?"

The witness raised his hands, which sported extra fingers that were not of Dryth design. "I am merely a Vassal of Its Immensity, the Marshal. I am neutral in your petty affairs."

The mention of a Marshal gave me pause—I knew of them, of course. Vast, planet-eating macro-organisms, the most powerful beings in existence. It seemed that these rituals—this Holy Law that Amoth had spoken of—had greater beneficiaries than merely the Dryth Houses.

"You're the Tohrroid!" the assassin said. "You killed Amoth, took his place! That's…that's incredible!"

"Now I am going to kill you and take your place," I said, making my body walk forward.

The witness—the Vassal—blocked my way with an upraised palm. "This is not permitted. It is a violation of the Tenet of Hospitality, the second Tenet of the Holy Law."

I did not turn my face to look at the Vassal. "Then I challenge according to your Law."

"On what grounds? What dispute is to be resolved?"

"She took away my home," I said, Amoth's simulated voice flat and even.

"Wait!" The assassin raised her knife in defense, balanced herself on the balls of her feet. "There's another way this goes down."

"How?" I asked, my body loose, knife at my side. To her, I probably looked as though I wasn't ready—that I had relaxed my guard. How wrong she was. "You stole my life. You robbed me of food and security and warmth. Now where will I go? Back into the gutter? For that alone, I am going to kill you."

The Vassal spoke to the assassin. "Do you wish to name a champion on your behalf? A different location?"

I stepped around the mutant. I had had enough of their rituals, their games, their Law—the various ways they made their crimes palatable to themselves and to their victims. Murder was simply murder—I had done it often enough to know that its central nature could never be concealed.

The assassin shifted her position, altered her hold on the knife. I saw the hesitancy in her eyes—she didn't know how to fight me and she knew it. Any battle we engaged in would be a blind one on her part. She had no way of knowing whether she would live or die. "You killed Amoth, so you're entitled to the fee for doing it. It's a lot of money, friend."

"Friend?"

She remained tense, ready. "I don't know what else to call you, okay? Listen, you can walk out of here with me or as me. *As* me and you wind up in the gutter; *with* me, and…maybe there's more than that in your future. In *our* future."

She made a good point. I could always kill her later. "What do you propose?"

"Where is Amoth's body?"

I gestured to the pond.

Slowly, carefully, she slid her knife back in its sheath. "I'm going fishing."

It took her a few minutes to find Amoth, but when she did, she dragged him onto shore and stabbed him a few times before rolling him back in the pond. I didn't know how convincing it would look, but it didn't matter. The Vassal made that clear as he watched: "This crime shall be reported. You will be caught."

The assassin patted her back. "Hop on. Disguise yourself— we'll walk right out."

"I don't trust you," I said. "At all."

"If you don't trust me, then trust my Code—I have no standing to kill you, now that Amoth is dead. I've no right to the fee, since you are the one who killed him."

"Codes can be broken."

She smiled at me. "Not when I plan to profit from them, *partner.*"

She was right—it was the gutter or her. I made myself look like a backpack, wrapped around her shoulders, and kept my fancy knife ready. Good as her word, the assassin walked right out. The Vanyi Dryth were shocked to see her alive. They blubbered questions at her, none of which she answered, but they let her go. I was amazed—amazed at the power of ritual, of convention. There was much I didn't know about the world.

An hour later, I was sitting across the table from her in a local commissary, watching the desert winds cake dust on the windows. She had bought me something called "zar"—a soup made with fungus and oily cheese. It was more delicious than the dead by a significant margin, if less filling.

"My name is Ada," the assassin said. "So, what *should* I call you?"

I was in the form of another Dryth female, a variation on her own frame and body type. My skin pigmentation was green with white accents, my eyes a deep shade of blue. I wondered how long I could fool the world this way. It occurred to me that the rules and systems of behavior of the Great Races might have cracks I could ooze between—just like Ada had. For the first time in a long time, I wondered how far I, a faceless blob in the crowd, might go.

That was it—my name.

"Call me Faceless," I said.

Tool Consciousness

Thraad Consortiums governed according to a kind of genetic inertia—whoever had the most disciples got to dictate to other Consortiums what was done. If there were lots of Consortiums and no clear hegemony, they combined into larger and larger Consortiums until one of the newly coalesced Consortiums had clear authority. At some point, I was given to understand, this would all break down into chaos and then the various members of the Consortiums would wander off and form new ones. And so on and so forth.

The only reason I knew all this garbage about how the snails arranged their society was that I was now an integral part of their stupid plans. It involved sneaking into a Thraad hatchery, disguising myself as an egg, and irradiating a specific percentage of the *real* eggs there with a rad-gun so that they wouldn't ever hatch and, thereby, prevent them from strengthening their parent Consortium.

I was uniquely suited to this task, as my body is amorphous, and forming myself into a gray-ish sphere was among the easiest shapes to assume. The main problem was, ultimately, the weight. I can change *shape* but not *mass*—I was just using the strength of my muscular outer membranes to clench myself into a smaller volume, but I still weighed ten times as much as your average Thraad egg. This was especially evident in the intense simulated gravity they maintained in their hatcheries, where they did so to mimic the forces present on their flat, muddy, and probably really depressing homeworld. Long story short, no Thraad was going to *carry* me into a hatchery without finding me out.

The hatchery existed in the business end of a huge centrifuge that dominated the center of the Thraad colony on Gorsurai—a dimly lit moon of blue-white sunsets, magnesium-salt oceans, and glittery purple sand that I had no particular affinity for but that the Thraad liked well enough to establish a major outpost, complete with an orbital strand to facilitate some fairly lively interstellar trade. The building that housed the centrifuge looked like a huge wheel, a couple hundred meters in diameter, and all the local Thraad Consortiums used it—it was, officially speaking, neutral territory. It was also guarded by well-paid Lhassa mercenaries with high-tech weaponry and limited senses of humor that made its neutrality somewhat more concrete.

Getting *into* the hatchery was one of those things that seemed complex at first—and probably would be complex if you weren't me—but was actually fairly simple. I just mailed myself inside a plastifiber box and some gormless Thraad from the Consortium for the Facilitation of Harmonious Trade carted me right into their mailroom. They'd scan the box, sure, but since I am not an explosive or a plague, all it really registered on the scanner was "unknown biologicals." This got me put in a *special* part of the mailroom—a sealed chamber—which, actually, was a lot better. There were never any personnel or drones in that part of the mailroom, so I could just climb right out, whenever.

Also, the rad-gun I needed to do my job I *also* mailed and was *also* put in the sealed part of the mailroom, so, you know, *convenient*. I just got out of my box, collected my rad-gun, and oozed up into the vents. About the only hard part was removing the filtration unit from the vents so I could easily slip inside. This required a mag-wrench, which I mailed with the rad-gun. I was spending a lot on postage, but it beat the hell out of trying to fight armed mercenaries every time I did this.

Which was a lot.

Anyway, the vents led to all the various Consortiums' specific hatcheries; they were deliberately designed this way, the thinking being that if you tried to poison one chamber, you would have to poison them all. They also, I'm guessing, didn't imagine that I—a Tohrroid—would be oozing through the ten-centimeter-by-ten-centimeter ducts with a gun and a wrench. As far as the Thraad and all the other Great Races of the Union of Stars were concerned, Tohrroids were disgusting, slimy blobs that couldn't even think, let alone speak or interact with the postal system.

There weren't usually any guards in the hatcheries, but there were Thraad nurses, and they stuck to a complex schedule I could never quite figure out. There was always one of them, their broad, slimy foot propelling them smoothly down the rows and rows of eggs nestled in little bubbling pools of mud. This was when making myself look like an egg came in handy—I'd plop into the mud and wait for my chance. All of my outer membranes are light-sensitive, so I can see in pretty much every direction. If a nurse was coming or going, I'd see them before they saw me.

My job was to decrease the Thraad birthrate in this or that Consortium so that they wouldn't overtake the others in the nonstop race for dominance of this stupid, placid moon of a completely boring gas giant. I had to dodge the nurses on their rounds and then zap eggs at random and for a very precise period of time, so as to make the whole thing look like some kind of natural occurrence as opposed to active mischief. My clients always had a very specific number of eggs I had to zap—thirty-two, fifteen, twenty-eight. It never made any sense to me, but I suppose the Thraad had their data. I probably had to stay below some kind of margin of error that would trip suspicions.

After I was done, I would crawl back through the vents, seal myself back inside my box, and wait a few hours before nobody claimed my package and it was shipped return-to-sender. Whole thing would take the entirety of a Gorsuraian daylight cycle—about seventeen standard hours.

I had done this now twelve times. As the birthrate of this or that Consortium dropped, the Consortium with fewer little Thraad-poles on the way would contract with my partner, Ada, to do the same thing I'd done to *another* Consortium. And so on and so forth. My life, it seemed, was just one delivery box after another. The money was steady. The job was pretty easy.

I hated it.

"What, you feeling bad about frying eggs?" Ada looked at me over her plate of steaming gardo noodles—a Lhassa staple that a lot of Dryth were obsessed with. I'd already finished mine and was hoping she was full so I could finish hers.

"It would be one thing if you let me eat them, but this? I feel like an accountant," I said through the simulated mouth of my simulated face. I'd assumed the form of your run-of-the-mill Lhassa lowlife—dirty flight suit with the sleeves ripped out, grandiose boasts shaved into my arm fur, one horn broken. The kind of Lhassa male who might catch dinner with a professional assassin without arousing much interest.

We were in a café on the top floor of one of the spiraling towers that had a great view of the city—a forest of ivory buildings nestled on the shores of a still, blue-green ocean. Behind us, a Dryth soloist was singing something upbeat, meant to bring up the mood without overwhelming conversation. This was the first time I'd been here. It was a nice place, and nice places always made me itch.

Ada met me in a different place each time, and I always looked different when we met. She, in her body armor and with her obvious sidearm, was the face of the operation—she was contacted by the Consortiums for the job, and as far as they were concerned, *she* was the one doing the work. So far as I knew, none of the Thraad Consortiums on-planet had figured out how she was doing it. I knew this because the Thraad had yet to change any of their security measures in the hatchery, and somebody obviously would have done something if they'd put it together.

"How do you even know what an accountant is?" Ada asked.

"I know how to *read*, Ada."

Ada snorted. Dryth don't have much in the way of noses—just sort of a vague bump where their snout might be—but their nostrils do a lot of emoting. "I don't think I'll ever get used to how scary you are." Ada had a tendency to treat me like I was radioactive. Like I could kill her at any time. This was technically true—I could—but that fact that I *hadn't* after all our time together I felt should have earned me more trust than it did. "How long are we going to do this?"

"Faceless, we've been over this," Ada said, twirling her noodles with a slender little fork. "This is a good job. We are keeping this society stable and functional through the Recovery and Peace period, like good assassins should. I am earning a real reputation in the right circles. The next War period is in another twenty standard weeks. Once that happens, the Thraad won't need assassins anymore—they'll just kill each other the old-fashioned way. We'll scoot off-world with a pile of trade credits, a good reputation, and the galaxy at our feet."

"I'm bored," I said.

"I didn't think you *could* get bored. When I met you, you'd just spent a year as a potted plant."

I hadn't been in a pot. I also didn't feel like being pedantic. I mostly didn't relish the idea of experiencing the efficiencies of the Thraad mail system *again*. "That was different. I was *content*. 'Content' is different than 'bored.' I think."

She gestured to my empty plate. "Hey, feel grateful. This place is beautiful, peaceful, and even the food is good. How often have you had it this good?"

That was a fair point. I had spent a good chunk of my life in places like prison camps and slums, eating refuse and carrion—typical staples for a scavenger like me. Eating this far up the food chain should have been nice. Instead, I was on edge, like any second a trap might spring. All around me were fat, satisfied aliens eating expensive imported food, and I felt like it all was too good to be true. As a being that traditionally fed on garbage, I could tell when something should stink. The fact that it didn't was…weird.

Ada slid a credit chit across the table—pay for the last egg job, some of which, no doubt, would go towards the *next* egg job. "This time it's the Beepers. They need seventy-one."

The Beepers—the Consortium for Efficient Air and Ground Traffic Infrastructure. Somebody didn't like how smoothly traffic flowed in this place, I guess.

"Faceless," Ada said, grabbing my fake hand and squeezing. My membranes compressed like a water bladder. "I can still count on you, right? No going behind my back?"

"Yeah," I said. It was a weird thing to ask me, and even weirder that she touched me. It made me wonder.

Ada nodded. "Good. It's hard to read your expression sometimes."

That's because I don't have one. Not really. Ada was always looking for something that wasn't there—some kind of body language she could recognize. Stuff like that always reminded me of how little we had in common. We were both out of our depth in this relationship. I didn't understand the world that well, and Ada didn't understand me.

I didn't understand me, either, but that was wide of the point.

Ada got up. "Your eye is drooping, by the way. See you at the next place."

She left. I watched her go without turning my head. I looked at my reflection in the windows overlooking the city and tightened my membranes around my simulated eye. Took me a second of adjustment, but then I had it. Perfect.

Nobody would notice me. Not ever.

Maybe that was my problem.

The thought of going through another egg job—another box, another interminable wait in the dark as I was shipped by some slow-moving Thraad, another ooze through the sterile ductwork of the hatchery—made me even more restless. Ada was right by every logical measure. The egg jobs were easy, steady money. I didn't care about the politics of it all, and I certainly didn't care about a couple of fried snail eggs. I never really got along with the Thraad as a species, anyway. So, why did this feel worse than living as a plant in a garden?

I didn't know. I guess I could try to have that conversation with Ada, but I was still not comfortable with the idea of confiding in someone else. Ada and I still had a…challenging working relationship. I think. I know less about relationships than I know about being bored. From what Ada had explained in the past, a partnership was where we shared labor and split the profits and was predicated upon trust for one another. It was complicated—just like the quiet prosperity of Gorsurai, I always felt like the floor was going to drop away beneath me.

At least when I was a plant in a garden, I didn't need to think about things so much. Everything just sort of made sense. Maybe. I don't know—my memory was sort of spotty. Probably too much time using a rad-gun—radiation was bad for my memory, for my ability to even form thoughts. A trick of my physiology.

If Ada was so concerned about me going behind *her* back, was Ada playing straight with *me*? How would I know if she weren't?

I decided to wait on the street outside the restaurant and find out—I had time.

The streets in Gorsurai City were slick and polished, like glass. Thraad hovercrafts, traveling on cushions of forced air-pressure differential, slid along at a crawl while Lhassa pups in bright capes whizzed between them on their single-wheel scooters. There was no direct ownership of vehicles in the city—the Beepers had built them all and left them open for free use. In other places I'd been, this would have resulted in knife fights and hovercraft piracy. Among the snails, it was all very civilized—most of the dome-shaped hovercrafts had four or five snails glommed on to their sides, like barnacles, all waiting for their ride to swing close enough to their desired destination for them to disembark. Thraad cruised on and off at will, and when a driver hopped out, one of the passengers took over. About the only problem was the traffic congestion—the city was growing faster than the Beepers could get roads built, and it showed.

In the shadows of an alley, I shifted my shape into that of a courier drone—a brightly colored metal ball with a series of slots where passers-by could deposit things they needed transported along with a nominal fee of trade credits. I made myself look shiny and brand-new so I'd blend in with all the other polished equipment the colony had in abundance for some reason. I sat there in the alley across from the tower where Ada kept an apartment.

She came down the building's broad entrance ramp with her trademark swagger, wearing a long loose coat with bright yellow zigzag stripes over her body armor. She hopped onto the nearest hovercraft, and the driver didn't even react. They drifted along in traffic and I rolled after. The traffic and the natural Thraad disinclination to rush made it easy to keep up. I could see Ada chatting away with the driver as they went, gesturing wildly, telling one of her hyperviolent stories that always made herself look good. The Thraad kept one eyestalk fixed on her, the other one on the road.

Ada looked behind her once every block, trying to spot tails. She didn't notice me, a courier drone. Like most bipeds, she was mostly looking for things she thought of as people, and I wasn't that. There were a hundred other spherical drones on the roads such that I'd never stand out, anyway. Ada was good but not that good.

She got out of the moving hovercraft in a solar-farming district belonging to a different Consortium, predictably nicknamed "the Solars." Here, the roads narrowed and the traffic all but vanished. The large panels above blocked out most of the sunlight from Gorsurai's distant star, like the canopy of some tropical forest. Ada turned down an alley lined with coolant pipes and carpeted in discarded circuitry and puddles of denatured nano-goop. I ditched the courier-drone shape and became something close to my natural self—something formless and dark, at home in the shadows. I followed after her.

Where was she going? Who was she meeting with? I started imagining all kinds of nefarious rendezvous—a Lorca tyrant, perhaps, or maybe some Dryth House looking to muscle in on Thraad territory. The Bodani Collective, trying to make a move to become interstellar for once. The possibilities were endless. I was excited to see the underbelly of this place at last. To see the peaceful veneer pulled back to show the rot.

Ada stopped in a shaft of uninterrupted daylight in an intersection between solar-panel farms. She looked relaxed. She'd been here before, *done* this before. To think I'd trusted her.

A shadow detached itself from the gloom—a Dryth, judging from the muscular build, the thick neck. I couldn't tell the gender from that distance, in that light. Gender was largely cultural affectation among the Dryth, anyway—they didn't produce offspring through sexual intercourse, apart from some weird fringe fetishists. Ada faced the stranger, dug in her pockets, and pulled out a couple of trade-credit chits. She dropped them in the guy's hand and he gave her a package. A weapon, maybe? Who would she be *paying*? That wasn't the direction money flowed in our business—shady people paid *us*.

The Dryth took off, leaving Ada alone, so far as she knew. She stepped out of the light and opened the package. It contained a series of cylindrical auto-injectors. I'd seen things like that before—germline genetic-engineering treatments. Housed Dryth had almost exclusive access to them; unhoused nobodies like Ada had to get what the black market could supply. I watched as she injected herself, one after another, her body shuddering with a mixture of pain and clear relief.

A drug deal. That was it. A regular, boring old drug deal.

I felt like an idiot, wasting my time. I was tired, hungry, covered in the filth of the streets and the alley. I could taste the grit of the planet's purple sand all over me. I left Ada to her vices.

I got something to eat.

The Thraad diet consists of small living fish and tough, coarse vegetables, usually as raw as can be managed. I had flopped myself on the ground next to a roadside stand run by a snail in a very practical shell covered with pouches of various seasonings. None of his food was fresh—the fish, in particular, looked long dead and probably not native to this planet—but the snail threw enough spices into the metal bowls he served them in that most probably couldn't notice. For my form, I'd chosen an

unhoused Dryth. I was exhausted, and I had no doubt my features and proportions were drooping—it took a *lot* of energy to compress my membranes into something resembling a biped, and I'd been at this all day. At least, at a Thraad place, nobody expected me to stand. The Thraad, as a species without legs, were a little unclear on the idea of "standing" and "sitting," anyway.

As I ate my pickled fish and dry weeds—sucking them into internal vacuoles where my internal digestive fluids would dissolve them—I revisited the idea of boredom. I was bored, I decided, as a side effect of my own agency. Prior to fairly recently, life was just a struggle to survive. Boredom isn't possible if death is a constant threat. I hadn't been bored because I hadn't been free. Oh, sure, I had *thought* about myself as free—no rules to follow, no relationships to maintain, no obligations to fulfill—but that wasn't freedom, it was the state of nature, and nothing is more restrictive than struggling for every meal.

Now? I had money, I had power (after a fashion), I had *awareness* of myself and the world around me. And what was I using it for? Dead fish and Ada's gene-tailoring habit. Nothing interesting happened here. There was no challenge, no new horizon. Ada talked ambition, talked "big plans," but what were those plans, anyway? Nebulous, vague things. Promises she either meant to break or didn't know how to keep.

I felt like I'd been given a set of tools by which I could change the world but then told I wasn't supposed to use them. Here I was, the most talented killer in this whole colony, and nobody even knew I existed. I was a nobody, a nothing. A shadow on the wall, unappreciated. It was making me crazy. *That* was boredom.

Maybe. I don't know—this whole thing was new.

I staggered back to the alley where I'd been squatting since we'd arrived on-planet. I had a hexagonal trash receptacle that was very comfortable after I stuffed it with old seaweed and discarded insulation foam. The other two receptacles had my stuff, such as it was—the rad-gun, some synthesized Dryth ration bars, a wide array of knives, a pile of credit chits, and not a whole lot else. With the money I was making from my work, I could have afforded a tiny apartment somewhere, but I didn't like the idea of being so traceable as to have a clear address. Squatting suited me better. I dropped my bipedal form and poured myself into the comfy trash bin, leaving a little bit of myself at the top to take in the early-morning air.

As I rested, I considered the traffic, the tall buildings glowing lavender in the waxing but distant sunlight, the smell of bromine and magnesium salt in the air. The world was bustling but quiet. Beautiful but aloof.

I felt like some noise.

I mailed myself again, except this time to a different office inside the hatchery. I wanted to talk with the administrator.

From Ada's research into the hatchery's organizational structure, I knew that while each Consortium maintained a separate hatchery, said hatcheries were maintained by a neutral party—its own Consortium but one *without* a hatchery of its own. They were called the Consortium for Secure and Transparent Breeding Practices, but everybody called them "the Eggers." Consortiums educate their own young communally—they didn't have defined family groups in the fashion of, say, the Dryth or Lhassa. If you were born into a Consortium, you were raised to value the things the Consortium did—efficient transportation infrastructure, plentiful power sources, good noodles, or whatever. Thing is, of course, not all the little snails wanted to stay doing things the way their Consortium did them. When they earned their shells (which meant "ditched the inferior calcium shells they grew naturally for synthetic replacements"), they

could just…leave. Just push themselves along on their carpet of body slime to some other Consortium and just, like, join.

I had spent too much time among the Dryth, with their rigid social hierarchies, their autocratic House structures, and their exclusive clubs to find this arrangement normal. It seemed completely chaotic, and the fact that it wasn't was the source of so much of my frustration with this stupid planet. Just when I thought I'd figured out how the larger world worked, it dumped some water on my circuits. None of this *should* work, but it did.

All Eggers were Thraad of the type that wandered off from their original Consortium to join. This made them true believers, not like some Thraad, who just sort of went through the motions of being a Beeper or a Solar because it was too much effort to leave. This meant my conversation with the administrator of the Eggers was likely going to be intense. I hoped so.

I wanted to make an impression. I wanted this snail to think about our conversation for cycles to come.

My previous postal journeys to the hatchery were sent to the facility as a whole, not to any particular individual. That put me in the communal mail room and its convenient sealed secure chamber. This time, though, as a package sent to the administrator specifically, I went through a different system. Security was pretty much the same—a basic scan, and me being labeled as "unknown biologicals." I heard one Thraad grunt a question to a Lhassa security guard: "Who keeps sending us this junk?"

I waited until I was placed somewhere that wasn't moving and until I couldn't hear anybody around. Then I slipped a pseudopod out the corner of my little box and took a peek. I was in a domed chamber with a notably curved floor—the severity of the curve indicated I was closer to the axis of the centrifuge that gave this place its artificially high gravity. The floor was slick with a greasy sheen that indicated a lot of Thraad "foot" traffic. There were low tables at comfortable chin-tentacle height and shelves loaded with spherical data repositories. An office, basically. Or a small library. I was alone.

I opened my own box from the inside and oozed out. Now, what form to take? I was terrible at simulating Thraad—they were too bulky and I couldn't actually manage to ooze the same kind of motile slime they used to get around without dehydrating myself. It would have to be a Dryth or a Lhassa. Who would the administrator *have* to talk to? What conversation couldn't they pass up?

I decided; I made myself into Ada—the assassin responsible for all those fried eggs. She was tall for a Dryth, which made it fairly punishing in the heavy *g* of the hatchery, but I was well rested after my trip in the box, and Dryth facial composition— big eyes, smooth, thick skin, nostrils, and a flat mouth—were always pretty easy. I may have skimped on the eyelashes, but Ada's never were much to pay attention to, anyway. She was pretty sensitive about it, actually. Used a lot of cosmetics.

I "sat" cross-legged on the floor of the room by one of the tables and waited patiently for my meeting to begin.

The administrator was big for a Thraad, which meant it was old. It was wearing a shell of creamy white with pockets built in for various tools of a medical nature. Its four chin-tentacles drooped, but its two eyestalks were active, darting here and there. When it spotted me, they stopped darting and fixed their gaze. It stopped at the threshold of the room, door still open.

I gestured to the fake multipistol I'd formed at my side. "Come in. I've come to talk, not shoot, but I'm flexible if the need arises."

The administrator didn't call my bluff. It slid into the room and closed the door behind it. "What do you want?" Its voice was squeaky rather than guttural—this was a female.

I gestured with my hand to the spot across the table from me. The Thraad moved to the spot slowly, her eyes never leaving my face. Her chin-tentacles were stretched out straight and quivering—she was terrified.

"How are your fertility numbers doing, Administrator?" I tried to adjust my facial expression into something nonthreatening, but I don't think it worked. That's the problem with faking a face—it's all puppetry, and I wasn't perfect at it. Not in situations like this. I probably looked very cold, very still—Ada called it my "sociopath" look.

The administrator twiddled her tentacles. "I don't understand—is there some kind of problem? I've been doing like you ask! I've been sending you the numbers! The Consortiums all think it's some kind of radiation leak, like I promised! No one knows!"

My expression didn't change—no indication of surprise—but inside I felt suddenly alight. I chose my words carefully, all in a modulated imitation of Ada's voice. "*Who* doesn't know? Be specific—I want to be sure my instructions are being followed."

She told me.

She told me everything.

My next meet with Ada was on a boat. I had never been on a boat. I did not like it—nowhere to escape to, nowhere to hide.

I brought several knives to compensate.

This specific boat was a roving crustacean restaurant—the bottom decks had all the nets and booms and machinery and such to haul Gorsurai's aquatic bounty from the depths and then clean, de-shell, and prepare them. The top decks were open to the salt breeze, beneath a cheery orange canopy. There were long tables intended for Thraad to eat off of and bipeds to sit on.

Ada was late. I sat on the bench in the form of a Lhassa mare, slurping shellfish soup from a deep bowl but watching everywhere.

I saw her coming—being run out on a hovercraft, standing atop the dome with her arms folded behind her back. There was something about her posture. She knew. She knew *I* knew.

She came up to my deck and sat at the other end of the bench, not recognizing me, of course. She was looking left and right, studying features and proportions and body language. Trying to find me out.

I didn't look at her when I spoke. "You were paying the administrator six thousand trade credits for each tip. You paid me, the one *doing the work*, a lousy five hundred. You are paying the black market who knows what for those restricted genetic mods."

Ada put up a hand in surrender. "Faceless, listen—"

"Then there are the meals. I asked to see a menu at that last place—those gardo noodles cost a cool two-fifty trade credits. So, who is paying *you*, Ada? That's what I want to know—who am I working for?"

Back on shore, an apartment tower buckled and collapsed in a cloud of purple dust, surrounded by a phalanx of Beeper demolition drones. People on deck rushed to the rails to watch. Some people screamed—it was their apartment. Their stuff. Their lives, being torn down to relieve traffic pressure on some downtown avenue.

Ada stood up, her lips pressed into a grim line. "What did you do, Faceless?"

"Nothing. I did nothing at all."

"You didn't do the job!" she shouted, facing me. "Faceless, do you know what you've done?"

"Given the Beepers hegemony, from the looks of things." Over the rail, another building was coming down. More people

screaming. I ignored them—not my problem. "I didn't realize they could borrow influence according to their birthrate. Administrator Phraxlythantri was surprised I didn't know." I simulated the hatchery administrator's voice: *"Tomorrow's Thraad are today's power!"*

"Look what you've done!" Ada gestured to the rising dust clouds coming off the waterfront. Emergency drones were circling over the demolition zones, their lights flashing—not everyone had gotten out in time, it seemed. "A careful balance is essential, Faceless!"

"Important to who, Ada? Important *why?*" I looked at her then, rotating my head in a way that demonstrated there were no bones in my long Lhassa neck. "Explain it to me. Like I am a child."

Ada glanced at the crowds around us, pushing and jostling. Thraad eyestalks, extending upward to see over the shoulders of the taller Lhassa and Dryth. "Do we need to do this here?"

A knife appeared in my hand, sliding out of a vacuole in my simulated arm. It happened fast enough to make even Ada flinch. "We do it here. We do it now. Or there is no more *we.*"

Ada took a steadying breath. "You don't want to kill me, Faceless. You'd be lost without me."

I stood up. "Been lost before; did just fine. Talk."

Ada gave the crowd another glance and then walked away from that side of the boat. I followed her to the opposite rail, where we were alone. She kept her distance, and I noted how she loosened her multipistol in her holster. If I was going to strike, I would have to make it quick—she was a fast draw.

"The Beepers are going to tear down fifteen percent of the buildings downtown, Faceless. People are going to die because of this little stunt. *Innocent* people."

"Spare me." I pointed at the chaos growing on the shore. "*This* is the first time something has happened on this stupid planet that makes sense to me. You're never going to make me upset that their weird little peaceful society is about to fall apart. I'm *relieved*, Ada."

Behind us, another thunderous crash as another building came down. The dust clouds were reaching us now. I could taste the concrete dust and the synthetic powders; I could smell plastic burning.

Ada watched, her nostrils tight and small. She was judging what to say, how to act. She looked at me as something dangerous that she didn't have control over—it was true, she didn't. She should have remembered that the entire time. "There's no profit in this for us, Faceless. This will hurt our reputation."

"Who are we working for, Ada?"

She closed her eyes for a moment—surrender. "A Lhassa cartel is moving in once Peace is over. They are paying me—paying *us*—to prepare the ground. They've got enough numbers that the Thraad won't put up a fight, so long as no larger coalitions form out of the current Consortiums." Ada gestured to the city across the water. "It was supposed to be a peaceful transition of power, Faceless. Minimal disruptions. Thraad Consortiums are never permanently stable—they inevitably break down into chaos, and all the things they build during their times of prosperity have a tendency to be destroyed. This would have avoided all that—the Thraad Consortiums would keep doing their thing, but the Lhassa cartel would call the shots. You've messed that up now. The War period will feature an *actual* war. Way to go."

The plan made a kind of sense, but there was something about it that I hated that I couldn't quite clarify. Instead, I asked the obvious. "And how much were you being *paid* by these Lhassa?"

"So, this is about the money? Was I shortchanging you? Yes! But how much money do you even *need*, Faceless? What do you even buy? You live in a slagging alley!"

I held still. Ada must have read something in that gesture. "Yeah, I've followed you too."

I felt like an idiot, like a *tool*—a common implement, a *thing* used by Ada to get what she wanted. I had it now—understood what I hated about this planet, about this job, about all of it. I growled at her in a voice that didn't resemble any she'd heard before—it was my anger, formed into words. "Who are *you*, biped, to tell me what *I need?*"

A trio of rescue drones squealed by overhead, their lights flashing, injured people in their suspension pods only silhouettes through the viscous medi-nanite goo.

"Where would you be without me, Faceless?" Ada asked, taking a step away from me, hand hovering over the butt of her gun. "Don't be stupid—you *need* me. Everything you have, I gave to you. Without me, you'd still be in that garden, doing nothing with yourself, *forever.*"

And there it was. Not partners, then—never had been. No trust. No equity. Just another of the so-called Great Races treating a Tohrroid like a shit-eating blob. Same thing with the poor Thraad—too stupid to manage their own affairs, they needed somebody like Ada or a Lhassa cartel keeping them from their baser natures, from their worst selves. *That* was what I hated about this place, about this whole society. A colony full of people thinking they knew what was best for everyone else, and me, right there in the middle, doing their dirty work.

The worst part about it was that she wasn't wrong.

Ada's hand was still resting on her multipistol. "Are we fighting...or what?"

I could kill her now—she knew it, I knew it—but she'd put a few clouds of fléchettes through me before it happened. Didn't know if I'd live, but I knew I wasn't ready to die.

I walked away, back to the opposite rail, where everyone watched with silent horror as the focused destruction of the

Beepers unfolded. Ada followed me, still at a distance, still watching, knowing full well that I was watching her, no matter where my "face" was pointed.

The waterfront was a cloud of dust—a fog of sudden destruction, the lights of rescue drones and demolition machines flashing orange and blue in bright patterns.

"Look at what you've done," Ada said. I couldn't place her tone—somewhere between horror and awe.

At that moment I felt large. Felt *powerful* in a way I never had frying Thraad eggs in a nursery. "Remember what I'm capable of, Ada. If you're very lucky, I might just take you with me."

Ada licked her lips. "So, we're still friends, is that it?"

"We weren't *friends* before—I was your pet. Now? Now we're stuck with each other."

"Yeah, I guess so," Ada said. The fight was out of her—she was plotting, figuring out her next move. Something I probably couldn't fathom or see coming. She had a serpent by the tail and dared not let go. Me? Same thing—I was more dangerous in a fight, always would be, but didn't have the contacts or the resources or the *knowledge* to go it alone. Ironically, we were sort of like a pair of Thraad Consortiums now: the two of us, balanced against each other by mutually assured destruction.

I gotta say, it seemed exciting.

Brood Parasitism

I'd been wearing the hostile environment suit for less than an hour and I already hated it more than anything. It tasted terrible—all sweat and grime and bits of urine and feces and protein substrate all mixed together in one noxious cocktail. I suppose, had I been a Lhassa like the original owner of this thing, it might not have bothered me as much since my taste receptors would all be conveniently tucked inside a mouth cavity. My outer membranes are *covered* in taste/smell receptors, and so wearing a suit like this was sort of like licking every square inch of the previous owner. And, sure, I'd done similar things in my past—digesting whole bipeds, I mean—but this time there was something about the enclosed nature of the suit that made it worse.

Or maybe my time in civilization had made me pickier about my meals.

The taste wasn't my only complaint, though. The other problem was that I felt *blind*. The only place I could see was through the transparent visor. For a biped, this offered a pretty good field of view, I guess. For me, it felt like I was seeing the world through the slats of a narrow air vent.

I reminded myself not to whine so much. It had been my idea to ooze inside the suit in the first place. I knew perfectly well the thing wasn't designed for a Tohrroid to wear. This was my fault. Well, sort of.

All around me, the hollowed-out city crumbled under the silent weight of a few million tons of nanite-infused dust. I'd never seen snow, but I'd heard the comparison made between the aftereffects of nano-weaponry and the morning after a blizzard. Everything was muted, quiet, and covered in a thick layer of feathery gray-blue fluff, light as clouds. A soft breeze whispered down the street, picking up the dust and twirling it through the air, only for it to drift back to the ground in spinning little flakes. You couldn't see the sky. You couldn't hear your footsteps. There was just the dust and the dead city and the headlamps of my companion, just slightly ahead of me.

My companion's name was Ormas—a tall Lhassa mare with a surveyor in her hand and a hand flamer dangling from her hip. Like all Lhassa, she was tall and lithe, her feet naturally balanced on the balls of her toe-joints, which made their gait difficult to match—it had taken me years to get it right.

"You all right, Parditt?" Ormas asked over the microbead. It was disorienting, hearing her voice echo through the sides of the helmet rather than hitting me straight on, as it would if I weren't in this suffocating suit.

"Yeah," I said, pulling the suit into a semi-upright posture. "I'm fine."

My name is not Parditt. This was just Parditt's suit. Parditt was a bloody lump of dead flesh in a warehouse two blocks back, getting slowly disintegrated by whatever nanites were still active. Ormas had no idea, though—I had changed the shape, texture, and color of that part of my outer membranes to match that of Parditt's now nonexistent visage, and I had his vocal patterns down to near perfection, seeing as he wouldn't shut up just before I killed him. My mastery of the Lhassa dialect they used wasn't complete, but I had the accent down. I was trying not to do too much talking, though.

Ormas looked me over. "Well, keep up. Zand wants us back at camp before sundown."

I turned my helmet right and left. Sundown? I had a hard time believing it was still daylight.

Ormas gave me a companionable nod and turned back to her work. I shuffled along behind her. I was exhausted—keeping a bipedal shape took a lot of my energy to maintain, especially when I basically had to balance on such a small portion of myself. I was leaning a lot on the exoskeletal functions of the environment suit to keep me upright. This meant when I moved, I looked like I was stumbling, and when I held still, I swayed. Perfect for somebody who was supposed to be injured, as I was.

We crossed a street clogged with groundcar traffic, the vehicles now just inert humps of dust in the road, as though abandoned. A few had crashed into each other or light poles or the walls of nearby residential towers, reminding me of just how quickly the nanites had done their work. I remembered the sound, mostly—the otherworldly keening of the snail-like Thraad as they all died more or less simultaneously. But not too quickly, no. It took a minute or two for the nanites to eat their way to some kind of vital organ. The whole thing had taken five minutes, maybe ten, every second of which was pure, agonizing terror for the victims. Their friends, their families dissolving in front of their eyestalks even as they themselves melted away. I'd seen a lot of terrible things in my life, but nothing else had ever come remotely close. It had been a week and I still was turning it over in my mind. What did it mean to me, that the Thraad who had once populated this city no longer existed? Only their shells remained, looking like discarded helmets scattered all over the place—each one a life cut short in a few moments of spectacular violence. There was a time, not too long before, when I told myself that it wouldn't have mattered to me, seeing something like that. Now? Now I had no words to explain how it made me feel.

Ormas tripped over something—some piece of groundcar debris, half-hidden by the dust. She cursed. "We're gonna have to clear a lot of these machines out manually. The structural nanites aren't cutting it. I hope Father's budgeted for that."

I grunted agreement, mostly because I didn't want to express an opinion. I believed her about the structural nanites—those were dusted through the atmosphere around the same time as the weaponized ones designed to eat the Thraad, except they were tailored to eat things like concrete and structural polymers and glass and stuff. They worked slower, and the basic idea I guess was to make demolition easier once the Lhassa cartel moved in. Because of them, the city we were moving through looked like it had been crumbling for several decades instead of just a matter of days. Ormas and Zand had been complaining about their progress ever since I met them—the things were especially slow at eating the synthetic shells of all the people they'd murdered. I think they were discomfited by the vivid reminder of their atrocities, but then again, maybe I was giving them too much credit.

Of course, I didn't give even the most infinitesimal shit over "our father's" finances. You go and murder an entire city in an afternoon, I couldn't see complaining too much about cleaning up the mess. If "Father" didn't want this kind of hassle, maybe he should have left the Thraad alone.

Zand was waiting for us at the next intersection, his surveyor out and scanning the crumbling buildings all around. He was a male—a bull—and his helmet had a bulge just above the forehead to accommodate his antlers. Parditt's helmet was much the same, but at that exact moment, I wasn't bothering with parts of the body the Lhassa couldn't see.

I remembered this street corner pretty well. There had been a food cart…where—there! I spotted it, just a corner protruding from a drift of dust, the metal corroded and rusty. I'd eaten there often, the food cheap and a bit stale but flavorful. The vendor had been a cheery old Thraad, his shell draped with a harness for all kinds of sauces and seasonings that his chin-tentacles would whip out and toss into the wok as he fried up your fish and then plopped it on a bed of dry vegetables. I was a regular, coming in the form of two or three different bipeds— sometimes a Dryth, sometimes a Lhassa. He recognized all my forms, knew their order, and would have it ready for me by the time I got to the front of the line. He wasn't a friend—I didn't really have those—but he was the closest thing I could think of in this city that fit the bill.

He had probably died right there. His shell, probably buried in the dust, was all that was left of him.

Zand looked up from his surveyor and addressed us. "Finally caught up, eh? Parditt, you look terrible."

"Found him in one of the warehouses. He's injured." Ormas said. "He says a piece of debris fell on him."

"A piece of debris *did* fall on me," I snapped at them both.

Zand and Ormas fell silent. I remembered Lhassa family protocol. Zand was what was called an "uncle"—a sibling of my "father," who was my biological sire. He was afforded a degree of respect and couldn't be directly addressed by someone as young as Parditt had been. "Sorry," I said. "It's been a long day." I sat down on the curb, leaning back against a crumbling light pole.

Zand ignored me. "Your little brother has a manners problem, niece."

Ormas shrugged. "He's still upset about Father's decision to dust the snails, that's all."

"Well." Zand said the word in a final kind of way that I thought indicated a lot of unpleasant things he might have said but refrained from actually voicing, again for some kind of elaborate etiquette-based reasons. I realized I hadn't fully anticipated how difficult it would be, integrating myself into an extended family group. I'd never done anything like this before.

"This neighborhood has some excellent topography," Zand said finally. "I can see why the Thraad chose it to build it up. We'll be able to put a spaceport here and a large marketplace without even having to level the ground or reinforce anything. I'm picturing the control tower *there.*" Zand pointed into the dusty gloom with a surveying laser, sending a line of red light across the square to an apartment building where maybe about three thousand Thraad had lived no more than six days before. "And right where we're standing could be a food commissary and a shopping center."

This had *been* a food commissary and a shopping center. Right here, six days ago. They'd gone and killed everyone and ruined the city just to build the same thing all over again.

I felt cold. Not like I was actually hypothermic—the suit was keeping me well insulated—but that kind of coldness I felt when I was plotting someone's death.

I was going to kill these fucking Lhassa.

I just needed to wait for my chance.

It was eight days earlier that I'd accepted the last job I'd do for the Thraad of Gorsurai City.

The Peace was ending—a single thirty-hour standard day left before the cycle ticked over into War. You couldn't get away from it. A clock was counting down in every shop window, in blazing orange holograms above every intersection: War was coming.

I'd known about the nature of the Cycles, but this was the first time I could remember actually experiencing them in any way that mattered. The Union of Stars—a sort of loose interstellar confederation of shared economic and cultural norms—had decreed that galactic time would be universal and segmented into three sections: four sidereal years of War followed by four of Recovery and then four of Peace. This was done to prevent the endless ravages of interstellar conquest. Or so I'd been told. How they managed to maintain unified time across the vast reaches of interstellar space was complex and mysterious to me—something to do with a pulsar and a lot of math. The way it played out didn't seem to work the way it was intended, either—the conquerors just bided their time for War to come or, more commonly, acted in secret.

Because a would-be interstellar despot only had four years to conquer something as vast as a planet, campaigns had to be decisive, hence the nano-weapons. As an assassin, I was part of that calculus too. Assassinations didn't count as "warfare" and so weren't proscribed by the tenets of the Union's so-called "Holy Law." In my professional career to date, I'd worked for a variety of parties all trying to unbalance the other, all trying to set the ground for the next period of War. There was money in that kind of work, assuming you had the stomach for it. Me? I was mostly stomach. I was born for it.

With War rolling around, my partner, Ada—a Dryth who'd brought me into this profession, taught me the ropes—was advocating for evacuation. She was pinging my Q-link every few hours with the itinerary of starships bound for safer ports. Everyone knew the Zhonto Cartel—the Lhassas—were going to attack. Their fleet was in low orbit already, their firing solutions probably already locked in. It didn't seem real to me, though. My food cart was still open. Thraad were going about their daily business. The traffic bustled.

"Why don't we ride it out?" I sent to her. *"How bad could it be?"*

Her reply was curt: *"You don't know what you're talking about."*

"Just one more job," I said. *"A big one. Then we'll go."*

Ada had set up the meet. She had a good reputation in Gorsurai; nobody knew anything about me at all. I went disguised as her assistant—a skinny, undernourished adolescent Dryth with a bloated oaglan sac on the back of my neck. The oaglan was a fatty organ that stored water, an evolutionary holdover from the Dryth evolving on an arid, almost-waterless homeworld. Most Dryth who could afford it had it removed; that fact that my disguise seemed to have one marked me as wretched and poor, and therefore the kind of person to be ignored. I liked this form and used it often—nobody expected a fat-necked Dryth kid to be dangerous.

As for Ada, she cut a figure that drew the eye. Her oaglan had been surgically removed in childhood, leaving her neck with nothing but smooth, hard muscle. She was tall, broad-shouldered, her skin pigment in an asymmetrical blue and white check pattern, like a kind of urban camouflage. She wore a cloak of zagan-silk, a smart "fabric" that was actually an electromagnetic field chaining drops of mercury together rather than any kind of textile. The mercury flowed and shimmered in the sunlight reflected from the broad, lavender face of the gas giant around which Gorsurai orbited. She was conspicuously armed—a multipistol on each hip, both elaborate pieces carved from the wood of some tree that grew on some distant planet. This was traditional in a meeting with an assassin—the prospective employers wanted to know if you had the means to fulfill the contract.

The employers in question were an array of snail-like Thraad representing the six least powerful Consortiums on the planet. Their shells were lacquered in bright colors, and the environment—a boardroom high up in one of Gorsurai's taller towers—implied wealth, but they weren't fooling either of us. These were desperate people. Anybody with the means had evacuated the city already.

I was standing just behind Ada, my simulated hands clasped behind my simulated back, and paid particular attention to Thraad body language. Their eyestalks were jumpy, bouncing around from the two of us to their companions. Their chin-tentacles darted in and out of their fleshy faces, snatching refreshments from the watery trough that ran around the rim of the table.

"Naythis Zhonto?" Ada repeated the name back to them. "The patriarch of the Zhonto Cartel?"

"He's no better than a pirate," one of the Thraad said. "Patriarch? It's a social aberration among the Lhassa—they're matriarchal."

"Regardless of his social status or sex, he's a Lhassa bull with a big warfleet and a stockpile of Dryth nano-weaponry at his disposal. Not an easy mark." I could tell by Ada's posture that she wasn't really considering their offer. She was just getting them to talk, getting them to demonstrate to me how stupid this job was. Even if we killed Naythis before the War period started, nothing was going to stop the attack by his cartel now. He had a half dozen daughters who would succeed him, not to mention a number of well-positioned mates who would slide into the role in an emergency.

"We'll pay a hundred thousand," the Thraad countered.

Ada stiffened. That was a big number. Evacuation contracts must have gotten very pricey if that much money couldn't buy these snails a ticket off this doomed rock.

"You understand that, even if I take this job, I can't guarantee I'll kill him before he attacks." Ada leaned forward, tapping the table carefully with one finger. "His cartel will still take over. You will still die."

One of the Thraad knew Dryth body language well enough to nod slowly. "We know, assassin. This is not salvation we seek. It is malgra."

Malgra—Thraad revenge. Slow, inexorable doom. Thraad folk tales were full of seemingly meek doctors and scientists who were humiliated and slaughtered by raging beasts or wandering barbarians, only for the barbarians to discover lesions they could not cure or tumors that would not stop growing, dooming the villains to a slow, agonizing death. A parting gift from those they had wronged.

The Thraad wanted this planet to be a poison pill. They wanted the poison to be Ada.

She stood up from the low table and arranged her glittering cloak. "I am sorry, friends, but I am not malgra. Not even for five times that much. I won't work that way."

The Thraad deflated, almost literally. Their heads retreated into their shells, their tentacles and eyestalks retracted. They were considering their deaths, now denied their last act of defiance.

I stepped up to the table. "I will."

Their eyestalks emerged slowly, all of them fixed on my simulated face.

"But you pay in advance," I said.

They agreed.

Ada hadn't been happy about it. If I accepted the money, that meant I had to attempt to complete the contract—professional ethics. It meant we were stuck in this system for the time being. She confronted me later. "Faceless, even assuming you can do it, there's no way to escape. It's a suicide mission."

This was the last time I'd talked to her, via Q-link. She was up in orbit, entertaining bids from some independent contractors with the desire to bump off competition but not enough guns to declare open war on them.

"I can do it. Don't underestimate me," I'd said. I was sitting in an alley, in something approaching my natural form—a dull, gray-ish lump of fleshy tissue. I was eating fried fish on skewers, dissolving them—skewers and all—in a vacuole inside my body. I felt good.

"It's a *public* job, Faceless. Naythis will know you're coming."

She was right about that part. Most assassination jobs were public—had to be, really. If an organization hired an assassin, they announced that they'd done so. They even had to announce who they were planning to have killed. Only the assassin's name was kept out of it. This was something that was part of the tradition—part of the code we assassins lived by. It kept us from being the target of revenge, you see. It wasn't *us* who killed you; it was our employers. We were just tools. Weapons, like any other. No remorse, but no rancor, either.

That was how I felt, anyway, *before* I watched the city I'd lived in for years scream and die in five minutes of pure terror.

Now?

Let's just say there was some rancor involved.

The Zhonto Cartel's base camp was a large floating platform in the harbor, protected behind a particle field that incinerated the dust particles and nanites that intersected with it, creating a dome of sparkling lights over a kilometer in diameter. A fat, rectangular decontamination chamber penetrated the edge of the field—the only entrance to the base camp, assuming you didn't want the particle field eating you alive. The three of us trundled up the metal gangway from the beach to the chamber door, Zand in the lead and me staggering along in the rear. I was nearly spent. It had been hours; the suit was suffocating me, pumping air to only one end of my body, and by now, I was feeling it all over. My membranes burned with exertion and hypoxia. I looked forward to Parditt's private quarters, where I could lock the door, sink into a blob in one corner, and rest for a while as I planned my next move.

The decon chamber's job was to isolate and destroy any stray nanites that were hitching a ride on our bodies. I didn't know *that* much about nano-weapons, but what I did know is that they could be tailored to attack specific genetic markers, making them a vastly superior mass-deployed weapons system when compared to chemical or nuclear explosives—which made a mess—and much easier to control than chemical or biological agents, which were less predictable. Nanites had a built-in lifespan—they would consume resources (in the case of living targets, their flesh and blood), reproduce for a certain number of cycles, and then go inactive. The more your genetics matched their targeting, the faster the process went. What killed a Thraad in seconds might kill a Lhassa in a couple hours. My physiology was so profoundly alien that they didn't do much to me at all.

When I had been waiting to spring my ambush, back in the ruins of the city, I could taste them constantly in the air—an acrid, metallic tang, sort of like tainted blood. I had a lot of them in my system—they certainly weren't *good* for me, but I wasn't in any immediate danger. Having them inside me was like getting a sunburn. The decon didn't do very much to get rid of them, either, since it was a radiation bath designed to incapacitate the nanites on the suits and clothing while not penetrating the body. All my nanites were already *inside* my body, trying but failing to find something worth eating among my weird fluids and fleshy membranes.

This all meant I was walking into their base camp with a little population of microscopic killer robots, gradually concentrating in little vacuoles between my outer and inner membranes— the place in my body where I dumped stuff I either couldn't or didn't want to digest. Oil and water, me and those nanites.

We stripped off our hostile environment suits. I watched the other Lhassa's movements carefully, making sure to mimic the ways their arms and spines worked to shimmy the things off. I stretched and compressed my exhausted membranes to mirror Parditt's utility coveralls, complete with the Zhonto seal and mission patches up and down one arm. I also added the stumpy little antlers protruding out of my forehead. The hardest part was mimicking the injury I'd claimed. You could break a biped's bones and not necessarily see that they were broken, so this was what I was going for—a sort of *swelling* in my chest and shoulder, some discoloration. I wasn't sure if I'd gotten it right until Ormas flinched at the sight of me. "Ugh! What did you *do* to yourself, Pard? You look *awful*."

Zand looked over and frowned. "You certain it was just falling debris? It almost looks like you have an infection." He came close, his hand out. He intended to grab my chin, turn my head—something.

If he touched me, the game would be up—I might *look* like a Lhassa, but I was too tired to make myself *feel* like one. I shrank away from him. "Leave me alone! I'll be fine!"

Zand stopped. "You are to go to the infirmary for an examination, Parditt. That's an order, now."

"Yes, Uncle," I said.

Zand cocked his head. "What, no back-talk? No grumbling? You *must* be injured."

I resisted the urge to make a rude gesture, but I did make a face that would convey as "irritated" to Zand. I got out of the decon chamber as soon as I could, leaving Ormas and Zand behind to talk business.

The Zhonto platform was almost kilometer on a side, with the central area dominated by a large landing pad sufficient to support a small transorbital freighter. The decon chamber and command center and comms array were all in the same complex at one end, and everything else was modular habitat blocks and cargo containers that had been stacked up all around the fringes of the landing pad. One of those had to be Parditt's quarters, but I had been counting on a sign or a map or some kind of…I don't know, a *concierge*, I guess, to point the way. No such luck—the Zhontos had splurged on nano-weapons but had cut costs when it came to amenities for their personnel. Nevertheless, I needed somewhere to lie down and rest before I collapsed into a puddle somewhere in public and my masquerade would be over.

The deck of the platform was frigid, the metal deck plating burning my membranes with how cold it was. I shivered involuntarily—the kind of shiver that would make it clear I was not a biped but instead a very clever pile of gelatinous goo.

There were Lhassa all over the place. They seemed…cheery. Congenial. They smiled and waved to me and called me by Parditt's name. I realized a lot of these people were related to Parditt—cousins and second cousins and whatever else. Genocide was apparently a family business. They were just so *excited* about this new world they'd stolen. In a matter of a year or two, all memory of the Gorsurai City I remembered would be gone, regardless of whether my mission here succeeded or failed. I'm adaptable; I've come to accept that life is change. This change, though, struck me as unwarranted. *Pernicious*, even.

And here the culprits were, asking me to come by their quarters for a game of cards later. Like it was nothing. Like the dust being incinerated by their particle field wasn't the remains of countless living beings who would have *gladly* played cards with Lhassa if it meant not being eaten alive by microscopic death robots.

I didn't know any of the people who greeted me, but I smiled and tossed my long Lhassa neck and did my best not to look like an imposter. It worked well enough in this casual setting, but as soon as I had to have a conversation with someone, I knew I'd be found out.

I looked for somewhere warm where I could hide out, recover.

I found a commissary—a long, rectangular cargo container with a long table along one side, lined with stools. Above, a drone-operated extruder spat fleshy-looking paste into bowls for a dozen or so Lhassa workers to shovel down between whatever busywork the cartel had them doing. I dumped myself onto the closest stool and leaned over the table, letting my body rest without totally abandoning my disguise. I just looked tired.

The worker next to me—wearing a shuttle pilot's uniform—swiveled on his stool to look at me. "Say, friend—you okay?"

I didn't answer except to grunt in the affirmative, figuring that would be enough to get him to leave me alone. It wasn't.

"Hey, you're Parditt Zhonto, aren't you? Suns and stars, you look terrible!"

"No, I'm fine," I said, not moving. That was probably my mistake.

"C'mon, let me get you to the infirmary. You maybe swallowed some nanites or something." He reached out, took my "arm," which at that moment wasn't distinctly detached from the rest of my body and was too exhausted to come off as being firm and muscular and cored by a calcium-based endoskeleton. My fake bicep jiggled when he touched me, like a kind of dense gelatin. He pulled his hand back, horrified.

I lurched out of the commissary before he could ask any more questions. I heard him call out to me, but I kept going. The cold, sunless air of the deck stung all over. This wasn't going to work—there were Lhassa everywhere, staring at me as I staggered around. Why did the damned things have to reproduce so often? Did they really *need* two hundred people to man this stupid metal plate they had floating in the ocean?

There was nowhere out of sight—the place was too crowded.

I elected to collapse on the ground, still in Parditt's shape. Let them think there was something deeply wrong with me. If they thought I was really sick, maybe they wouldn't touch me. Maybe they'd even leave me alone long enough for me to rest and maybe slip away.

Maybe, maybe, maybe—the word meant death and failure to an assassin. Rely on dumb luck in this business, and you wound up dead. That was what Ada always said, anyway.

I was beginning to see what she meant.

This mission had been a mistake.

My plan, such as it was, had been simple. I always preferred plans with as few moving parts as possible, even if that meant they were high-risk. Fewer variables meant less that could go wrong, and if I have to pick between dire peril that I knew about and modest peril that took me by surprise, I will pick the first one every time.

Getting aboard Naythis Zhonto's flagship was basically impossible and, even assuming I could do that, getting into his *presence* would be even harder. I'd never been aboard a Lhassa ship, but the way it was explained to me is this: people *everywhere*, all the time. Lhassa reproduced very, very rapidly—chances are if you saw a Lhassa mare, she was pregnant or carrying young in her marsupium. Every Lhassa was part of a vast and complex network of family obligations. The world, to them, was nothing but cousins as far as the eye could see. They all *knew* each other.

This was honestly horrifying to me. I hadn't chosen the name "Faceless" because I enjoyed personal connections with others. Whereas in other places I had used my mimicry to infiltrate all kinds of organizations, it was mostly based on the idea that there was always somebody around that *nobody knew*— an anonymous courier, a low-level employee on their first day, a contractor come in for a one-time job. When everybody in an organization was *related* to everyone else, this became an untenable plan. I could fool you into thinking I was somebody you never knew, but fooling you into thinking I was your sister? Fat chance.

So, I decided that sneaking onto the flagship was a no-go. But what if I could bring Naythis *to me?*

I knew, from intelligence Ada had bought from one of her contacts, that a couple of Naythis's *children*—his direct genetic descendants—would likely head up the scouting mission after "deployment" (or, in another way of putting it, the "screaming deaths of a hundred thousand people"). My plan was to ride out the nanites, ambush a scouting team, go back to their base camp, replace one of the children, and then find a way to call Daddy to the surface for a face-to-face meeting. Then, when we were in private, execute the contract, mimic Naythis, and commandeer some kind of trip off the planet's surface to a rendezvous point I'd set up with Ada ahead of time. It was about as straightforward as I could get it.

I've already described the nanite attack; I don't feel like doing it again. Understand that it isn't like the Thraad on Gorsurai were my *friends*—they regarded my species with the same disgust and disdain as everybody else—but, like all good scavengers, I had a healthy dislike of pointless *waste*. Killing everyone was unnecessary. It was, I guess, *cruel*, though that was a weird word for me to use, given how many people I've suffocated to death over the years. Anyway, it started with a sudden, hard rain as the nanite deployment in the upper atmosphere screwed with the clouds, and it ended in the gutters being choked with slimy gore. If I *were* a social being—something with what qualified as a "normal" amount of empathy for my fellow living creatures—seeing that go down probably would have scarred me psychologically. I might have gone insane.

Fortunately, I'm more cold-blooded than that. I don't even *have* blood in a conventional sense. I was just…shocked, is all. Surprised.

When it was finally over, I found a likely spot to hide out and I waited as things dried out and the dust started flying. All assassinations involve a lot of waiting, and I am good at it. I collected a few crude weapons—things the structural nanites wouldn't easily compromise, like a couple heavy rocks to be pushed off ledges—and ate my fair share of Thraad effluence before the nanites could. I was functionally invisible in anything other than infrared scanning, and I kept a low profile when the Lhassa scout drones cruised through on their initial survey, searching for movement or signs of life. They weren't scanning for me, anyway—I have no doubt a fair number of my cousins survived in the sewer systems, and this raised no warning flags either. Tohrroids were waste-disposal organisms. We weren't threats; we were part of the sanitation infrastructure.

I waited some more.

After six days, Parditt's inspection patrol happened along. I waited until one of them (Parditt) was apart from the others, investigating the rubble, and I called out in a Lhassa voice: "Help! Help me!"

Parditt, dutiful pup that he was, came running. I had taken the form of an injured Lhassa mare, pretending to be trapped under the debris. He leapt to my aid, holding my simulated hand, telling me I would be all right. Babbling on and on about how sorry he was. His eyes were big and bright behind his visor, round with concern.

"I didn't want this to happen," he said, tossing rocks aside as he tried to dig me out (I was not actually trapped—it was all a shapeshifter's illusion). "It was my father. All this death, all this violence—I can't believe you survived!"

"The nanites," I said faintly. "I thought...they were meant for the Thraad."

He stopped digging. "Well, yes, but they are probably deep inside you, too. You probably have a lot of internal bleeding. Who are you? What are you doing here?"

"The Thraad," I said, "they were my friends."

He looked terribly sad through his faceplate. "I'm sorry. I'm so sorry."

He seemed like a nice kid. Honestly, he did. "Can...can you...open your visor for a second. I can't...can't understand..."

Parditt Zhonto, dutiful rescuer, popped open his visor and willingly breathed in likely a couple active nanites so I, the apparently dying stranger, could hear him better in my final moments. "It's okay," he said. "Everything will be okay."

There was genuine compassion in his eyes. I wondered what he might have looked like if I had been a dying Thraad or Dryth. Or even a Tohrroid. Maybe he would have stayed just as compassionate—maybe he was one of those mythical "good ones" who actually believed in the sanctity of all sentient life.

I never found out, because a half-second later, I smashed his face in with a rock.

The good news was they threw me on a stretcher rather than carrying me to the infirmary slumped over someone's shoulder or something. The nice flat surface of the stretcher meant I had a lot more ability to look at least *mostly* like a young Lhassa bull. The bad news was that they were taking me to the infirmary, where there was literally *no way* I could convince anybody I wasn't actually a Tohrroid with extreme delusions of grandeur.

Even now, the stretcher was performing some basic diagnostics, throwing up holographic diagrams above my body that indicated, in no uncertain terms, that something was wildly amiss. "I'm not getting any heartbeat!" one of my helpers yelled—the shuttle pilot from the commissary. "His body temperature is way too low!"

The crowd of people rushing me across the platform was joined by Ormas, who I saw elbow her way to the back of the stretcher. Her voice was frantic. "Pard! PARDITT! Can you hear me? What happened to him? Somebody tell me!"

They told her, sort of all at once and not in any cogent order, but she got the idea pretty quick—I looked sick, I'd collapsed, and that something was wrong with my skin. Everybody was assuming nanite infiltration.

"They must have gotten in his blood after the accident," somebody else said. "Injecting with medical nanites now." They pushed a button on the stretcher.

Beneath me, a needle popped out of a little hidden alcove. If I had been a Lhassa, it would have stuck me right in the rump. Since I wasn't, I let the thing inject the medical nanites into a little vacuole inside myself and kept them there; they burned like a hot coal, but that was it.

"They're not working!" Ormas yelled, looking at the hologram of my "body" and its extremely uncooperative biometrics—no pulse, low temperature, no blood pressure to speak of.

If there was a way I could change my own body temperature or convincingly mimic a heartbeat, I didn't know it. I was trying to make little ripples in my body in what I figured might be important places, but all that did was confuse the stretcher's medical scanner. At this rate, they were going to assume I was *dead*.

Hey.

Hey, wait a minute.

Being dead would be easier than being alive. They didn't pump dead bodies full of medical nanites, for one thing. They also didn't expect you to walk around and probably left you alone. They *also* might get certain *important visitors*.

So, I died. I just held still, with only the respiratory action of my outer membranes drawing in oxygen beneath me and out of sight. Since the medical nanites hadn't worked, that seemed to be their only move. I made the color drain from my ersatz face. I made my tongue loll out—the whole thing. I looked very dead. The medical scanner concurred.

Ormas didn't take it well. She screamed at me and slapped my face a few times. She howled up at the sky like an animal. Her howls were joined by a couple of the other Lhassa who had brought me to the infirmary. Shared grief, I guess.

They parked me in an isolation chamber—a cube-shaped room with a cot, a counter beneath which were a bunch of cabinets on wheels, and a door that could be environmentally sealed. It was bitter cold. Ormas didn't want to leave. She kept grabbing at my hand, and a doctor kept preventing her from touching me. "Don't," she whispered in Ormas's ear. "We don't know what killed him. It could get you, too."

You bet it could, lady. Just give me a good nap and a solid hunk of masonry.

And then it was finally quiet and I was finally, *finally* alone.

The room was freezing, so the first thing I did was throw off the sheet they'd covered me in and crawl off the cot to access the environment controls, bumping the temperature up enough so that I wouldn't freeze to death while awaiting my next opportunity. I snagged a laser scalpel from a drawer and slithered back under the sheet. Then I rested.

Outside the room's thin plastic walls, I could hear Ormas—she hadn't left; she was just in the hall outside. She was arguing with somebody about something. She was still howling, too. It grated, her grief. She has lost, what, only *one* of her dozens of brothers and sisters and was despondent, and yet she was involved in the wholesale murder of an entire society and felt *nothing*? It didn't make sense. Not caring that all the Thraad were dead should mean she could keep it together when her brother keeled over—that would be consistent. If she was this sad about one dumb pup croaking, she ought to be even more despondent about the stacks of empty shells littering the streets of her would-be new home. You couldn't have it both ways. It was offensive.

I knew a doctor—probably Zand—would be coming in to examine me before too long. The stretcher might not be smart enough to tell the difference between a dead Lhassa and a living Tohrroid, but the stuff they had in here *would*. The medical nanites were still burning a hole in that vacuole between my inner and outer membranes. All the weaponized nanites I'd breathed in over six days of waiting were concentrated together in another one—the little robots were still active and hungry. I wondered what would happen if I merged the vacuoles and made the medical nanites fight with the killer ones. I didn't risk it.

More waiting. More resting.

I heard a lot of noise outside—the thunder of a shuttle's landing jets, buffeting the roof of the little makeshift infirmary they'd stashed me in. I was pretty sure I knew what it meant. Somebody had told Naythis his son was dead. He was coming down. My plan, such as it was, was showing results.

My attitude soured somewhat when Zand, Naythis, Ormas, and an armed bodyguard filed into the isolation chamber, wearing hostile environment suits. Zand was armed with a double-barreled shell-gun—the kind of thing that could spit plastic fléchettes in a wide arc. The kind of thing that could kill me instantly. He looked angry. Not good.

The bodyguard had a stun baton—fifty thousand volts of electricity per strike. The kind of thing that would scramble my membranes, make me lose my shape. Very, very not good.

They sealed the door behind them.

Naythis was larger than any of them, his body built like something from a xenobiology vid about herd alphas and preferred mates. Even beneath the suit I could make out the corded muscle and recognize the animalistic grace with which he moved. His helmet was a custom job, with extra forehead space for his impressive antlers. He stood, feet apart, chest thrust out, hands on his hips. It was pretty clear he wasn't here to mourn.

"What have you done with my son?" he said through his suit's external speaker. His voice boomed in a kind of artificial way that made me think he'd actually put an echo effect on that speaker. I'd guessed he was vain—this was confirmation.

I kept playing "dead Parditt," just to see if he was bluffing.

The Lhassa patriarch nodded to his bodyguard, who then lunged at me with the stun baton. I didn't have time to react; the voltage coursed through me like liquid fire. Any attempt to keep my disguise was lost as my outer membranes spasmed uncontrollably and I flopped off the cot and onto the floor with a wet thud.

They could have kept on beating me. Zand might have killed me with a single shot from his roomsweeper. Instead, Naythis held them back. He was grinning, pleased with his discovery. I'd hated him in the abstract before this—any shit who would dust a whole city just to rebuild it in his own image deserved contempt—but now my hatred was much more personal. Watching him gloat made me want to lunge, but I hadn't lived this long as a Tohrroid because I was impulsive.

"What *is* it?" Ormas said, her eyes wide behind her faceplate.

"It's a smack!" Zand said, the slur rolling off his tongue easily from frequent use.

"Isn't it fascinating?" Naythis said. "See how it doesn't make any sound when it's hurt? A survival mechanism. The Tohrroid never wishes to reveal its location. The perfect scavenger, the perfect ambush predator."

"Th-thanks," I managed, using not Parditt's voice but my own—the one I'd selected for myself when I first learned to speak. I spoke in Dryth Basic—not their language, but one all of them would know, since that was where they bought all their weapons of mass destruction.

Zand's eyebrow tufts shot up at the words. Ormas squealed in surprise and disgust. "It *talks*?" she asked.

Naythis nodded. "Don't worry, my dear—it's quite helpless now that its little ruse is undone. I'd heard about this one—this assassin with no face, killing its way through Gorsurai. At first, I didn't believe my spies, but, well…seeing is believing."

"*This* is the assassin the snails hired to kill you?" Zand gaped at his brother and at me. "The *insult!* The *indignity!*"

"They were desperate. Grasping at straws. They couldn't afford the famed Deadeye Ada, so they trawled the gutter until they found *this* thing." Naythis shook his head. "Pitiful. Do you see now, smack?" he said to me, speaking extra loud, as though I didn't have better hearing than he did. "Do you see how outmatched you are? Now, *where* is my son?"

Second time he'd asked that. Interesting. "He's hurt but still alive. He wasn't my target."

Zand leveled his gun, finger on the trigger.

I stayed where I was, on the ground in a little blob of grayish flesh. "Kill me and you'll never find your nephew, Zand."

"How do we know he isn't dead already?" Naythis asked.

"You don't," I said. "Truth be told, even *I* don't know. I hit him pretty hard. The more time you waste trying to figure out if I'm lying, though, the more likely it is that he's dead."

He was definitely dead, by the way. I had made sure of it. Good thing I'm an absolutely perfect liar.

"Tell me," Naythis said, "and perhaps you will get to live."

"I'll take you to him," I said. "Let's take your shuttle."

Zand snorted. "We can't possibly trust it to tell the truth. I say we kill it."

Naythis stood up, frowning. "We will not abandon my son."

"So, we send out drones. We look for him our own way!" Zand pointed at me. "It's a killer, Naythis. We shouldn't take it anywhere."

"It almost certainly hid the body so that the drones would miss it," Naythis said.

He was right about that.

"If it dies, it might take us hours to find Parditt!" Ormas chimed in. "Now that we know where it is, it's powerless to hurt us. Father, we have to go! Even if…even if he's gone, my mother would want his body."

Naythis Zhonto, conqueror of planets, looked down at me—the shapeless blob on the infirmary floor—and made an assumption based on his unshakeable belief in his own superiority. "If it betrays us, it will die. It won't commit suicide for some dead snails. Zand—get the shuttle ready. I want to leave as soon as possible."

Back into the wasteland that had been my home, this time seen from the cockpit of a transorbital shuttle. They'd induced me into a clear plastic jar as a kind of holding tank—sealed but with breathing holes, like I was some kind of fun insect for a science class. They had me up in the cockpit so I could give convenient directions. It was hard to get my bearings, though, even with the full weight of the shuttle's advanced sensor technology at my disposal. Even the last few hours had seen the city deteriorate significantly—most of the taller buildings had fallen, very few of the streets were clear or even distinct.

It didn't really matter.

I wasn't taking these shits to Parditt, anyway.

While they were all around me, their helmet visors open and their eyes looking out the transparent canopy of the shuttle, I used the laser scalpel to cut a hole in the side of my little aquarium. Then, with a barely audible cough, I released all the weaponized nanites I'd collected into the air. A killing concentration, even for Lhassa. They didn't notice.

They wouldn't notice, either. Not until the nasty little things were well and truly lodged inside their lungs.

When we landed, I wasn't given a hostile environment suit. They carried me inside my jar instead—on a litter between Ormas and Naythis's bodyguard. Nobody noticed the little hole I'd cut. They were too worried about finding young Parditt.

The wind was high out here in the ruins. The dusted remains of a hundred thousand Thraad and the nanites that killed them swirled in the air, hampering visibility. The heads-up displays in their visors were lit up, their sensor suites scanning the area and laying a wireframe animation over their field of view, identifying obstacles.

"How far?" Naythis yelled at me over the howl of the wind.

"Hard to say," I said. "That way, though."

So, we walked. Or, well, *they* walked, me suspended between them. The dust caked on the side of my jar so that I couldn't see any better than they could. The bodyguard stumbled, as did Ormas, as they trundled over the piles of Thraad shells blocking their way.

Zand and Naythis were ahead of us, calling into the gloom. *"Parditt! Parditt!"*

Ormas was coughing, struggling to stand in the rubble. "I thought," she said, stopped, tried again. "I thought you assassins didn't kill innocent bystanders. I thought that was in your code or something."

"Your brother wasn't innocent," I said.

"Yes, he was! He didn't want any of this! He tried to *save* the Thraad! Fought for it!"

"I know." I remembered the look on his face in that warehouse. The look of anguish at the destruction his family had caused. Ormas wasn't lying.

"Then why did you *kill* him?"

She knew. She knew better than all of them that her brother was dead. Clever mare.

"You social organisms," I said, watching her cough and founder in the half-dark. "You need to make up your mind. Are you a group who acts in concert, or are you a collection of individuals who have no responsibility to each other?"

"It's not that simple!" Ormas said.

Behind me, the bodyguard was on one knee, wiping at her visor. "Ormas!" she said, "I can't see. My eyes...they sting like acid..."

Nanites, eating her corneas.

My moment.

I cut a larger hole in my jar and slipped out. Ormas tried to grab me, but I cut one of her hands off at the wrist and left her howling. The sound was obscured by the wind.

Then, pulling myself upright into a Lhassa-like silhouette, I headed onward, stalking my true prey.

I found Zand first, squatting down, his back against a crumbling old pillar, his gun across his knees. He was panting for breath. "Something...something's wrong..." he said.

The laser scalpel cut through his suit and his throat in one clean arc.

I picked up the gun and walked onward.

Fifty meters farther on, Naythis Zhonto was on his knees, feeling around in the dust. "Parditt? Parditt, is that you?"

"Yes," I said in Parditt's voice.

"Oh!" Naythis whirled in my direction, his arms outstretched. "My son! I'm here! I came for you!"

I took Parditt's form, even as the wind made the nanites sting like acid against my outer-membranes. I took Naythis by the hands. His eyes were cloudy. Blood was leaking out his nostrils and caking the hair around his mouth. "Are you all right?" he asked.

"Yes," I said. "I know where we can go—this way."

I led him on, away from the shuttle, until we came to a steep embankment. This used to be an amphitheater, if memory served. I was so hard to see the city as it once had been. It was almost entirely erased.

"Where are we?" Naythis asked, coughing up a spatter of blood on the interior of his helmet.

"The end." I pushed him. He tumbled down the slope, arms and legs flailing, until he landed in a heap at the bottom. The suit was too well padded to permit much injury, but the nanites eating him from the inside out were enough to keep him down. "Parditt!" he yelled. "Parditt, help!"

I took my time slithering down the incline. We were slightly sheltered from the wind, now. I could see more clearly. "You should have listened to your son, Naythis," I said in my own voice.

"You!" The patriarch fumbled for a weapon, but I'd disarmed him when I helped him stand—the advantage of being able to form as many pseudopods as I wanted. When he realized I had him, he sat down in the dust again. "You're a hired killer! You can't tell me you *care* that the Thraad are gone!"

"A job is a job."

"I can double your fee! Triple it!" he said, backing up slowly in the dust, hacking and wheezing.

"It's not about the money, Naythis," I said. I was alarmed to discover I meant it.

"They're dead!" Naythis sounded desperate, his breath coming in rapid wheezes. "Why even do this?"

I leaned over him and whispered, "Malgra."

I turned.

I left him alone with his handiwork. He would not die for hours. Not long enough for him to be found and saved. More than long enough for him to suffer.

Malgra.

I was the only one who found my way back to the shuttle—the rest of them were lost, dying. Not justice, but a version of it.

I entered the rendezvous coordinates into the autopilot and sat in one of the big padded seats as the expensive shuttle went through its launch sequence. Outside, the dust buffeted the hull of the ship. It made no sound.

As the ship rose through the atmosphere, I looked back at Gorsurai one last time—once a city, now a tomb. I was glad that I could do this last thing for the Thraad here. It wasn't about proving myself. It wasn't about the money or my reputation—it never had been. I resolved never to tell Ada about this revelation—it was important, she always said, that an assassin not get personally involved. But I was. I had been. Had to be.

I would never have a family, of this I was certain, but I now felt I had some idea what it might be like.

It hurt.

Part 3:
Discourses on the Great Races and their Discontents

The Great Races are thusly named because they, among all other lifeforms in the galaxy, have guaranteed their own survival. They have spread their genetic code, or its equivalent, across such a vast area of space that exterminating the species as a whole has become an impractical, if not impossible task. No irate Marshal can destroy the entirety of the Lhassa species, for instance, no matter how it tries.

We would be remiss, however, if we were to accept the self-serving myth that states that the Lesser Races are, by nature, inferior. Survival, while being the only metric of worth that the universe respects, is not and should not be the only dimension of worth that we, the thinking beings of the universe, accept. While it is well known that none of the Great Races wish to have more company among the stars, this is to their detriment, for above all things, this remains true: the universe remains vast and there is much to learn.

—excerpt from *Meditations on Physical Reality* by Rantothorianak, Scholarly Elder of the Consortium for Universal Wisdom and Knowledge

Vestibular Dysfunctionality

In my natural state, I am amorphous—a blob of fleshy, muscular membranes full of caustic goop. I have no set color or size, assuming my mass can support it. I can be whatever I want to be.

You would think this an advantage, but you would be wrong. It's terrible. Every single moment of it.

The way I have come to understand it, evolutionary adaptation has enabled most species to find their niche and thrive there. Their ancestors were the ones that suffered, dying so that those that survived might find a way to shore up their defenses against the world and live, comfortable and safe, behind the walls of their genetic superiority. But not me, no—I, along with my whole wretched species, am forced to adapt again and again and again, without pause. There is nowhere we are at home, where we are safe. We Tohrroids are forever on uneven footing. Even the word—*footing*—is given to us on loan. We only know what it means when we become someone else.

On Barsaylus, this is perhaps the truest it has ever been. Literally everything I do on this horrid planet is a miserable struggle. The ground, you see, just won't stop *moving*.

"Ground" is inaccurate, I guess. The correct term is the "deck," because I am not standing on the ground in Barsaylus. No one is. There *is* no ground. This is because the entire planet is one gigantic ocean, and everyone who lives here does so on one of a series of incomprehensibly huge boats that sail along as part of this huge armada, cruising all around the planet forever.

Why do they do this? Fucked if *I* know. I didn't ask and nobody bothered telling me. All I really knew was that there was a person I was supposed to assassinate here and, assuming I did that, I would get to leave again. I was determined to do that as quickly as possible and then never, ever come back.

What made Barsaylus so bad was simply a function of my physiology as it intersected with the general culture of the Union of Stars and their attitude vis-à-vis Tohrroids. To move among the so-called Great Races of the Union required that I contract and shift my outer membranes such that I *looked* like one of them—a trick I had gotten quite good at during my time out here among my "betters." The problem was that I couldn't actually *balance* a fully upright body when the floor beneath my simulated feet kept shifting and tilting. When taking on the form of a Dryth or Lhassa, I staggered and flopped like a blind drunk. Rather than blend in, I drew all the attention, and none of it was good. You can't very well infiltrate a place if you keep bumping into the walls.

There was more to it than that, though. Stuff that was less concrete, that I was less able to articulate. I spent time deep in the bilges of these city-sized boats, surrounded by my own species for the first time in ages. I felt my cousins sliding and smooshing past and over me, vibrating with simple messages that I understood from my distant past—things that meant "danger" and "food" and "warmth." I hated it deeply, being among them. It felt like I had spent my entire life climbing, only to fall down at the last.

I could move around more easily after the sun set beneath a horizon the same color as the sky. I could creep down alleys like a pool of shadow; I could ooze up the rigging of the huge, wind-powered vessels, winding my way around the cables like a serpent sneaking up the stairs. I made my way from ship to ship across long rope-bridges that bobbed and rattled with the action of wind and waves beneath.

I could see in all directions at once (my outer membranes are all light-sensitive, making my body essentially a giant eyeball), and beneath me I could gaze into the frothing, dark blue chill of the endless Barsaylian ocean. They said it was ten kilometers deep, often more. Of the bipeds who fell in, either by accident or malicious intent, very few were saved. Almost none of them knew how to swim. Me? I was a natural in the water—I lived in a pond for years, once, disguised as a big floating flower—but falling in would only make this mission last all the longer.

I wasn't looking because I was trying to concoct some kind of plan, though. I was looking because there were *lights* down there, in the crushing, frigid deep. Something—maybe some-*one*—was alive far beneath us. I was curious.

But I wasn't being paid to be curious. I did my best to ignore the lights, forget about them. What did I care if there were glowing fish in the sea? How was that even relevant to *anything*? Any one of the Great Races could wipe this whole planet out tomorrow and it wouldn't matter. No one would even notice. I knew—I'd seen it happen. With any luck, I wouldn't ever see it again.

So: work. The sooner I was done, the sooner I was gone.
The target was a Lorca with his own ship, way out at the end of the fleet of floating cities. Lorca are solitary creatures—you never find more than one in any one place, except if they're mating or fighting to the death. Possibly both. They didn't generally have a problem socializing with *other* species, though—you usually found Lorca with huge retinues of servants and sycophants from all kinds of different species—but this *specific* Lorca, my target, lived alone except for a series of drones for defense and maintenance of his giant yacht. The idea was to go

to said giant yacht and murder him, for which I would be paid enough money to get off this damp stain at the edge of known space and head for more *stable* territory.

My clients were a group of ship administrators—"captains" was the word they used, I guess—who had all pooled their money to pay for a public assassination of this Lorca, known as Kimbrol the Sheentest. There were all kinds in that room with its irritating...*surging*—that steady rise, that steady fall, that gentle sway. The Dryth and the Lhassa and the Thraad and the Voosk flocks all sat there on their perches or in their chairs or on the floor or whatever and just looked perfectly at ease. Meanwhile I, disguised as an unhoused Dryth mercenary, kept changing height and lurching to one side or the other as we spoke. They noticed—I *knew* that they noticed—but for whatever reason, they never brought it up.

"Why do you want him dead?" I asked. It was an impertinent question for an assassin to ask—it was really none of my business—but I'd had enough bad experiences now that I made a point of asking. If they wouldn't tell me, that in itself was a clue as to what I was dealing with.

The captains didn't seem eager to answer, or so I thought at first. Eventually, though, the Voosk flock spoke up, one of its members saying, very rapidly, "He is very insulting."

They all made their various nonverbal cues for agreement—the Dryth nodded, the Lhassa tossed their heads, the Thraad bobbed their eyestalks. I asked them to elaborate, but they couldn't quite agree on what "insulting" meant in this context. The Thraad described "inaccurate depictions" of their Consortium's aims. The Dryth called him dishonorable and crass. The Lhassa said they worried how he might affect their population's overall mental health. The Voosk flock, all members speaking with one voice, just said he was an asshole. They all seemed very agitated, so I didn't pry any further.

"And you're certain you don't want my partner to do it?" Ada, my Dryth partner, was the one who'd found the job in the first place. She was right now on a trans-stellar starliner in orbit, probably drinking too much.

"No," the Dryth captain said. "We want you—it has to be you."

On this they also all agreed. They said it had to be me, and I was reasonably certain they knew what I was, judging from the way they kept their distance from me, the way they declined any physical contact and offered no refreshments. I—a filthy, sewer-dwelling Tohrroid—had to be the one to kill Kimbrol the Sheentest.

They just hated him *that* much, I guess.

Kimbrol the Sheentest's private yacht was a three-hulled affair with three huge airfoils attached to each by thick cables that pulled it along in the persistent, never-ending Barsaylian wind. Kimbrol kept his ship about a kilometer from all the other ships in the armada—close enough to easily get supplies but not so close that you could easily get aboard without his say-so. The only physical link between his ship and the closest massive city-vessel was an extendable EM tunnel—a series of triangular frames suspended in open space and anchored to generators on either side. An ellipsoid capsule full of supplies and, maybe, a guest could be shunted back and forth in a tunnel of electro-magnetism in this way, but it wasn't always connected. Kimbrol liked his privacy. It made sense for someone with a public target on his head.

I lurked around the terminal for this EM tunnel and got a sense for what he had delivered. It was food, primarily, shipped in every few days. Lorca are big carnivores and they need to eat kilograms of meat a day, and I guess Kimbrol didn't like eating the synthesized stuff. A floating drone would emerge from the capsule when it arrived and would use a little scanner to inspect all the foodstuffs for purity before loading them inside and heading back.

It was a relatively simple matter to replace one little sack of gooey protein for another, but *after* the scan was done. I chose a windy, rainy day where visual sensors would have trouble parsing detail. I pushed one of the sacks of food over the edge of the platform and took its place. The drone, being a drone, didn't really notice that I jiggled in the wrong way. All it cared about was that the inventory was complete, and then off we went.

Once aboard the yacht, the drone started unloading things and bringing them down to the kitchen. I went for the ride, taking a good look at everything there was to see. It was raining, the water smelling strongly of the chlorine that soaked the Barsaylian oceans. It was cold and dismal, with the swelling ocean the color of dark slate and the sky a vacant, empty blue-gray.

Belowdecks, the passageways were broad and clear—large enough, no doubt, to accommodate a full-grown Lorca who wanted to move around. There was limited artificial light, everything being lit by windows and portholes and skylights that admitted natural illumination. On this particular day, it all looked muted and abandoned, like ancient ruins or the vacuum-scoured remnants of a starship on the drift.

The kitchen was a huge, circular chamber with stone-tile floors and a large firepit in the center, currently cool. All along the edge were counters and stasis chambers for keeping things fresh before preparation. I slipped away from the drone before it could pack me into one of these things, where I would clearly suffocate and die in short order. I made myself the color of the floor tiles and just sort of...*melted* onto the deck, spreading myself out in a thin layer that was visually identical to the tile pattern beneath. The drone, figuring it had mislaid something somehow, turned around and floated off, tracing its steps back to the EM-tunnel terminal. I had a few minutes to make myself scarce.

I figured I would ooze into a vent somewhere—I love vents, since nobody looks inside of them and they take you literally everywhere. The ventilation ducts in the kitchen, though, were covered by plastic vent covers with a mesh too fine for me to ooze through. I'd brought a laser with me—a compact military type—but it was intended for bisecting Lorca skulls and not cutting through vent covers. It would probably cut straight through the cover and the vent behind it and cause who knows how much damage along the way. Not exactly subtle.

So, new plan—creep out of the kitchen and find a vent cover I *could* ooze through.

This led to a new problem: the floor outside the kitchen *burned.* The second my outer membranes touched it, they started to sizzle. I recoiled by reflex, the white-hot pain blinding those parts of me that were affected. Even after I withdrew, it didn't stop! The vicious…whatever it was made my whole body quiver in agony. I flopped awkwardly to the water basin on the floor in the corner of the kitchen and sank into it. The water was cool and clean, and after a moment of sitting in it, the pain subsided.

That burn wasn't from heat—that was a *chemical* burn. The floor around or outside the kitchen was coated in some kind of chemical that burned my membranes on contact. I had never encountered anything like this before, to my memory. My memory was admittedly pretty bad, but still. What was *that* about? I cursed in every language I knew, if only internally, while I cooled my singed body.

That's when I saw the other Tohrroid.

Unlike me, it wasn't bothering to try and hide. It was just rolling down the middle of the corridor outside the kitchen, its outer membranes mimicking the neutral color and fuzzy texture of the deck carpeting. I don't know if it saw me—probably did—but if so, it didn't seem to care. Why would it, anyway? We weren't a social species. Technically speaking, as we reproduced asexually, this Tohrroid was essentially my clone. Since *I* wouldn't feel the need to say "hi" or even acknowledge another Tohrroid, why would it?

Whether it saw me or not, it slowed down as it neared the kitchen, stopping about two meters from the entrance. It made itself into a kind of carpeted trapezoid and reached out with a half dozen little pseudopods, which jerked back into its body when they were scorched by whatever was laced through the carpet. It was confirming the barrier was still there.

I couldn't help but sit there and watch. I knew exactly what it was up to—it knew the food had just been delivered, and it was trying to poach a snack. I wondered what bilge it had wriggled out of. I wondered how it had evaded the drones. It was pretty big—almost as big as myself—which meant it ate pretty well. Maybe this was a regular trip.

From a vacuole inside itself, it produced a pair of plastic container lids, each only a couple centimeters on a side. It placed them flat on the ground and then pushed itself up so its entire bulk was balanced over them. Then it started to shuffle—one lid would get pushed forward, then the other, then the first one—as it kept its body weight balanced overhead. I could tell it was tiring quickly—its outer membranes quivered and shook. Rather than a tight little bolus, it was drooping, and the subtle movement of the ship on the waves wasn't helping. It wasn't going to make it.

I considered helping it, though mostly as an intellectual exercise rather than an actual impulse. As I said—we aren't a social species. It wouldn't stick its neck out for me any more than I would for it. Besides, what would I do? Cheer it on? Like as not, I would burn myself again. No, thank you.

The Tohrroid made it a meter before the plastic lids slid apart beneath it and it fell onto the tainted carpet with a thump. There was a sizzling sound and it basically leapt away, retreating. It rolled back the way it came, this time a lot faster. It probably would keep burning until it could find some water to wash off the chemical, whatever it was. Sucked to be that thing.

I gave it some credit, though—that was reasonably clever. All it needed was bigger lids or more of them.

Fortunately, I had access to both. I took a few of Kimbrol's meals out of their sacks and, using the sacks, made for myself three boots, basically. I *walked* out of that kitchen and found a hiding place—a closet containing a variety of pipes and pumps related to the ship's plumbing system. I made it in just before the drone came humming back down the hall. It was probably reporting the missing package to its owner. I wondered just how paranoid the Lorca was—given the chemical barrier he put around his kitchen, probably pretty paranoid. Either that or he just hated sharing his food.

I quickly noticed I wasn't the only Tohrroid in the plumbing closet. There was another one—different from the big one using the lids—and this one was pretending to be a pump and doing a pretty good job of it. The only reason I noticed is because I was thinking about looking like a pump myself—somebody had beaten me to it.

We didn't speak—we don't have a language, not exactly. Besides, nothing to say. Its presence did interest me in one way, though: two Tohrroids, abovedecks, in daylight? My Lorca host was running what my clients might refer to as an "unsanitary" ship.

It was also a ship that was unusually difficult to hide in. Because of the windows and skylights everywhere, there weren't any good shadows. Because the corridors were so broad and clear, there weren't any narrows spaces for me to dive into. And then there was that horrid chemical scattered across the floor in some places. I got burned twice shuttling around that stupid boat. It was starting to piss me off. I couldn't wait to put a couple laser tracks through Kimbrol the Sheentest's spine and be on my way.

I found him abovedecks, near the back of the boat (the "stern" was the term, apparently, though the word was strange—it felt alien even in the tongues it was spoken in). The stern was comprised of a broad platform surrounded by a very low fence of taut steel cables. On all sides was the endless ocean, which rose and fell around us like living mountains. I had never felt so exposed in my life, crawling onto that deck—nothing on all sides, and only the airfoils that formed the vessel's propulsion overhead. Beyond it, the gray sky.

At least it had stopped raining.

Kimbrol the Sheentest was at least three meters tall, probably taller. Lorca were hexapods—two muscular hind legs, two taloned forelegs, and two arms above that. They walked with their four hindlimbs on the ground, mostly, though the forelegs had opposable digits. Their bodies were gray and scaly and thick with boulder-like muscles. Their heads were dominated by their jaws—wide and rimmed with razor-sharp teeth. They tended not to wear very much, their hide thick enough to account for a very wide range of temperatures they found comfortable. Kimbrol was wearing a harness across his chest, though. It was full of loops for various hand tools. I saw chisels, hammers, awls, cleavers, axes. All primitive, though—nothing powered.

Kimbrol was working on something—some big hunk of resin or concrete. He was chiseling at it, rubbing it down with abrasive gloves. Poking at it with his clawed forelimbs and then moving around it, examining from multiple angles.

Kimbrol was *sculpting* something. Whatever it was had yet to take shape, but it was getting there. What had probably started as some big cube was now a series of interconnected lumps. I wondered what it was meant to become.

But I wasn't curious enough to let him live.

I drew my laser, powered it up with a faint whine that I hoped would be swallowed by the steady howl of the wind and the slap and chatter of the sea along the hull. I crept closer.

The good thing about lasers such as the one I carried was that they could penetrate almost anything—and certainly a Lorca—but the bad thing was that they were almost *too* precise. If I started cutting from way back here, I might not kill him right away, and I didn't want to give this eight-hundred-kilo monster the opportunity to splatter me if I could help it. Despite my job, I am not a particularly good shot—my depth perception degrades quickly over distance—so I got closer and closer until I was certain I couldn't miss. Kimbrol never turned around.

I took aim at his back, planning to cut him (and his unfinished statue) clean in two. I hit the activation stud.

Nothing happened.

I looked down at the weapon—a Thraad model—its power source was in the green, but…but nothing doing. I hit the stud again and again. Nothing. What the…

Kimbrol turned his torso to face me. He pointed to a hemispherical device attached to his harness. "An EM inhibitor, quite powerful. Your device—indeed, *all* electrical devices in about a twenty-meter radius or so—won't function. I am also likely irradiating you, but as you are a smack, what do you care, eh?"

This was bad. Very, very bad. I scurried away from him as best I could on the lurching deck, cycling through colors that would make it hard for him to see my outlines.

He was quick—much quicker than me—and before I could properly react, he loomed over me like a tidal wave of muscle. I tensed for a fight—if he grabbed me, he was in for a rude awakening. Nobody and nothing could out-wrestle me, the amorphous bag of hostile muscle. I'd stab him to death with his own chisels.

He didn't grab me, though. He threw a net over my body—a fine, mesh net. I tried to escape it, but he had me trussed up like fish in a fraction of a second. Almost like he was used to dealing with Tohrroids. So used to them, in fact, he knew how to keep them out of his kitchen.

I suddenly felt very stupid.

He hung me in my mesh sack from one of the cables leading to the airfoils floating so far above and ahead. Then he sat on his haunches and gave me a good look-over. "You're a big one, that's for sure. Pretty close to splitting, I shouldn't wonder. Exciting for you, or terrifying?"

I didn't say anything, but I desperately wanted to. Me? Reproduce? I'd rather die. It seemed a kind of death, anyway— losing half of myself all at once. Half my knowledge, half my skill, half my memories. I'd no longer be myself.

"They say you can talk. Is this true?" Kimbrol asked.

I said nothing. Screw him.

He picked up my laser where I'd dropped it. "Regular smacks don't go carrying these around, friend. You're the Faceless Assassin, yes? No need to be shy. What's the point, eh?"

"Fuck you," I said.

Kimbrol grunted his laughter. "There, see? Isn't that better?"

"Just kill me," I said. "Better that than listening to you talk."

"Who said anything about killing you? How could I pass up the opportunity to converse with a Tohrroid? It is an unparalleled opportunity. For us both, yes?"

"I see that your Lorca sense of superiority is intact."

It did nothing to dent his good mood. "That is only because we Lorca are, in fact, superior. You do not recognize this because you are so low to the ground. You have never seen the world from the heights—physical, intellectual, financial, *cultural*—that I have. We Lorca are the lords of the galaxy, though unacknowledged and much depleted in recent ages, admittedly."

Pretty soon, he was going to start reciting his lineage, I was sure of it. I tried desperately to find a way out of the net, but the mouth of it had sealed itself somehow—more tricks of chemistry, I guess.

"Ah," the big Lorca said, "I can see you are not in a listening mood. Very well, then, little one—stay, watch me work. We will converse again soon, and at length." He patted me gently with one of his big hands and then casually tossed my laser over the side and into the sea.

I stayed in that net for days. We did not converse. I was forced to watch him work on his stupid statue, chiseling it down centimeter by centimeter, chips of rock clattering on the deck only to be swept out to sea by the wind and the errant wave. Not for the first time, I wished for eyelids. For a pair of eyes I could turn away. I hated that he was forcing me to see something I didn't care about. I hated how easily he had taken me into his power. I wished for a storm, a rogue bolt of lightning—anything—to appear and destroy his work, just so I wouldn't have to watch it happen.

The sculpture was a series of figures, gathered together doing something, though I couldn't see what, as that part hadn't been finished yet. I did get the basic outlines—a Thraad, a Dryth, two Lhassa, and a many-headed thing that had to be a Voosk flock. In other words, the captains of the city-ships that had hired me. They stood in a semicircle, very close together, all looking down at some figure in the center that wasn't fully fleshed out. I couldn't see what purpose it served. These people all wanted him dead—why carve their likenesses in stone? Why do it here, bobbing around an endless ocean?

I didn't ask. Kimbrol was counting on my curiosity getting the better of me. He was counting on my Tohrroid nature winning out. The arrogant scum-sucking slime.

At night, I was alone on the deck. Rain and surf would lash the surface of the ship, soaking me and making the material of the net cling to my membranes. It was suffocating and cold. Struggle as I might, there was nothing I could do to get out of the net. Whatever it was made of, I couldn't digest it, so I couldn't eat my way out. I needed a tool—something to cut or burn.

One night, the sea was relatively calm. Still the great, endless swells of water that we slid up and then down, but no chop, no spray, no rain. Even the wind seemed calmer. The neon light spilling from the city-ships to the west filled half of my vision, overpowering the stars and shooting columns of pure white into the endless night sky. To the east, though, all the lights were *beneath* the surface. I could see them, floating along, keeping pace with the great armada. What were they? Who were they? Could they help me? Did they even know I was there?

My interest was not mine alone. Other Tohrroids came up on deck, clinging to the gunwales and hanging from the rigging, changing their body color to match the lights in the deep sea. If I didn't know any better, I would have said that constituted communication.

By the fourth or fifth day, when I was cold and dehydrated and sluggish, my stubbornness finally outweighed Kimbrol's patience. It was early—just after sunrise—when he stood back from his handiwork, clapped the dust off his hands, and sighed. "What do you think?"

The Thraad figure on the end was nearing completion. His eyestalks were carefully rendered, floating at different heights. It was clearly meant to represent the Thraad representative on the council of captains, but it was...exaggerated somehow. The flesh of the sculpture's face was pocked and dull—an effect created by some acid and various kinds of abrasive tools. The result was that the Thraad looked sick, disoriented. The effect was compelling, though I did not say so.

"She has a wasting disease, you know. It affects her memory, her judgement. She has grown more erratic in recent months. Like all Thraad, though, she will not admit to weakness or confusion, even though her ailment will eventually kill her and, I suspect, many others as a result of her deteriorating judgement."

Now I could see his play—he wanted me to see who I was working for. Wanted me to doubt my mission. Could he be this dense? "I get paid either way," I said.

Kimbrol glanced at me, surprised I'd spoken. He smiled, showing his many rows of teeth. "Not if you can't kill me, you don't."

I said nothing to that. Eventually, they'd hire another assassin, maybe even Ada. Ada would probably do it the loud way—a railgun, set up on the top deck of the nearest city-ship, punching holes in this little tub until it sank to the bottom. I'd initially said no to that plan when she offered it, but time was making me regret that decision.

"They want me dead for things like this, you know." Kimbrol pointed at the sculpture with a foreclaw. "It's what I do."

"Make statues that drones could make faster?" I asked.

"No—I tell the truth. The whole, uncompromised truth. I capture it, lock it in stone, and then show the world. Holographic images capture motion, capture *change*, but they don't capture truth. The eye misses what the heart needs to know. I draw it out. I display it."

"They want you dead because you made ugly statues of them?"

Kimbrol smiled again, as though I'd walked into another trap. "You think it trivial, this work? And yet here you are, being paid a large sum to put an end to it. Doesn't seem to make sense, does it?"

"I don't ask questions. I just do the job," I said.

"Not good enough," Kimbrol said.

"What's that supposed to mean?"

He came close and prodded my net, inspecting it, I guess. "I don't mind dying, assassin. I will in fact embrace it when the time comes. I will not be killed for some petty sum, though. I insist my death be worthy of the name."

"Who said you got a choice in the matter? Who said this is a negotiation?"

Kimbrol tugged at the net, making sure it was still firmly secured. "I did."

The smart play was to wait things out. A good assassin was a patient assassin—the mark always made a critical error eventually, leaving them vulnerable. Wait long enough and you could kill anybody. In this instance, however, there were several factors working against this as a strategy.

In the first place, I was starving. Kimbrol had no apparent interest in giving me water, let alone food. I was a large Tohrroid, and so I had a lot of "me" to burn before I died—my species doesn't so much starve as *wither*. But for every kilogram of myself that I cannibalized, I lost more and more of my sense of "self." My neurological system—my "brain," such as it is—is not concentrated in any single organ but dispersed throughout myself in a big network. As that network shrank and became less complex, I would forget things, lose skills. Eventually, I'd wind up like the rest of my cousins—wretched, mindless, and impotent.

Though starvation wouldn't kill me, dehydration definitely *would*. I was keeping myself hydrated mostly through rainwater—it was raining more and more often. I did not know exactly why, but I got the sense it had something to do with the yacht's (and the entire armada's) course. As we drifted up and down the mountainous swells of the endless Barsaylian oceans, heading *wherever* it was we were going, the air grew warmer and the day/night cycle became longer. I presumed we were moving to a different climate zone of the planet. Even with the increased rainfall, though, I was not getting enough water to sustain my mass. I was losing flexibility and strength every day I was left to dry out in the sun on this pole. If I didn't do something soon, I wouldn't be able to.

The final problem, though, was more worrisome. The EM-scrambler thing—the thing that Kimbrol always wore on his work harness, every time I saw him—he said it gave off radiation. I didn't know *that* much about radiation (or maybe I used to and then forgot?), but I seemed to recall one important fact from somewhere in my past: radiation interfered with the Tohrroid ability to think and form memories. I could survive it—much, much longer than a Dryth or a Lhassa or even a Lorca could—but it quite literally made me *stupid*.

I could feel it working, too. I found myself unable to remember things I obviously should be able to—what Ada looked like, for instance, or what planet we had been on before this one. I always felt a step behind Kimbrol. Felt outsmarted. And, honestly, that was nonsense. Lorca just *weren't* that smart. All they were was *rich* and *big*. That's not the same as smart. Of course, here I was saying that while hanging in a stupid net from a pole like today's catch.

All I needed to get free was access to something sharp. While I couldn't pull the fibers of the net apart, certainly not with my lack of leverage while inside it, I felt certain it would cut easily. And, each and every day, there was a big Lorca literally *covered* in sharp metal objects, not five meters away from me, working on his idiotic crafts project.

If I was going to do this, I was going to have to sucker him in. And, sure, my mind might've been going, but even the stupidest version of myself knew how to get a Lorca to let down their guard: you just asked them about themselves.

The only thing he wanted to talk about was his sculpting, so I decided to take up an appreciation of the art. It wasn't that hard to fake it—Kimbrol the Sheentest was very talented, or at least was to my untrained and deteriorating senses. His sculpture of the captain's council was coming along nicely. He had roughed out all five figures at this point and, at my prompting, told me everything he was hoping to show about them.

"They are greedy and fragile beings," he said as he carved the first Lhassa captain's thinning mane, drawing attention to the artificial extensions she'd had put in to make her look younger. "They have been here too long. They put forth an image of vitality, but they lack it in every way that matters. Here, on the surface of a planet that is ever-changing, they are stagnant and calcified."

"And once everybody sees this statue of yours, you think that will change something?" I asked. I wasn't trying to sound sarcastic, but the idea of a fine sculpture causing the power structure of a whole planet to collapse was absurd.

Kimbrol smiled at the question, the sunlight glinting off his muscular flanks, the small steel file looking dark and filthy in his huge hand. "The truth always changes things, smack," he said. He didn't look up from his work. "Show a tyrant his works of tyranny, and he will still be a tyrant. But he will be a tyrant without excuses any longer."

"I think you underestimate how delusional tyrants can be," I said. Again, I wasn't *trying* to be sarcastic, but it was hardly my fault that everything he said was so…I don't know. I'd forgotten the word. Stupid?

Let's go with stupid.

The Lorca looked back over his shoulder towards me. "You think me a tyrant?"

Yes. "No."

"I am trying to set you free," Kimbrol said. "Without me—without *this*"—he gestured to my prison and the yacht and the rolling sea all around—"you will never be anything other than a *mirror image*. A replication. A copy of a copy, enslaved by the visions of others."

I could think of a half dozen ways in which what he said was complete idiotic garbage, but that wouldn't work with the plan. Instead, I said, "Maybe you're right."

Kimbrol turned back to his sculpting. "I think you are lying to me. But that doesn't mean I am wrong. You will see, in time."

But how *much* time?

That night, I watched a totally extraneous murder from the one I was trying to orchestrate. One of my cousins, a Tohrroid, was on deck again. I'd tried signaling to them, calling to them—anything to get their attention—but the only things they seemed to care about were the things beneath the waves and their array of lights and ever-shifting patterns. This time, a Tohrroid was way out on the ship's left-side outer hull, hanging down from the netting, trying to reach the water. It had made itself a reflective orange color, like your standard safety vest. "Look at me!" it was basically saying. "Save me!"

There was a splash; something shot up from the deep. A harpoon of some kind, or maybe just a barbed tentacle—I couldn't see clearly enough in the dark to tell. The Tohrroid wriggled in pain and what I guessed was terror and then was yanked beneath the waves. And that was it—no more Tohrroid.

Beneath the waves, the colorful patterns shifted and changed again. This time, they were bright orange, just like the Tohrroid had been. They were signaling back, but the message had been lost. It had been asking for rescue; they thought it was served up for dinner. Easy mistake to make, I guess. I spent an hour or two thinking of how I might use this to my advantage. Nothing sprang to mind. Things were having more and more trouble springing anywhere in my thoughts, I realized. If only I knew what Kimbrol wanted from me.

The next morning, I found out.

The sculpture of the council of captains was almost complete on its edges. They were arranged in a semicircle, each of their figures exaggerated such that their worst qualities could be clearly seen. "The Truth laid bare," as Kimbrol put it. But what were they surrounding? I had assumed he was going to sculpt some kind of table or holodisplay (somehow) and show them gathered around it, but this was not so, apparently.

Instead, he grinned his predatory grin at me and pointed to the as-yet-undefined spot. "This is you," he said.

"I don't understand," I said. "There's nothing there."

Kimbrol laughed. "That's because you *aren't* anything. You are undefined, inchoate. *What do I carve here*, I ask myself, day in and day out. But I can't answer it, because there is nothing *to* you."

"What does that mean?" I had trouble following his problem. He didn't know how to carve me…why? Because he didn't know what shape I was then, when I met with them. "A Dryth, I think."

"No, no no—that is what *they* saw, or wanted to. That was a reflection of what they wanted, what they *are*." Kimbrol came close and prodded me. "What are you *really*?"

"A Tohrroid," I said.

"And what is that? You eat trash, you hide and you skulk and you steal—is that you?"

I didn't have an answer that I could articulate. He'd hit on something there. What *was* I? It was the central question of my existence. I was genetically identical to the pathetic blobs scooting around this yacht, to the untold millions of them trapped in special chambers in starships, eating offal. But I was *not one of them*. Not anymore. I made that choice a long time gone.

But I wasn't an assassin, either, was I? Ada was the real thing—she had the look, the swagger, the weapons. I was just another weapon to her, wasn't I? One trapped and broken in a little net hanging from a rope on a sailboat. Pathetic. Ridiculous.

"Yes," Kimbrol boomed, his great body blocking the rising sun. "You are beginning to see the problem, smack. You are like a block of stone yourself—malleable, able to take on any shape—but unlike the stone, you have no center. No mass. No way to orient yourself in relation to the world, and that is most important—orienting yourself in relation to the world. Who are you? What is it that you offer?"

"I'll offer you a quick death if you let me out of this bag," I said.

Kimbrol wasn't worried. "You hate me, but even your hate is the reflection of another's *idea* of hatred. You cannot hate on your own—no Tohrroid can. Look around? You've seen them, yes, squirming through my yacht. I let them stay because I wish to understand them. To understand *you*, who have no form and yet claim a profession. It is perverse. You, and your whole species, is a perversion."

I felt like changing the subject. "There's creatures under the water. Did you know that?"

Kimbrol shrugged. "Fish, cnidaria—things that feed on microscopic organisms in the sea. Mere animals. What of them?"

"One of them harpooned one of your pet Tohrroids last night. Yanked it right off the deck."

"No, that's impossible," the big Lorca said, turning back to his sculpture. "They aren't thinking beings like you and I."

"A lot of people don't think Tohrroids are thinking beings, either."

The Lorca took out his tools, considering his sculpture from this or that angle, shaving off a few chinks of stone here and there. He grinned at me over his shoulder. "Are you then pleased that I have acknowledged you? That I have recognized the *potential* in your species? Gratifying, is it not? Now I only ask that you *achieve* it. Do so, my little assassin, and my life is forfeit. This I swear."

It became clear to me then. I knew what he wanted. It was obvious, really—it was what all the Great Races wanted, in the end. He wanted to dictate the shape of the world. He wanted to categorize and draw borders. He wanted to take a piece of something in nature—a block of stone, a vast ocean—and *bend* it to his will. Have it bear him along, ambitions and all, because that was what it was all about, in the end—himself.

He even thought he could dictate the terms of his own death.

We'd see about that, now, wouldn't we?

The next night, as I watched the clouds overtake the stars above, I made myself bright, bright orange. The most orange I could be. Because fuck it, that's why. Come and get me, lights—too much longer, and I would be dead, anyway.

I made noises—chirping sounds, clicks, howls—all the things I'd seen my cousins do when trying to contact the lights beneath the sea. The other Tohrroids were nowhere to be found—the death of one of them seemed to have warned them off appealing to the kindness of aquatic aliens. That left only me—the only Tohrroid crazy enough to court one death just to potentially stave off another. Was this a mark of my intelligence or a sign of my declining faculties? Who could tell the difference anymore. Nothing about this whole arrangement was "smart," from a bunch of captains telling me to kill someone over some rude statues to me getting caught in a net like a crustacean, to some Lorca deciding to live alone on a *boat* in an *endless ocean.*

The lights appeared at length. Unlike their last snack, I wasn't really hanging over the edge of the boat—if they wanted me, they would have to come and get me. They'd have to climb out of the ocean and get me in my little net where I was hanging down, like a ripe fruit ready to pluck. And unlike most of my cousins, I was *big*. A solid meal.

The lights grew brighter, larger. They were right beneath the surface now, causing the sea to undulate over their forms. Tendrils shot up, grabbing the edge of the boat with flat, broad pads. The whole ship lurched to one side—wait, how big were *they*?

No, no—not *they*. This was an *it*. One creature. One gigantic sea monster. Oh…oh, no.

I had just messed up, and big-time.

The thing that appeared over the side of the ship was not the whole creature, I am sure of it, but just the eating end of it. A jawless, circular mouth, almost five meters across, ringed with tentacles and lined with bright, dagger-like teeth, all facing *inward*. The tentacle pads had dark spots at the end—eyes, I guess. The teeth in its mouth? They were barbed, like harpoons. From what I could make out about the rest of its body, its skin was translucent, beneath which a riot of bioluminescence was put on display. Some kind of megafauna, luring its lunch with pretty light shows.

I stopped being orange and started being the least noticeable color I could manage, which was a very dark gray-green. The giant thing didn't like this, and from its huge mouth shot one of its harpoon-like teeth, attached to a tendril that would yank me back into its mouth like an elastic rope. This had been my plan all along, just…well, not quite like *this*.

But you know what's sharp? Harpoons. Harpoons are sharp. When it speared me right through one end and my world erupted into a rainbow of pain and shock, that was the one thing I had fixed in my mind—it had cut through the net. I was free.

Well, assuming I wasn't eaten in the next five seconds, anyway.

The barbed tooth on the end of the tendril yanked back on its meal (being myself). The pain made me blind for a half-second, but the good thing about having so much conscious control over my amorphous body was that I could relax my membranes around the barb, letting it slip out of me, along with a significant amount of my vital and digestive fluids. Now the barb was simply tangled in the net rather than me *and* the net. One of the holes it had speared was open. Shivering with agony, I forced myself through the opening and fell with a plop onto the deck.

The wind was increasing and rain began to fall. The airfoils that had pulled the ship in all the time I had been on it began to shudder and jump in the squall. The sea monster pulled and pulled against the net, finally shredding it. Its eye-tentacles waved in all directions, trying to see the dark little spot that was me. I expected to see the beast to slide back into the abyss at any time, but no—it was hungry, and it wasn't leaving without a snack. I crawled across the deck, increasingly slick with both rain and my own bodily fluids, trying to make the hatch and escape belowdecks, but my body not wanting to fully cooperate.

I was dead several times over. If I didn't get eaten by the beast, I would bleed to death. If I didn't bleed to death, Kimbrol would rip me apart with his huge, taloned hands. There was no escape and no way to complete my mission. I didn't even have any way to call for help.

Or wait…maybe I did.

Slipping and sliding on the deck, ducking under probing tentacles, I positioned myself on the opposite side of the yacht from the creature, at the extreme end of its reach. Sitting on the outrigger hull, I made myself yet again that delicious orange color the creature favored. It spotted me almost at once, regardless of the rain. Three teeth-harpoons shot out even as I rolled and returned to the bland neutrals that the creature couldn't see. It missed me.

It didn't miss the outrigger hull, puncturing its carbon-fiber frame easily. As it pulled and pulled to retract its teeth, I heard the carbon fiber crack and shatter. The whole ship sank deeper in the water, even as the huge waves, whipped up by the wind, broke over the bow in a thick sheet of frigid water. By this time, I had rolled myself to the hatch and vanished belowdecks, not so much with grace but with the desperate thump and smack of a deflating balloon trying to plug its own leaks.

Belowdecks, an alarm was sounding. The structural compromise of the hull, the seawater pouring over the deck as the prow tunneled rather than crested the top of a wave, the airfoils in disarray—the ship was clearly in distress. I rolled down the corridor, swaying with the motion of the storm and leaving a viscous trickle of my fluids in my wake. I had trouble thinking, had trouble recording what was happening. The idea I had had—my brilliant plan to escape this whole thing alive—was lost to me almost as soon as I'd hatched it. What was I doing? Why?

All I could remember was that I needed to find Kimbrol the Sheentest and stay close. This might have been some plan of mine, or it might have just been survival instinct, as I was joined by a dozen of my Tohrroid cousins, all of them oozing along in search of the master of the ship, who almost certainly had a plan to avert this catastrophe.

We found him on the bridge—an elliptical chamber with a huge divan at its center surrounded by workstations manned by hovering drones. The Lorca was splayed out on the divan, peering anxiously through the rain-spattered windows that formed the forward part of the ellipse. He was barking orders to his drones and, I noted, that if his drones were functioning near him, his EM inhibitor device was not nearby or switched off.

"Structural integrity at 65%," one of the drones reported, its single manipulator arm poking at a holodisplay.

The ship lurched upward on one side—the weight of the sea monster coming off as it slipped back beneath the waves. This was timed with another massive wave, this one breaking over the bow and flowing up and over the bridge itself. For a moment, no one could see except for the light of the instrument panels.

Some of my cousins tried to enter the bridge, only for their membranes to sizzle on the chemical coating the floor.

The ship shuddered again. "Main hull breach in the hold, port side. We are taking on water—chamber is being sealed."

Kimbrol cursed in the Lorca tongue. "We'll never last the storm. Send a distress call to the nearest city-ship." He sounded more annoyed than afraid—sea monsters, mountainous waves, vast storms were nothing to a being whose ancestors had conquered the stars before any other. He was mourning his art. His work unfinished. The *audacity*.

A drone with a shock prod preceded Kimbrol off the bridge. It cleared a path with the rest of the Tohrroids—he never spared any of us the slightest glance. We followed him at a safe distance as he headed up on deck.

On deck? I didn't want to go there! That was dangerous—the monster, for one thing, but I could just slip off into the sea and be lost in the storm. Every instinct in my body tried to hold me back. My cousins—my genetic copies—followed suit. They quivered and sighed at the thought of going out beneath the now-black sky, from which dropped sheets of cold rain.

But...no—I followed. Injured, alone, unsure, but I followed. Because I was not a creature of instinct, not any longer. And if I once had a plan to stop my host, I had to trust myself to follow it through. I dragged myself onto the deck, my whole back half engaged in clenching my wounds closed. What was the plan? What was the *plan?*

Then I watched him unpack the big, hexagonal raft with the emergency beacon. And I watched him strap on a series of floatation devices.

And then I knew.

Everything was the same shade of eye-searing, rescue-me orange. I wanted to laugh, but laughter is not what I am—that's something I imitate, as Kimbrol so rightly pointed out. Instead, I did what all good scavengers do: I waited, I watched, and I hoped for misfortune.

Kimbrol in his big raft pushed off from his floundering yacht, leaving me and who knew how many Tohrroids behind. We were all on deck now, all watching. We do not speak, as I said, but a ripple ran among us. A ripple that spoke of excitement and anticipation. We all knew what it was about, knowing it more deeply than any spoken word could convey.

The Lorca had not gone twenty meters in the water when the great lights returned, seeming to flicker beneath the churning ocean. We on the yacht clung tightly to what we could, our colors dark and neutral even as the battered ship lost its airfoil and shuddered up and down the great swells. Kimbrol, however, lit his flashing beacon and sounded his rescue pulse—a sharp klaxon that pierced even the roar of the wind. He defied the storm's claim—Barsaylus's claim—over his life, while we Tohrroids resigned ourselves to its mercy.

Six ropy tendrils pierced Kimbrol's raft. He roared in surprise as it crumpled beneath him and he sank. The rescue beacon went beneath the waves, joined by larger and more ancient lights that understood well what it meant to be clearly visible in a sea of predators. There was a flicker of color, and then the beacon went out.

Kimbrol the Sheentest was no more.

The yacht, in the end, didn't actually sink. It capsized and it filled with water, but the Tohrroids and myself managed to cling to the hull until the storm broke and the sun came out and we were left, baking in the heat. My cousins clustered at the edge of the ship, half-submerged, looking for all the world like a thick bank of algae. When little fish came close, they snagged them and ate well. They avoided bright colors. They were learning.

The rescue skimmer came a few hours later, when the sun was at its peak. They were looking for Kimbrol, but I noted that they hadn't bothered rushing. Was that because they honestly didn't think anything would happen to the Lorca, or were they bribed by my employers to hang back? No way to know. Not my business to know.

I was weak, even queasy. I managed to make myself into a crumpled, injured Dryth youth, clutching her wounded abdomen (which was my real wound). It took all of my strength to manage it, and I wouldn't have bothered if I thought the ship would stop otherwise.

They hovered over me, forcing the water down around me with great jets of unnatural force. The Tohrroids clenched into balls and held tight to the edge of the yacht. Me, I could feel my form blurring, flattening. I hadn't the strength to maintain it.

The hatch at the back of the skimmer opened and a tall, svelte Dryth in an armored bodysuit drifted down to the hull on an AG harness. I knew who it was before she retracted her visor—Ada. Thanks to Kimbrol's actions, I didn't know her by sight anymore, but I did remember her methods. She was here to see if I was still alive—her favorite little tool.

"Faceless?" she asked, standing over me. "That you?"

I could scarcely speak. "Yes."

"Did you get him?"

"Yes," I lied.

"What happened? Are you alone?"

I thought of the sea monster, eating what it could with its food all pulled up by the massive fishing nets of the city-ships. I thought of my cousins, all hiding by the waterline, free from Kimbrol's indulgences. Ada could have seen them—seen all of it—if she looked. She never looked. I thought what would happen if I told Ada about it all. I thought what would happen if I didn't. The end result seemed much the same. The only question was which answer the sea monster and the Tohrroids and the rest of this planet deserved.

"I did it. All by myself. Let's go."

Ada smiled in that restrained Dryth way, showing her blunt teeth. "This is a big score, Faceless. People will really know who we are now."

She picked me up and I let myself sag into jelly in her arms. I didn't have the energy to say anything, but I wondered as she carried me up and away from that endless sea: what was I? What were "we"? It seemed arrogant to presume to know, when so much in the world could be changed.

Rates of Acceleration

When the Dryth Houses feel like showing off their technology, it feels a lot like contempt. Contempt for living things. Contempt for nature. Contempt for the entire universe writ large. Anyone who can reconstitute a whole asteroid field into a single gigantic torus just for the fun of racing through it doesn't just *not care* about your problems, they don't even acknowledge you as a thing capable of *having* problems. To them, you are a mote of dust. Who cares if you have anxiety?

The torus was something like a million kilometers in diameter, which made its circumference a bit over three million. The diameter of the tube itself was comparatively tight—a mere five hundred meters, only three hundred of which was hollowed out entirely. It was like a hair-thin hollow noodle of inert minerals, stretching out in an empty corner of the Hainar system, orbiting that red dwarf at a happy, healthy distance, well beyond the range of the worst solar radiation storms. The structure of the thing was not stable—not at all— and I guess that was part of the point. Racing through that basically infinite tube meant wildly changing gravitational and topographical conditions. Not just a challenge but a suicidal one.

Racers died all the time. The thing is, when you're backed by a Dryth House and can afford to have a half-dozen clones of yourself on tap for any kind of emergency, winding up a scorch mark or a splintered icicle in the middle of a vast, artificially constructed suicide course just wasn't that big of a deal.

The race took thirty standard days to complete. My partner Ada and I arrived on the observation cruiser on day three. As a well-known assassin and an unhoused Dryth, Ada drew a lot of attention. She was tall and muscular and wore matching multipistols on her hips—ornate, handmade weapons, with stocks made of an organic material called wood. They get it from trees, as I understand it. I don't know much about trees.

Anyway, the point is that when Ada swaggered off the interstellar transport and onto the main concourse of the observation cruiser, her semi-chameleonic skin rendered in fractal spirals of white and blue, everybody *looked*. Assassins might be part of life in the Union of Stars, but ones of Ada's caliber, with a laundry list of high-status corpses appended to her file, were both uncommon and glamorous. I'd seen some of the hype-vids about her. A shot of a gunfight on Oswen IV where she took down six Lhassa bodyguards in five seconds, or one of that spear duel on Cadria that had her chasing down the arch-regent on a grav chariot and harpooning him on the steps of the senate. Ada was big-time. There were weirdos out there whose fondest hope was to be important enough someday to draw her on a contract. As she walked down the broad corridor of the cruiser, Dryth kept coming up to her and asking for her thumbprint on little blocks of indelible semi-organic gel shaped like her head.

Of course, all this attention meant that absolutely no one noticed me, walking by myself at the back of the pack of fawning admirers, my outer membranes formed into the shape of a humdrum, run-of-the-mill Dryth laborer, unhoused and poor. The kind of guy who hitches a ride on an interstellar transport with his last trade credit in the hopes of starting over somewhere new. I used this form fairly often; I was comfortable in it. This guy was short and wide and that made him much, much easier to maintain. In my normal form, I don't have any shape at all. I'm a fleshy blob, a ball of extremely sophisticated muscular membranes and stomach acid. And anxiety.

I liked not being noticed. I liked that Ada got all the glitz and glamour. And Ada?

Ada liked how good I was at killing people.

Oh, sure, she was a talented performer and she really *did* harpoon that regent that one time, but when it came down to it, if she needed a hard target taken out—I mean somebody who *literally* watched their own back and didn't do things like accept duels from professional killers—Ada turned to me. Because I didn't care about glitz or glamor or reputation. All I cared about was the money.

We'd come up in the world, Ada and I. After we met, we spent a cycle or two of eating condensed ration bars and sleeping in coffin-sized bunks, snagging grunt-work contracts for Thraad Consortiums and other low-bid losers. Now? We were living the high life. The best food, the best accommodations, the best weapons, and did I mention the best food? I mostly liked the food.

Our reason for coming to the Hainar Death Loop was financial. Here, the combined resources of five Dryth Houses were invested in a spectacle the rest of the galaxy could only dream about. The prize for winning was more than just money—it was literal power. A quantum tap on Hainar itself—all the blazing energy of a red dwarf star, accessible at will and without end. The winner wouldn't just be rich, they would ascend to rank of Solon—a demigod of the Dryth race. Ada and I were betting that people—very, very wealthy people—would be willing to kill each other over a prize like that, and that meant professional assassins would be in high demand.

As I moved through the concourse, well behind Ada and

her gaggle of fans, I could see our competition all over the place—assassins with less flash and bravado than Ada, maybe, but their rad guns and plasma throwers worked every bit as well. None of them spotted me. Since I can see every direction at once, they had no idea I was looking. I committed their descriptions into a little data recorder I had stored in a vacuole inside my simulated head. I resolved to keep tabs on them, as best I could. Not because I was worried they would take a run at us—assassins didn't take jobs against other assassins, as it violated our code—but because some clients weren't above double-booking a target and only paying the one who bagged them first or, more common, some assassin took out your meal ticket before they could pay you off. That had happened to Ada and me more than once.

Eventually, I met Ada in a public viewing holosuite, sometime after the day's race had begun. Dryth of all ages and houses were sitting in high-backed chairs and reclined so they could look up at the panoramic holographic representation of the Tube, racing by at over ten thousand kilometers an hour, the uneven landscape a whirring blur of icy crags and venting gasses. The display helpfully highlighted the engine signatures of a few dozen different racers, here at the front of the pack, their names and statistics available for display based on a little console built into the viewing chair. The racers themselves were all piloting skimmers—antigravity hovercraft not capable of true flight—that were strapped to starfighter-grade antimatter engines, streaking through the Loop like meteors careening through the outer atmosphere of a desolate planet. I imagine for the average biped with all their visual organs built into one end of their bodies, the sensation of blasting along with the racers was deeply immersive. For me, whose depth perception worked differently and who could see the dirty floor and the worn upholstery of the chairs at the same time as the absurd multimedia display above me, it was just chaotic and noisy.

Ada saw me. She was wearing goggles that saw into the infrared spectrum—a pretty reliable way of identifying me, assuming you knew what the heat signature of a squat Dryth was *supposed* to look like. She held out a carton of some kind of freeze-dried legume. "Hungry?"

I was always hungry. I took the carton and absorbed the little spheroids through my hands in tiny vacuoles that would soon be flooded with my digestive juices. The things were sickly sweet with just a touch of heat—they were delicious. "Any leads?" I asked.

There was no one near us, and the noise of the race above would likely foul everything but the most sensitive of microphones. Even still, we kept our conversation vague.

"Just one. Solid pay. Covert job."

Covert jobs were assassination contracts that weren't made known to the general public. Most jobs were public—if somebody put a contract out on your head (or whatever body part you considered most integral to your continued existence), that contract would be posted somewhere everyone could access it, including yourself. When the job was completed, the assassin would get paid, and the organization or individual who *ordered* the job would be the one held responsible. The assassin was the tool, not the wielder.

A covert job threw all that out the window. There was no cover for the assassin in that instance—the death was considered "illegal" insofar as laws applied—but there was also no warning to the target given and the pay was often better. You got covert jobs when somebody didn't *want* anyone to know who killed the target. In fact, they didn't care if anyone took responsibility at all. All they wanted was the target *dead*.

There were always complications, though. "Who is it?" I asked.

Ada looked up at the screen, her goggles shining with the reflection of the holographic light. "Here she comes now…"

The race holo was tracking an exhaust plume—a flare of light streaking through the jagged, alien, semi-darkness of the Death Loop, passing competitors and dodging attempts to foul the skimmer's course. Two such competitors slammed into rocky outcroppings in spectacular fashion—*RETIRED* appeared next to their names on the leaderboard.

The pilot of the skimmer, who was climbing the rankings for the day's race fast enough that her trajectory was hard to track, was a Dryth female by the name of Yatka. No surname, which meant no house affiliation. She was an Unhoused Dryth, playing against pilots with a stack of clones and infinite funds behind them. And she was winning.

Even I, the perennial cynic, was impressed. The Dryth had courage, that's for sure. "Her?" I asked.

"She's giving the Houses a rash," Ada said, munching on a handful of spicy-sweet spheroids.

"Sure, but…" I looked at the race list. Half the field was listed as "retired," which meant "very, very dead." Their clones, assuming they could be properly decanted, would take over the next day, but for an Unhoused Dryth without any chained clones backing her up? "There's no way they expect her to *live* through this, do they?"

Ada showed her flat teeth, which glittered white in the riotous holographic light. It was a Dryth smile. "Enough to pay us a quarter million."

For a full ten seconds, I forgot to make my assumed shape blink. "What's the catch?"

"The catch is that we can't kill her now. Or tomorrow. Or the next day. We have to kill her on day thirty, and we need to make it look like an accident during the race."

"What if she doesn't *live* to day thirty?"

Ada shrugged. "No money."

I could see how the angles worked in this job—it wasn't quantum mechanics. Our employer, House Saishinn, was finessing the gambling odds. The longer this Yatka lived, the more she showed up the Great Houses, the better the odds of her victory became and the more money she drew. Then, on the last day, when the most betting action was at play with her as the heavy favorite, they would guarantee all the bets predicting she'd win, see her taken out in grand fashion, and walk off with a huge proportion of the trade credits changing hands. Now, for the post-scarcity economics of a Dryth House, all that would really mean is trade *leverage* rather than wealth. They were trying to get their competing houses over a barrel by appealing to the masses. They wanted to make this Yatka into a folk hero, kill her off, and make all the profit. Not a bad plan.

I also didn't see how we were going to do it. "Ada, there will be a public contract on her head by the end of the day. She's going to have assassins stalking her at all times, she's going to get challenged to duels, not to mention surviving *that*." I gestured to the race still raging above. Another driver clipped a stabilizer on a piece of falling ice and cartwheeled into a ravine before exploding. "How can we possibly do this?"

Ada took a sip of some frothing beverage that smelled like disinfectant. "Two ways—first, let's see if we can get some business on the back end." This meant approaching a target of an assassin contract and getting them to pay you to put out a contract on the person who targeted them. Basic assassin business. It might thin out the number of contracts, but it wouldn't be enough.

"And the second one?" I asked.

She reached over and patted my head, which jiggled in a way that clearly demonstrated I had no skull. I knocked her hand away. She kept grinning. "We get her a bodyguard."

A bodyguard? "Who?" I wondered aloud.

Ada just kept smiling at me.

It took me a second. Then I got it. "Oh. Oh, great."

Ada passed me a dossier on a data card. "I've got your persona *all* figured out, Faceless. You're going to love it."

I did not love it. In the first place, Ada had clearly fashioned my new identity off of her own image—a tall, unhoused Dryth female, generously muscular—and had spent a *lot* of time detailing this fictional bodyguard's face—long lashes, eyes of violet flecked with green, slender nostrils. "This is you, only prettier, am I right?" I asked her after I'd looked it over.

Ada snorted, which meant I was right. "Focus on the backstory."

I didn't. My experience infiltrating biped societies had told me that people judged with their eyes far, far more than they did with their brains. All I needed was a loose narrative—I was a bodyguard looking for work, and Yatka seemed like somebody everyone would want to kill. There, done. Unhoused Dryth never liked to share their backstories, anyway. I'd been hanging around with Ada for more than a cycle now and I still had no idea where *she* had come from, did I? Yatka and I weren't going to trade stories about our childhoods or talk about what our emancipated clones were up to. Gross.

For a long-term infiltration like this, the physical toll on my outer membranes—holding myself upright, keeping the shape and color and *texture* consistent, etc.—was prohibitive. Thankfully, I'd designed a little gadget to help me with that. It comprised one of my very few possessions—an internal frame, roughly in the shape of biped's skeleton, minus the ribcage and the fingers/toes and stuff, made out of a series of lightweight and flexible struts. It was designed so that I could let *it* support most of my weight as I moved around "upright," increasing my stamina and also letting me focus more on the finer details of shapeshifting, like eyelashes and blinking and breathing from where my lungs should be. It wouldn't let me last *forever*, but certainly for long enough to play the role of "bodyguard" for the Death Loop's most notorious racer for a full shift. All I needed to do was get the job.

First things first, I had to kill her current bodyguard. This was easy—I oozed through the ventilation system in the racer barracks while everyone was racing, jammed the ceiling fan so I could slip through, and cut his throat while he slept. I left the same way, unjamming the fan as I went. Very professional, very quiet. The local gossip networks speculated at length about who could possibly be responsible. He was Unhoused, though, so nobody did anything about it. Everyone knew that Yatka, currently the race leader, was going to have to endure this kind of thing more often. Old race aficionados—Housed Dryth who lived on the cruiser and watched the races every cycle—clucked their tongues and muttered about fate and inevitability.

Yatka, though, seemed unphased. During off-race hours, you'd see her in the commissary, holding court among a throng of her wild-eyed fans, dancing on the tables and getting fall-down drunk, as though the world weren't a nest of sharp-toothed predators just waiting for a chance to make her a snack. She got in shouting matches with her competitors and even got in a fistfight with a House Ghiasi Dryth over some smug remark. Knocked two of his teeth out. My initial assessment of her stood—she had a suicidal amount of courage.

"I like her," Ada remarked during one of our recon outings.

"You would," I said.

"I like her for the same reason I like you," Ada clarified. "The world is designed to screw you both over, and neither of you give a single fuck."

At that moment, Yatka was puking next to an airlock while

two of her engineering team held her up. None of them were keeping watch. "I don't have a death wish, Ada."

"Faceless, you're a Tohrroid—a trash-eating vermin—who walks around pretending to be a Dryth and kills people for a living. That is the craziest shit I have ever heard of. Compared to you, our girl here is positively *tame*."

I saw motion out the back of my "head"—two figures, dark coveralls, moving quickly towards the dead-end hallway with the airlock. I saw a glint of steel—they had blades. "Looks like our moment has come," I said.

Ada winked at me. "Go get 'em. Make it look difficult, remember? We want her to feel like it was a close one."

"Ada, if I need to get in a skimmer chase and harpoon princes, I'll ask your advice. Killing people in dark alleys? That's *my* specialty." I got up and ambled away as though I hadn't noticed anything. I paused in front of a closed-down shop window and perfected my face in the reflection of the glass, pulling my eyes slightly closer together, pushing myself up on the wireframe another few centimeters to get my height just right. The whole time, I was watching every second of the entire assassination attempt unfold out of my back.

The two killers were Lhassa geldings, judging from their stooped posture and shaved-down horns. The Lhassa only castrated bulls who had proven themselves too volatile for even *their* culture's generous tolerances, so these two slugs were definitely real winners. Probably just a pair of bounty hunters, taking a shot at a real contract instead of scraping undesirables off the concourse floor and pushing them out an airlock. Come to think of it, they *were* right by an airlock. Their plan—stupid and straightforward—laid itself out for me.

They stabbed the two engineers first. They revealed themselves as amateurs right away when they didn't slash the legs and instead went for the lower back, hoping to find their kidney. Two things about this: first, one of the engineers was wearing body armor, and the knife didn't penetrate so much as punch him in the back. Second, instead of one big kidney, like the Lhassa, the Dryth have something like six tiny kidneys, all distributed throughout their torso. Stabbing *one* of them just isn't that big a deal. That's what the second engineer got—a knife probably close to one of the other of his half-dozen minor organs. Both Dryth screamed.

Persistence, of course, makes up for a lack of skill, especially when it comes to stabbings. The two Lhassa kept poking away at their victims as I crossed the corridor. While there hadn't been a lot of people around before, *now* the corridor was completely deserted. The café where Ada and I had been sitting had closed up shop and locked the doors. I saw no sign of Ada. It was just me, the two killers, and their targets.

The guy who'd taken the knife in the kidney now had probably ten stab wounds. He might die, might not—depended on a lot of things I couldn't tell about from this angle, and, anyway, I didn't actually care. The other one in the body armor was now in a wrestling match for the knife with the other guy and rapidly losing. I watched the gelding reach inside a leg pocket of his coveralls and pull out a laser. Guy probably shoulda opened with that.

All of this took about eight seconds. In that time, Yatka had fallen on her face, puked a little, and was just starting to figure out what was happening. "Hey… HEY!" She grabbed the wall and tried to stand up. She was paying attention now. Good.

My turn.

If I didn't have the wireframe, my first move would have been to "spit" a knife out of my chest and into the back of that Lhassa with the laser. That, though, wasn't something a biped could do, so I had to resort to the old-fashioned headlock. I grabbed him around the throat just as he burned a hole through the engineer's face. I am not stronger than a Lhassa bull, no matter how muscular I make myself look, but I had other advantages. As he grabbed my arm and was probably wondering why my flesh was so squishy, I stabbed him through *his* single kidney by poking a knife out of my simulated stomach. He went rigid with pain. I gave the knife a twist, yanked it free, and dropped him so he could bleed out in peace. *That* is how you stab people.

Gelding number two had noted my arrival. He was covered in blood and cursing in whatever clan language he spoke. He held his knife out in a fighter's crouch, watching me. "Not your concern, lizard!" he shouted.

The Dryth aren't lizards. If I *was* a Dryth, I might have been insulted. Instead, I just showed him my knife, coated in his friend's blood. It was a nice one—triangular blade, black as charcoal, monomolecular edge. Ada had given it to me for some reason I couldn't remember.

The gelding backed away. He was thinking of running, which I didn't like. I put my "foot" over the other guy's laser and pulled it up through a vacuole into my simulated torso. When he turned to run, I made as if I was pulling the laser out of a pocket and bisected his spine.

Yatka was leaning on her knees, next to me. "Nice...nice shot."

"I was aiming for his head," I said, truthfully.

Yatka wasn't listening anymore, though. She was looking down at her friend, the one who'd had his back made into hash by that Lhassa's cheap plastic knife. She wanted to scream, I think, but she threw up instead.

I hate touching people, but I put a fake arm around Yatka and kept her from falling over, tensing my membranes to make them seem as firm as Dryth arm muscles. "It's okay," I lied. "It's going to be okay."

Ada, watching from a corner about twenty meters away, gave me a thumbs-up and a wave, knowing I would see it.

We were in.

I stayed with Yatka while cruiser medical drones showed up and pronounced both the two Lhassa and her two friends dead. We were sitting in the café across the way, right where Ada and I had been watching her. Race time—the thing around which the circadian rhythms of the fat passenger cruiser pivoted—was in a couple of hours, making it early morning.

Yatka sipped some tarry Dryth concoction that was served warm and bitter. She hugged it to her chest as she watched the drones hose the blood and puke off the walls. "It was a good thing you came along," she said. "You really know your way in a fight."

I didn't say anything. I focused on blinking the right number of times and mirroring her breathing rhythms.

"You never told me your name."

"Kura," I said.

"What's your story, Kura?"

"I was looking for you. I'm a bodyguard, need work."

Yatka sipped, watching me with golden eyes over the rim of her mug, "What happened to your last client?"

"Joined House Doonrue. Doesn't need me anymore."

Yatka shook her head. "Sellout. Fucking tourist."

"Excuse me?"

She held up two thick fingers. "Two kinds of Unhoused— the ones that wish they were Housed and the ones that wish that first group would fucking die in a fire. Which are you, Kura?"

I made my face smile. "That second one. Definitely."

Yatka smiled back. "Want a job?"

* * *

I watched the next day's race from Yatka's pit barge—a ship that flew along the perimeter of the Death Loop and kept in constant contact with her. The power plant, engines, and a bunch of other parts were all quantum-entangled with replicas inside the vessel, allowing a variety of repairs and modifications to be made instantly and remotely. The command center monitored her vitals, gave her information about upcoming conditions, and kept track of all the other racers as well. Every racer had a ship like this, creating a little fleet of ships, flying in formation around the Loop at speeds that, for starships, were extraordinarily slow. I was introduced to a bunch of different people whose names I didn't bother to remember. They all seemed relieved that I was there. They'd looked me up, apparently, with the cruiser's skennite core—a kind of living crystal that had a part time job as a database. The forged documentation that Ada had provided regarding my so-called existence was sufficient to not just fool it but make it particularly enthusiastic about my skillset.

I had nothing in particular to do while on board, so after getting some rest in my natural state (I hid in a vent in the lavatory, my wireframe folded up on the lip of the disposal chute), I found myself watching the race. I couldn't realistically avoid it—every holodisplay, every console, every *surface* in the pit barge was displaying the stats. Unlike bipeds, I can't "close" my vision off with a couple of handy sheets of skin or turn away—I *have* to see it, no matter how stupid I think it is. I was immersed against my will.

The displays on the pit barge were different from the aggressive light show that the spectators watched, though. This was a professional enterprise, shown with the clinical detachment of a well-honed organization. A day's racing was ten standard hours, more or less, during which time the racers would traverse over a hundred thousand kilometers of territory in relatively close quarters with the others. The pit barge was constantly compiling and updating data, plotting courses, getting information from and giving it to Yatka, who was strapped into her skimmer a hundred kilometers away and on whose reflexes the entire enterprise turned.

Or so I thought at first.

The more I watched, the more I started to see the *strategy* in Yatka's race. All the other racers were Housed Dryth, who knew perfectly well that a lost skimmer or an early retirement was, in some cases, an acceptable loss. They were willing to take huge risks, fly dangerous courses, working on the assumption that any losses would be offset by the losses of other racers. Yatka, though, had to *think*—she had to plot courses that were both survivable *and* optimal and fly them *flawlessly*. Her team wasn't navigating—*she* was. Her voice was always coming over the Q-link, asking questions about mineral compositions and torsional forces, and then she would nudge her ship into a slightly different spiral around the torus and, like a miracle, wind up blasting to the front of the pack. It was astounding. I couldn't believe how fast she could do it, and almost all in her head.

"What's her background?" I asked one of the pit crew at one point.

"She's a geophysicist," the young Dryth female answered, smiling up at me. "She's amazing, right?"

"Yes," I was forced to admit. "She is."

At the end of the day's race, Yatka placed third, which still kept her the overall leader by a few points. I was there to meet her as they cut her out of the cockpit and uncoupled her body from the control rig. She looked happy to see me. "Enjoy the show?"

"Looked dangerous," I said. "You're going to put me out of work."

"Funny." Yatka toweled the back of her neck and reached out to grab a water bladder.

I grabbed her wrist, concentrating on making my hand feel firm, strong. "Me first."

She looked up into my simulated eyes—I was taller than her by a good margin. She held my ersatz gaze for a few seconds longer than seemed necessary. "Are we going to have to share meals now, too?"

That actually was a good idea. "Yes."

She fluttered her eyes at me and tipped the bladder into my mouth. I drank. "Safe?" she asked.

I felt the nanites in the water start trying to break down my tissues, but the joke was on them—the composition of my body is completely different from a Dryth's. What would have devoured her esophagus from the inside out, I just found a little spicy. "No," I told her. "Not safe."

As the barge traveled back to the cruiser, I did my job and tracked down where the water bladder had come from. They'd been supplied them in bulk when they did their initial supply requisitions before the race began. They—all of Yatka's team—had been drinking them for days without incident, so the assassin must have put the nanites in just a few of the bladders rather than all of them. Pretty clever work, but good odds you'd miss your mark and just kill a random engine tech or something. A weird play. I had them space all the water and told them to buy only from a Thraad Consortium. I gave them a few suggestions.

"That was a close call," Yatka said. "That's two I owe you."

"It's going to get worse before it gets better," I told her. "And the only thing you owe me is dinner."

Yatka grinned. "Kura, you are one smooth operator, you know that?"

I wasn't sure what she meant. I decided to assume it was good.

It was three days of this—me escorting Yatka around, watching her race, tasting her meals—and in that time I foiled two other assassination attempts. These were clumsy things—a lunatic with a plasma thrower in his coat pocket, trying to blast her in a crowd as he passed (it would have killed at least six people and caused a monster of a fire), another one trying to stab her from behind in a bar. In both instances I had the assassins dead before they knew I was aware of them. It pays to be able to see out your back. Plus, now I had a new plasma thrower and a knife.

Yatka talked a lot, mostly about racing and the Death Loop. "The longer we race, the worse conditions will get," she said. "The Loop is already undergoing collapse. The checkpoint rings can't keep it in place forever, and gravity is doing its work."

"Good odds you'll get killed," I said. We were sitting together in the back of a dimly lit Lhassa restaurant, where I could see all the other tables. I had the plasma thrower in plain view, just as a warning for nobody to get any ideas.

Yatka slurped her noodles. "Maybe, but it'll be worth it."

"You want to be a Solon that bad?"

"No. But they do." She jerked her chin at a group of House Cholkos, sitting at the circular methane bar at the center of the place, taking hits off little plastic tubes. "And I'm going to keep them from getting it."

I wasn't buying it. "A tapped star, though. If you don't want to be a Solon, what will you do with all that power?"

Yatka looked up at the race highlights, being projected on a holo in the corner of the restaurant. "Destroy it," she said. "Nobody should have that much power."

I made my shoulders shrug. "Why not?"

The highlights were now showing a list of the retired racers from the day and the status of their clones, ready to be fed into the meat grinder. "Just look at what it's done to us," was all she said.

* * *

Ada met with us the next day, before racing had begun. She'd sent a courier—an actual living one, not a drone—and proposed the meet-up in a conference room on the outer ring of the cruiser with a big window providing a panoramic view of the Hainar system. She promised to come alone.

"Why would the top assassin on the cruiser want to talk to me?" Yatka asked me. "She's not just going to, like, shoot me in the face, is she?"

"She'd have to get through me first," I said.

Yatka grabbed my shoulder and hung off it with much of her weight. My outer membranes strained in agony to maintain their shape, but I think I managed it. She was always doing things like that—touching me at odd times, staring into my eyes. Not knowing what else to do, I just let her do it—let her hang, held her gaze. "I know you will," she said, "but this is Deadeye Ada. She could probably kill you bare-handed."

She wishes. "Ada is a pro who cares about her reputation. She wouldn't stoop to such a cheap trick if you were her target."

"You're sure?"

"I'm sure." In point of fact, Ada absolutely *would* pull that kind of trick. I'd seen her do it. That kind of stuff didn't make it into the legend, though. "Don't worry—I'll check it out."

By "check it out," that meant I left Yatka in a secure location and went to the meeting early. Ada was there, of course, wearing her trademark body armor and a long cape of some kind of color-shifting fabric. She'd laid her multipistols on a pristine square of crimson fabric, each disassembled into their various pieces. For one of them to fire, it would take her about ten minutes of tinkering, or so it appeared, anyway. I didn't turn my head toward her when I walked in, but I pointed at the display. "Nice touch."

"I'm trying to look nonthreatening," Ada said. "It's difficult."

The view out the window was…uninspiring. Just a field of stars, really. The Death Loop was so long and so slender, it was invisible to my membranes at this distance. As for Hainar itself, it was a muddy red blot at the edge of the window, its radiance dulled by the window's flare-reduction systems. "I trust you've been enjoying your time off?"

Ada snorted. "Being this conspicuous is work, you know. I've fought six duels since I've been here."

"Yeah, I've heard. Amateurs. Idiots out for cheap revenge."

"How's things on the inside? How is Yatka?" Ada came and stood next to me—we were, at the moment, the same height. "Think she suspects?"

"She's too busy with the race, too preoccupied with the other assassins on her trail. I'm guessing *you* put the nanites in the water. How'd you manage it? They bought that stuff before we got here."

"I got the contract before we got here, that's how. It was part of my prep work."

I turned my head toward her, just to let her know I was pissed. "And you didn't *tell* me? What the fuck?"

Ada smiled and backed away. "Faceless, if I'd told you, you wouldn't have come!"

"You shit." I hated when she did this—went behind my, well, when she wasn't straight with me. "What else are you holding out on?"

"Nothing! Nothing, I swear! I just got a little advance notice on this one—I took some liberties. Sorry!"

She wasn't sorry. She couldn't resist a big job like this—something spectacular, something to burnish her reputation in the right circles. To her, contracts with the major Dryth Houses *were* the right circles. I was never very clear on what Ada wanted out of it all—trade credits, *money*, but to do what? I guess I couldn't articulate what I wanted it for, either. A sense of safety, maybe. A sense that I, an invisible nonentity, *mattered* and the money proved it. Maybe she was the same.

Maybe that was why we made good partners—because we didn't know.

Yatka, when I brought her in, wasn't quite so indecisive. "So, you want me to pay you to take out the people who are trying to kill me?"

Ada smiled. "Yes."

"No."

I was surprised. "Why not? That might take some of the heat off. Make my job easier."

"If you're worried about them being replaced by their clones, they won't," Ada said. "I'll make sure their whole operation is sunk."

"But I don't want them to die," Yatka said. "I want them to see that they're *wrong*."

Both Ada and I were confused, but only Ada showed it on her face, what with it actually being her face and all. "I don't understand."

"Why aren't you Housed?" Yatka asked her. "You could be— any one of them would love to take you. Why not?"

"Because I belong to no one but myself," Ada said. "I don't do what I do for the glory of anyone but me."

Yatka shook her head. "But isn't that an *empty* reason? All that death and violence and bloodshed just so, what, people will think you're amazing?"

Ada folded her arms. "Empty to *you*, maybe."

Yatka leaned forward. "Don't you see that they're *laughing* at you?" She pointed back through the door, back at the observation cruiser at large and all the Dryth Houses, jockeying for supremacy. "The Great Houses aren't *impressed* by you. You're a tool! Just a knife in their arsenal—the sharpest one, maybe, but that's it. You'll wear out, you'll break, and then they'll just get another one. But while you're here? They make you dance by dangling trade credits in front of your face—money that's a *pittance* to them, a fucking *rounding error* on their interstellar ledgers—and you think you're special?"

Ada's eyes sparkled. For a second, I thought she might kill Yatka right there, and screw the contract. But Ada was, as ever, a professional. "I *am* special. And I'm sorry we can't do business."

Yatka got up. "I've got a race to prepare for. Come on, Kura."

Ada stood up as well. "Just remember to watch your back." She snapped her fingers over the disassembled multipistols and, with a hum of electromagnetism, the weapons reassembled themselves in the blink of an eye and were in her hands, pointing right at me. "The one that gets you, you won't see coming."

Yatka snorted. "Same to you, assassin."

The race continued. Just as Yatka had predicted, the farther the race went, the closer we got to day thirty and the last stretch, the worse the Death Loop got. Huge chunks of the ring would break off sometimes, leaving an uncrossable abyss that killed any racers that hadn't made it across before it opened. Volatile gasses spurted from fissures, some of which ignited on contact with a skimmer's exhaust plume, blowing the vessel off course and out of control.

The racers got more aggressive, too, particularly the ones in the back of the pack, which Yatka's team started referring to as "the Churn." Weapons weren't technically allowed to be mounted on the skimmers, but that didn't prevent some of them from finding creative ways to hurt each other—barrel rolls so their repulsor wash pushed nearby racers into the ground, armored fenders for aggressive side-swiping, and so on were common. One guy actually had his team *increase* his exhaust output, creating a streak of plasma fire that he used to burn through the cockpits of those he passed. Fortunately, he hit a magnesium pocket on day fourteen, and both he and his skimmer were incinerated instantly. After that, his successive clones didn't take the risk.

Yatka navigated it all with her trademark panache, all of it a front for her meticulous planning and extensive knowledge of the track conditions. At some point, I realized that the longer the race went on, the larger her advantage became.

It was because of the clones.

Every time a clone died on the track, the knowledge that racer had gleaned on the track that day—the skill, the tricks, the warning signs they used to notice danger—was all lost. The new clone only had knowledge from the backed-up copy the day *before*. They still knew most of it—*almost* all of it—but the knowledge was delivered as theory, not experience. I knew from hard years on the outskirts of the world that there was no substitute for experience, for *lived* experience. Muscle memory was about the only kind of memory I did well.

The clones didn't have it, or at least not as much of it as Yatka did, and it showed. Her top finishes became first-place finishes, day in and day out. Her lead in the rankings grew and grew. The gambling action on her races became a frenzy—everyone wanted in on this, the improbable victories of an Unhoused nobody.

The assassination attempts got more frequent, more professional. With me by her side, they stopped trying the direct approach—no more attempts to gun her down as she was coming out of a restaurant on the main concourse, no more knives in crowded rooms. Now they tried more esoteric methods. Poison, of course, but as it had become my habit to share meals with Yatka, that didn't get far—Tohrroid physiology is very, *very* different from that of a Dryth, and anything that would poison her did nothing to me and I would always detect the flavor. When you spend your life eating a thousand different kinds of garbage, you develop a *very* discerning palate.

Next was bombs. Bombs are not technically against the assassin code, but they're sloppy—too many bystanders to get caught in the blast—and so professional assassins don't like them much. Hard to make a case for yourself as a good hire if your record has a long list of property damage and collateral casualties. So, the kind of bombs I was dealing with were little ones—little concussive poppers, large enough to reduce anybody in, say, a public lift to soup but not large enough to actually blow up the lift. Here, again, I had an edge—bombs like that were hidden out of sight, but for me, very little is out of sight. Throw in a little scanner to check beneath floors and inside control panels and we were good. I had, by day twenty, foiled about sixteen attempts and taken down twenty assassins, most in dramatic fashion.

I was getting a bit of a reputation myself now. They hadn't come up with a catchy nickname for Kura, though they were working on it. "Kura All-Seeing" was being floated around, but it was pretty awkward to say in Dryth Basic.

It was also having an effect on *Ada's* reputation as well. Rumors were surging about when the race's most notorious assassin would take up Yatka as a target. There was even a betting line on it—who would come out on top? The omniscient Kura or the deadly Ada? Place your wagers!

"You two look a lot alike, you know," Yatka observed once. It was an hour or two after the day's racing, where her lead continued to grow. She had been starving coming out, though, and didn't want to wait for a table at some of the more secure restaurants on the concourse, opting instead for this Thraad selling fish and greens out of the back of a cargo container slapped down in the corner of one of the shuttle bays. I didn't like the wide-open spaces, but there was more cruiser security here than on the concourse—they didn't want their shuttle bay getting shot up, after all—so I had agreed.

I was trying not to look at the holos of Ada's face next to my own simulated face floating over the café with the words *WHO WILL WIN* between them. Currently, the odds were five to one against me. I tried not to be insulted. "I don't see the resemblance," I lied.

We got our food and sat down. I appreciated that the snail-like Thraad had realized that most bipeds like chairs. I especially did—wearing this shape day in and day out was exhausting. I wasn't sure how much more of it I could take. *Two hundred and fifty thousand trade credits*, I told myself. *Ten more days.* For some reason, that wasn't as motivating as it had been, weeks before.

Kura got that look that meant she had something private she wanted to tell me. She had done this more and more often—told me little things about herself, like how she always wished she was a Lhassa as a kid, and how her parents had forced her into university. She lowered her voice and leaned over the table. "I was biologically conceived, you know."

I tried to think how a Dryth was supposed to react to this. I knew, for instance, that the vast majority of Dryth were artificially conceived—almost all of them genetically tailored in a vat and gestated and decanted from same. I knew that there were a bunch of neo-traditionalists and weird religious cults and some sexual fetishists who did it the old-fashioned way, and that this was a rude topic to bring up in the wrong company. But was I—was *Kura*—the wrong company?

I realized that I'd not moved or blinked for too long when Yatka ducked her head into her bowl. "I'm sorry! I shouldn't have said anything!"

"It's okay," I said, though I didn't really know why. I mean, it *was* okay—who gives a shit about Dryth reproductive taboos—but I felt as though saying so was pulling off some kind of veil. I felt exposed. "Yatka, I don't care about that."

She breathed a sigh of relief. "I was worried about telling you. I mean, you were *obviously* decanted." She gestured to my body. "I mean, look at you. I never would have thought somebody like you would...well, would *believe* in me like you do."

I'll admit it—that stung. I was going to kill her in ten days, and she had no idea. Seemed almost...unsporting. Cruel, maybe, though I had little trouble thinking of things that were far crueler that I'd done, let alone *seen* done. "It's not going to work, Yatka. You aren't going to change the Houses by winning this race. They'll just crush you—crush *me*—and keep going."

"And *that's* why I'm doing it!" Yatka said, grabbing my hands. "And I think that's why you're doing it, too. I know you hate them—well, I don't know, maybe 'hate' is too shallow of a word for you. Kura, have you ever *seen* yourself kill somebody? It's...it's *contemptuous*. It's like those assassins and the Houses that hire them are the *vilest* things you can imagine, like some smack oozing out of the gutter, stinking like shit."

I pulled my hands away. "I don't like that word," I said.

"What word? 'Shit'?"

"No—'smack,'" I said, fully aware that, in all my life, I'd only verbally objected to that slur a handful of times. Honestly, at that moment, I couldn't even think of an instance. I just took it, internalized it, *accepted it* as the price of being alive. But there I was, in that café, across a rickety folding table from a short, craggy Dryth racer who wouldn't stop looking into my eyes, and I found myself talking. "It's disrespectful of them—the Tohrroids. Without them, we wouldn't even have the air we're breathing. The cities would overflow with trash. They... they're important. And then we call them nasty names."

Had I blown my cover? It felt kind of like I had. I expected Yatka to pull away in horror. To scream to everyone that here—right *here*—was the biggest, ugliest smack in the universe. Quick, somebody get a flamethrower!

Instead, she said this: "I hadn't thought about it before, but you're right. I'm sorry."

No one had ever done that before. Well, Ada apologized when she fucked up sometimes, but it wasn't like this. Yatka wasn't worried I'd quit—she was worried she'd hurt my feelings. She cared about me, as a friend. It occurred to my asexual self, very belatedly, that maybe she thought of me as more than that.

It was as I considered this shocking turn that Yatka and I got absurdly lucky, because the assassin who took the railgun shot at us from, I would later learn, four decks up, hadn't properly factored the density of the shuttle bay compartment into his trajectories. The rail—a blazing sunbeam of liquefied alloys—missed us by a little over two meters, punching a fat hole in the deck. The explosion knocked me and Yatka off our chairs and everyone else in the café, likewise. Then the vacuum of space started doing the rest—sucking furniture and people into that hole and into the deep, dark black that yawned beneath the shuttle bay and the outer hull that had just been pierced.

I was no longer Kura—the concussive force of the shockwave had made me into a more natural quivering pile of flesh, still awkwardly clinging to my now-misshapen wireframe. Fortunately, Yatka was dazed—her head had stuck the deck pretty hard. Maybe she hadn't seen what happened to me.

Alarms were going off. People were screaming. We were getting sucked toward the gap. Lights were flashing—they were going to seal off the shuttle bay because of the hull breach. I pulled myself together, quite literally, and dragged Yatka across the floor and out the door before it closed.

In the end, that little railgun stunt killed six bystanders—which made the cruiser authority mad—and compromised the structural integrity of five compartments aboard the ship—which made them *much* angrier. The assassin—a Lhassa mare—was apprehended and spaced. It had been the first and only time security had actually intervened in all of these assassination attempts. Killing people was one thing, but firing railguns *inside* starships was quite another.

Yatka was taken to the medical bay with a pretty bad concussion and a fractured skull, not to mention some burns and scrapes. She had to retire without starting the next leg of the race, giving all the rest of the field a whole day to whittle down her point total.

I spent the day at the side of her rejuvenation pod, doing nothing but think. I thought about those people at the café who had been a bit closer to the railgun's impact site than we were, and how they hadn't done anyone any harm and came to it anyway, and about how that was just the way the whole universe worked—you lived for reasons you invented yourself, you died for no reason at all. The Dryth Houses were supposed to be a solution to that, as I understood it. Shared purpose, shared drive, and a long, long life with as many descendants as you wanted. You could even make copies of yourself and live forever, after a fashion. Inside the walled gardens of the Houses was utopia. But look at all the wreckage they created in the process—whole stars tapped and yoked, whole oceans of blood spilled, all for their own notions of comfort and perfection. Their contempt was much, much deeper than anything my bitter insides could vomit up.

Ada came to visit. She wasn't in disguise or anything. The med-techs in the corridor saw me and saw her and they got out of there as fast as their legs could carry them. I wondered vaguely how this would change the betting odds.

"How's our girl?" Ada asked. "She gonna make it?"

"Yes."

Ada leaned against the wall next to me. She took out her pipe and lit it—some kind of Thraad fungal concoction. It smelled like a swamp. "You know, our employers are getting worried that we won't come through. This last one was too close, Faceless."

I thought about it. I found I didn't care. "We shouldn't do it," I said.

"What?"

"The contract—fuck it. We shouldn't do it. Let's not."

Ada grinned and took a few quick puffs. "We're in this, partner. No pulling out now. I can't be seen balking at—"

"I don't care about your reputation, Ada. You know that."

"But *I* do—you know *that*." Ada turned to face me. "You need me, remember? This partnership is good for both of us. The money we've made—"

"Screw the money. I'm *tired* of taking their money the same way I was tired of eating their shit. I don't want to be at the bottom of the food chain anymore, Ada."

"So, what are you saying? We get on top? That's impossible, Faceless." Ada gestured vaguely, unable to convey the shape of what I was asking. "We *can't* become Solons—you because you're, well, *you*, and me because…because the only way is…"

"Is to win the race. For real," I said.

"*We* aren't racing, Faceless—*she is*"—Ada jerked her thumb in the direction of the rejuvenation pod—"and what makes you think she'll share the bounty with us, the people who were paid to kill her? To you, the one who's been *lying* to her all this time?"

"She doesn't care about the reward. All she wants to do is kick them all in the teeth. To show them all that their stupid way of life isn't the only way."

"It *is* the only way," Ada snapped. "You might not like it, but it *is*. This job buys us our own ship, Faceless. It buys us freedom the likes of which we've never known. And you're going to pass on that on *principle?* Come on!"

"I'm not doing it. I won't kill her."

"You're just upset. The stress is getting to you." Ada tapped her pipe ash out on the floor. "We'll talk again when you come to your senses. In the meantime"—she pointed at Yatka's pod—*"do your job."*

She stormed out, leaving me alone. I reached up and put my fake hand on the cool front of the pod, right on top of Yatka's name and vital statistics. Oh, I'd do my job, all right.

The next assassination attempt was more insidious. It might not have been an assassination attempt at all, come to think of it, but somebody messed with the medical-bay software such that it took Yatka seven days to recover instead of just one. Seven days of her lead being cut, day after day, until she was no longer ahead on points—she was just behind. During that time, I stewed on what to do next.

Her team was in a panic. I realized then that all of them had thrown in hard with Yatka. Her losing was like a violation of an article of faith—she couldn't lose, because to lose would mean she was wrong, that Unhoused Dryth were worthless, shiftless no-accounts who would never amount to anything, and that the Houses were right to ignore them and exploit them. Maybe they *should* have unlimited resources and make slaved clones of themselves and live for the glory of their House and its specific, narrow cultural goals and affectations. Maybe they should turn their back on the universe and live in a place where everything was brought to heel for their own comfort.

They dragged me into a meeting, and I couldn't think of any real objection to not go because they held it literally in the corridor outside Yatka's rejuvenation pod. They vented their insecurities about their life choices for a while until one of them—I never really bothered to learn names, but this was one of the navigation team—floated an actually pertinent idea. "Could we get one of *us* to race? Get one of us to pass for Yatka and just, like, *not* finish dead last for a leg?

Then came the very sensible objection to that plan, from one of the engineers: "We could die!"

"Right, but if we don't die *first*, we still don't finish dead last." The guy was serious, too—his face very solemn, his nostrils slender, his eyelids drooping, his hands clenched into fists. What a lunatic.

They all looked at me. I made my face frown. "What?"

The navigation guy ticked off things on three of his four fingers., "You have exceptional reflexes, superlative spatial awareness, nerves of steel—need I go on?"

"I also have an aversion to fiery death."

"I think you could do it."

"What about the *g* forces—I don't handle those well." This was very true, in the sense that there was no way I could maintain my form while in that cockpit. I might even suffocate.

"We have dampening systems for that!" an engineer chimed in.

I looked around at them all—a ragtag team of Dryth outcasts, their skin a riot of colors and patterns, their eyes full of hope—and I said the next words carefully, so they would all understand: "No. Fucking. Way."

"I can't believe it," one of them muttered. "How could you do this to her? Aren't you two in love?"

"Aren't we in *what*?"

I got a lot of "are you a sociopath" looks right then. I get them a lot when I'm letting my inner sociopath show—I'm not cut out for this, working with others. Team play. Sacrifice for the larger goals. I didn't have larger goals. I didn't have a team. All I had was Ada, and I wasn't even talking to her just then.

The engineer told me he was going to make a plan anyway and send it to me via the Q-link. He said the implants required "trivial surgery" to install, still assuming I had a brain and a skull and all that other crap a Dryth was supposed to have. I ignored him and waited for him to stop talking and leave.

An hour or two later, Yatka's rejuvenation chamber finally blinked green. She was okay and about to be released. I stood there as the pod opened with a hiss of air and the vertical chamber slid down the wall to become a bed. Yatka was naked, but the bed thoughtfully furnished itself with a modesty sheet as she was lowered, as though I hadn't just seen literally everything for a solid ten seconds. Dryth notions of modesty are very, very weird.

I was the first thing she saw when her eyes flickered open. She smiled. "I knew it. I knew you'd get me out of there." She reached up and squeezed my hand. "How long was I out?"

I gave her the bad news. She took it rather well. "Might take some of the heat off, anyway. We're still within the margin—we can still win."

"We?" It was that same weird feeling I'd just had while sitting with the team. An assumption of inclusion, of *participation* in this ridiculous, suicidal enterprise.

"I've been thinking." She was still holding my hand, and I, meanwhile, was keeping up the pressure there to simulate the texture and density of a Dryth hand. "Something I wanted to tell you in that café in the shuttle bay, before…you know."

"What is it?" I found her trying to gaze into my eyes again. I didn't know what to do, so I made myself look away. This was getting too tangled, too thorny.

"I know you and Deadeye Ada have some kind of business to deal with. Something unfinished." I opened my mouth to lie, but she forestalled me. "I don't need to know about it— it's okay. I was just hoping that, when this is all over—win or lose—if you'd…well…if you'd stay with us. Stay with me."

"Once the race is over, nobody will be trying to kill you anymore," I said.

"I know. Kura, I don't want you to stay because you'll be *useful*. I want you to stay because I care about you."

I pulled my hand back.

Yatka sat up. "The Dryth Houses don't have a monopoly on happiness, Kura. Just because we don't accept them—because we won't *conform* to them—doesn't mean we have to struggle and be miserable forever. I feel like you've spent so long in the dark—so long killing and fighting and suffering—that you don't think you deserve love and acceptance. But you *do*, Kura. You do! We can be that for each other. We don't need a whole House, a whole culture—just the two of us and a few friends, the galaxy at our feet."

She meant it. To the extent that I could read Dryth facial expressions and vocal cues, she meant it. She loved me and wanted to stay with me. She was promising, what, a life together, or mutual support?

I wondered—did I have that with Ada? Is what we were doing *mutual*? I had asked myself that often over the years and never come up with a satisfactory answer. But at least Ada and I were honest with each other. Well, most of the time.

"I'll think about it," I said. This wasn't a lie, for a change. I thought about it. It was almost all I thought about.

The next two days of racing, with Yatka's triumphant return blasted over every holoscreen on the observation cruiser, were some of the most intense ever. The Death Loop was collapsing in earnest now as they neared the finish line—where the race had started, thirty days ago. There were few navigable pathways. Fire and ice and the harshness of hard vacuum assailed the skimmers every hundred kilometers. The retirement rate was outrageous.

Yatka outdid herself. Whoever had put her in that coma for almost an extra week had *thought* they were doing her a disservice, but I think what they actually did was give her a chance to recuperate from the physical and mental stresses of the race such that she approached this home stretch with a fresh store of energy and greater dedication to purpose. She made first-place finishes each leg.

The betting action was absolutely wild. No one could believe she had lived this long. She was the favorite to win by a light-year, even if the points totals were close. Her fame and notoriety made Ada's little cult of wannabe victims look tiny and sad by comparison. When we walked down the concourse, she was thronged by admirers—Unhoused Dryth, inspired to do more with their lives, other aliens just glad to see the Houses put in their place, and even a few Housed Dryth who were casting off their affiliations, blanking their Housed colors and going rogue.

I could see it now. I could see what made her dangerous. She made success—real success—look possible without having to submit to the hierarchical games every Dryth House played with its members. If Yatka—a biologically birthed, short, Unhoused *scientist*—could do it, anybody could. She had been right, *was* right. Her being in the race was a real threat to the Great Houses in a way Ada and I never could be.

It occurred to me for the first time that you could never kill your way into a better world. I'd been trying for years, I'd come a long way, but Yatka was showing me just how short my vision had been. Ada and I could have it all, but not so long as we played the Houses' game. They were rigging it, just like they were rigging the race. Just like everything else.

Ada had told me that, much like the booby-trapped water bladders, the means to sabotage Yatka's skimmer was already inside the pit barge. At the start of day thirty, I retrieved it from the hold, along with a bunch of other replacement parts. It was very small—enough to fit neatly in the palm of my simulated hand. It came with a haptic expert system for installation—the closer I moved it to where it belonged in the skimmer's engine, it would hum slightly with a pleasant vibration. I knew roughly where to put it; the expert system would do the rest.

It was a simple matter, sneaking my way into the hangar where the skimmer, in all its fearsome, battle-scarred complexity, hung ready for one more day of racing. It was a sleek, dark triangle, its repulsor skirts retracted, its armor newly patched and buffed. Printed on the side in blocky Dryth Basic was the word *Liberator*. An atrocious, ridiculous name.

I moved toward the main drive cone and I felt the little device hum happily—I was nearly there. Just reach out to where I felt it wanted to go, place it, and let the little machine do its work. Now was the moment of truth.

For the first time in my career, I didn't think I could go through with it. I held the little thing up—that deadly little cylinder—and…I just couldn't. I didn't want Yatka to die. No amount of money or promises would change my mind about that. I thought that maybe…maybe I *would* join her. Start a new life as someone else. I wondered how long I could keep it up.

My Q-link—the one I had with Ada and hadn't used, even once, since the mission started, buzzed to life inside me. I answered immediately, "Ada, we need to talk."

But the sound from the other end was nothing but a concentrated sonic blast. It made me stumble against the wall as my body vibrated in resonance with the frequency. I felt as though I might burst apart. Certainly, I was thrust off my frame and hit the deck in a quivering blob.

I managed to cut the connection. A sonic attack? Was it Ada, trying to kill me by remote? What was happening?

I heard footsteps coming up the corridor. Not enough time to re-form myself, not enough time to get situated on my wireframe. Instead, I oozed unsteadily into a mostly empty toolbox and closed the lid. There, in the dark, I tried to pull myself together. It took a few minutes.

My Q-link buzzed again. Ada, or another attack? I didn't answer. A few seconds passed—another call. It could be Ada, urgently trying to reach me. It could be whoever put that screamer on the line, trying for another hit. I weighed the risks.

I needed to know what happened to Ada, one way or another. If she was dead, if she was alive—the only way to know was on the other end of that line. Tensing myself for a quick shut-off, I answered the third call back.

It was Ada's voice. She was breathless and in pain. "F-Faceless…that…that you?"

"What happened?"

"The Saishinns…" she managed, naming the Dryth House employing us, "they…they took a shot at me. Sonic attack. J-just now."

I felt cold, and not just from the cool metal of the toolbox. They tried to double-cross her—to double-cross *us*. They assumed Ada had placed the device already, as the pit barge had already departed the observation cruiser for the Loop. They never intended to pay.

That kind of thing got you killed by assassins, but not when you were an almighty Dryth House. What was Ada going to do? Nothing, that's what. There weren't enough bullets in the galaxy to put an end to House Saishinn.

"The job's off?"

"Yes!" Ada said. The echo of her voice made it sound as if she were in some kind of crawlspace or something. I pictured her, low-crawling through the ventilation shafts, knife between her teeth, plotting vengeance. "Tell our girl to kick their asses. Meanwhile, I got some throats to cut. We'll meet up after."

By that she meant some kind of desperate escape, I guessed.

Her, multipistols blazing, as we fought our way onto a commandeered transport and jumped out of there to some out-of-the-way little planet where our enemies would take a while finding us. The kind of thing that had been the defining characteristics of my life to date.

But now I had something new lined up. "Yeah," I said. "Later, Ada."

I cut the connection. I oozed out of the box.

Yatka was there. She was holding the frame in one hand, the sabotage device in the other. When she saw me, she nearly screamed.

"Wait!" I said.

I said it in Kura's voice. Ingrained habit.

Yatka's expression was like ice when first struck by a hammer. She fell backwards onto the floor from shock. She pushed herself away from me. "No...*no*... You...you *can't* be!"

If she actually screamed, things would get worse. Her team would come running, I would be outnumbered, I would be unable to control the situation. The old self-preservation instincts, perfectly honed by a life of scavenging, came back online. I formed myself into Kura, my hands outstretched. "Please, let me explain."

Her face contorted in a kind of emotional pain I could only imagine. "You...you were going to *kill* me! You're...you're *it*! The Faceless Assassin!"

I hadn't heard that title before—was I...did I have a reputation after all? "I'm not going to hurt you, Yatka. I...I changed my mind."

"It was all rigged, wasn't it? The whole thing—the whole *race*—was just a cheat!" She banged her newly healed head against the wall. "How could I have been so stupid! So naive!"

"It's okay, Yatka—you're in the clear. Our employers double-crossed us..."

"*Our?!*"

I winced inwardly. A stupid mistake. I was losing my control, letting my guard down. Yatka had made me feel too safe, too willing to be honest. It was hard habit to break, once acclimated to.

"You and Deadeye Ada are a *team*!" Yatka scrambled to her feet, still backing away. She was looking all around the hangar, trying to find a way out or possibly try and understand how her life's goal—her great work here, on the Death Loop—could be undone so quickly, so easily as this. "You were going to kill me today on the track with this!" She held up the device. "And… and that would be it!"

"Right, but I'm not *going* to anymore!"

She moaned, "I can't believe you. Not anymore, I can't. Even if…even if I kill you, the Houses will never let me do it. I'll never get there. Who knows how many racers are on their side! How many were just *letting* me win, until this moment." Yatka's eyes bulged. She was in a panic.

I didn't know what to say or do. "Just…calm down."

She grabbed a plasma torch off a bench. "You're a monster, you know that? You thought you could crush people by using me, but I'm not going to let you. I'm never going to set foot in that skimmer, understand?"

"That's fine, Yatka! I'm okay with that! Let's think about this—"

She ignited the torch. "When I'm dead without racing, everyone will wonder *what could have been*. They'll wonder if I could have won. No matter how many times people tell them otherwise, they'll never stop *wondering*. That will be enough. That…that will *have* to be enough."

I kept my distance. "What are you talking about, Yatka? Put the torch down, please. I'm not going to hurt you."

"You and your masters haven't won. They'll never win. Because my people will be free! NO MATTER THE COST!" With a sudden jerk of her arm, she brought the white-hot flame of the plasma torch across the side of her skull. On the list of ways to die, it's a particularly unpleasant one. She had perhaps just enough time to realize that before she fell to the deck, her head a smoking ruin.

Shit.

I heard voices coming up the corridor. My instincts took over—step one: hide the body. There was a scrap chute—a place they threw trashed pieces of metal and glass and other materials to be melted down and reconstituted in the pit barge's furnace. I grabbed Yatka by the wrists, dragged her over, and dumped her in.

I felt heavy, suddenly. The magnitude of my betrayal, maybe. The sheer vicious stupidity of it all. The administrators and admirals and whatever in House Saishinn who were, right then, composing epic poetry about their giant fucking victory over the filthy, unwashed rabble.

I couldn't let it stand.

When the two engineers came into the hangar, I made myself into Yatka and mimicked her voice perfectly. "I need you both to reconfigure the skimmer controls. I'm going to fly without implants."

The two of them blinked at me for a second, but when they realized I was serious, they got to work.

The smell of Yatka's burned flesh still floated in the air. If the engineers smelled it, they gave no sign—they'd probably burned out their sinuses with toxic chemicals and gaseous metals years since, come to think of it. To them, Yatka was still alive, still fighting. To Yatka, she had died a martyr to her cause. To me, though, there was unfinished business.

House Saishinn and its fellow Houses had to be made to pay for all of this, and I knew of only one way how. It was insane, but there it was. I was going to race the final leg of the Death Loop, come what may. Maybe I'd die, but maybe I was okay with that.

In any case, there was no turning back now.

The speed of the race was something I hadn't anticipated. You didn't so much *see* the terrain as get a sense of it as a kind of background noise—a jagged, squiggly line of static that, if you touched it, you died.

The cockpit had a seamless, 360-degree view, rendered by the skimmer's onboard computer. The skimmer itself would have felt like an extension of the body, had I the implants. Instead, I could feel it in the four places my team had designed controls—one for each "foot," one for each "hand," and voice control for the rest.

I was wearing my wireframe to help give me some structure against the acceleration. It helped, but only barely. I felt like I was hanging on to a rocket bound skyward. It was exhausting, punishing. And yet I had volunteered for this.

The terrain was a simpler matter than it looked. Yatka's navigation notes were extensive, and the optimal path was plotted out in my visual spectrum as a broad green line. I stayed on the line—easy enough.

The other racers should have been the problem. As each joined the race following my start, I expected them to try any number of things to knock me off the course. I was not an able pilot, only a creature with a very good sense of three-dimensional space and good reflexes. My natural aptitudes would only take me so far against the myriad of dirty tricks I expected.

But the racers, instead, kept their distance. What should have been a desperate scramble was, instead, just me making sure I didn't hit the walls. I was just flying my own race.

There was only one explanation: they all knew I was going to explode. Maybe there was a leak in House Saishinn's operation, maybe Ada had blown the whistle, maybe they had all just figured it out on their own, but the word was definitely out. As I rocketed out ahead of the pack, untroubled by any interlopers, the odds in Yatka's favor must have skyrocketed. Trade credits and raw materials were flowing into the hands of stern Voosk bookies, and the Dryth Houses, knowing what they knew, took those bets and bided their time.

Except I didn't explode. I crushed myself practically flat with the power of that skimmer and I nearly careened into space a few times, but explode? Never.

By the time they collectively figured out something was wrong, it was eight hours in, and my lead was so large, they could barely catch up. It should have been a thrilling leg, but it hadn't been at all—it was a blowout.

I transferred out of the Death Loop as I shot through the final checkpoint and was sent directly to the victory dais in the center of the massive stadium in the center of the observation cruiser. The crowd—the crowd who had all just made modest money off a near sure-bet—chanted Yatka's name as I emerged from the cockpit after being cut out by drones. The great circular stage featured five Dryth ambassadors standing in tall pulpits so that they loomed over me, each of them wearing the traditional garb of their various Houses—Cholko, Ghiasi, Saishinn, Doonrue, and Atphos, all done up in long robes and absurd hats. They looked grim, those Dryth. They knew they'd been had but couldn't guess by whom.

There, on a plinth at the center, was a small device—a series of interlocking rings, spinning around a glowing core. The startap, a near limitless source of power, or so I was meant to think. I doubted it was real.

"All hail Yatka of No House, victor supreme!" one of the Housed ambassadors intoned in a booming voice. The crowd roared in appreciation.

"Now," said another, "claim your prize, child of the stars. Ascend to Solon."

I didn't approach the plinth, didn't claim the sphere. It wouldn't work for me, anyway—I wasn't a Dryth, and I doubt they'd bothered figuring out how to have a Tohrroid access a star-tap. Instead, I bowed deeply, and said, "No. I won't."

My voice boomed through the stadium—amplifiers on the stage. An uneasy silence fell. The ambassadors shifted in their seats.

I drew the plasma thrower—the gift from that stupid assassin weeks earlier—and took aim. A rustle of panic, but I moved too fast for anyone to stop me. One shot and the star tap, real or not, ceased to exist in a burst of sun-bright flame.

Silence.

Then the crowd—not all, but a sizable, loud part of it—was on their feet, chanting Yatka's name. I dropped the plasma thrower, spun on my heel, and marched right out the center aisle.

No one would ever see Yatka the loop racer again. But they would never stop telling the story.

The next two days, the concourse buzzed with the legend. I slipped into a booth across from Ada in that same Lhassa bar I'd sat in with Yatka when she told me what she was going to do with the star-tap.

Ada looked like death, her face puffy with bruises and her eyes discolored through her IR glasses. When she smiled, she was missing a tooth. "Now, *that* was some spectacle, friend. I'm in awe. Really."

I returned her smile, though I didn't share the sentiment. "I learned from the best."

I was back in my favorite unobtrusive-laborer form. Cruiser Security and Yatka's team was still looking for her, posting a reward of a couple thousand. Apparently, after she left the stadium, she had ducked into a lavatory and never come out. Some were saying she was dead. Those people were right, of course. But it didn't matter. Death was no longer a barrier for her message.

Ada slapped a datapad with a travel itinerary down on the table. "We leave in an hour."

"Ada, this says we'll be traveling as freight."

Ada shrugged. "Maybe next time, then, you should *accept* the offer of unlimited power and wealth."

"Maybe next time, we don't work for the Houses."

"I'm thinking you're right." Ada nodded, looking at Yatka's face plastered all over every single screen and holo projector. "It seems, right now, that the real glory is in fighting against them, not *for* them."

"Sure. Let's just get paid next time, too."

Ada lit her pipe. "Picky picky," she said.

Later, when we were shivering together in the corner of that dark freighter full of cloned livestock, I watched the dim red star Hainar out the slender little porthole. Now untapped, who knew how long it would last? Or would the Houses just tap it again? It felt futile, this course of action, this trajectory through the dark toward a destination I knew would never show itself. There was no money in going against the current, only glory. That, in the end, was enough for Deadeye Ada.

For me, I wondered if anything would ever be enough again.

I reached out to Ada, there in the vast dark, and took her by the hand. To let her know we were in this together, me and her.

Ada made a face at me and pulled her hand away.

Part 4:
On the Futility of Cosmic Agency

The galaxy is a system set in motion incomprehensible aeons ago with an inertia that defies measurement. It will continue to spin for aeons after we are all gone, after the records of our existence have corroded into interstellar dust, and no memory of us remains.

What is the point, then, of ambition? Of action on behalf of cause? Of yearning for progress? Of dreams, in the abstract and concrete senses of the term? If extinction is not just possible but certain, would it not be better to seek comfort where we may, bide our time, and die in peace?

We will become extinct, yes. Our planets will be swallowed by the long death of their suns. But let us live in accordance with our best principles, satisfied in the pursuit of purpose that, if yet unrealized, was the truest expression of our nature. This is our only task. Our only solace. It will not spare us the pain, no, but it will transmute it into something more than mere sensation. We are the observers of the Universe; we infuse the meaningless with meaning—let us infuse it with something we are proud to be and proud to know.

—excerpt from *Meditations on Physical Reality* by Rantothorianak, Scholarly Elder of the Consortium for Universal Wisdom and Knowledge

Planned Obsolescence

I climbed down into the dark canyons of Sadura with Hito Ghiasi's head in a mesh sack.

This far down into the frontier planet's abyssal crevasses, only a vestige of civilization was in evidence. Indelible spray paint marked the stone walls in Dryth characters—signs for construction crews, planetary geologists, and so on. Here and there was a seismic sensor spiked into a fault line—a little nub of steel with a blinking green light, reminding the locals that they were no longer alone.

Between these marks and strung between the canyon walls stretched kilometers of semi-organic cables, crisscrossing at crazy angles and fused together with crystalized binding agents in a complex network of webs. The work of the Quinix, the locals—the arachnids. The people paying me for the head.

My meeting with the arachnids wasn't for an hour. I always arrive early—best way to stay alive in the contract killing business. I found myself a little ledge that looked sturdy enough and formed my blob-like body into something that looked like just another rock, the sack with Hito's head neatly contained in a vacuole inside me. I sat still and watched.

My species are opportunists, and opportunists learn to pay close attention to the world. Even still, it was dark and my night vision, if anything, is worse than your average Dryth's. To tell if my clients were nearby, I had to rely on smell and taste (which, for me, get all jumbled together as the same thing) and the vibrations of the rock beneath me and those of a cable affixed to the wall nearby. Nothing.

The Quinix are giant spiders, though—stealth is part of what *they've* evolved to do. So is seeing in the dark. They can see far enough into the infrared spectrum that I wasn't even convinced my typical camouflaging and shapeshifting abilities would be much good. I can make myself look like a rock, but my heat signature is a little beyond my control. If they were planning to eat me…well, I wasn't sure if I could stop them.

The first of them I heard before I saw. It was chittering in its language to somebody. The pocket translator I had stored in another vacuole echoed the words in Dryth Basic. *"It is close. There was something climbing down the wall."*

More chittering, from a slightly different direction. Another one, I assumed. All Quinix voices sound exactly the same, especially through the translator. *"It is the assassin. It is early."*

So much for the element of surprise.

I shifted myself from something that looked like a rock into something vaguely bipedal—something based on the Dryth body type but without bothering with the little extras like eyes and nostrils and a mouth. I had considered mimicking the arachnids' own forms, but getting the hang of four limbs and a head is hard enough—the idea of trying to manage eight at once would take too much concentration, and I wanted to stay loose in case things went badly. It's a universal hazard of my trade, doesn't matter what planet you're from—if you're willing to pay some alien to bump somebody off, it isn't a big leap to suggest you might be willing to bump off that same alien to save yourself some money.

"Over here!" I called out, opening a little aperture in my "face" to let the sound resonate out across the cable-crossed canyon.

My Quinix clients dropped into view, their rearmost legs

handling the complex work of lowering themselves on strands of finger-thin fibers their massive abdomens produced. The Quinix, for some, are a living nightmare. Me? I'd seen worse. They were males, each of them about two and a half meters across, their eight limbs arranged with predatory symmetry. They were black, fuzzy, and with six big green eyes arranged around a mouth of quivering palps and sharp fangs. This deep in the canyons, they got much bigger than the ones I'd seen puttering around the city. That meant they were older, well past maturity. They possibly pre-dated the arrival of the Dryth and others from distant stars.

The two arachnids perched themselves along a couple of intersecting cables. They were close but not *too* close—maybe four meters away. Probably leaping distance for them. I could see one of them had a couple long knives sheathed up around his thorax. The other guy had an old-fashioned shell-gun cradled in two of his arms. They looked nervous, insofar as a pair of giant arachnids can look that way. I'm a good study of body language, and the way their palps were twitching, I think they were more scared of me than I was of them.

You know, *maybe*. They're spiders, so who knows?

I produced the sack with Hito's head in it and tossed it to the closest Quinix. "I made it look like an accident, as requested. His cable-car broke loose, took a long fall. They'll be looking for his body for weeks."

The lead Quinix peered inside the sack. *"This is good, but the job is not finished."*

"Don't give me that garbage. It's him. I've included his full genetic scan in a chip right there—perfect match. The guy's dead."

"Hito Ghiasi still lives, assassin. This we know."

I'd brought a pistol with me—a little plasma thrower, maybe a four-charge reserve—that was currently stashed in a vacuole inside my "chest." I moved it closer to the surface of my body, just in case I needed to pop these two goons. "I saw him die. I was there. I just handed you his head. Now pay up."

The two arachnids turned away from me and whispered to one another. I couldn't quite make out what they were saying, but whatever it was, I imagined it worked out to me being cheated. They turned back around. *"We appreciate the lengths you have gone to. You have successfully killed Hito Ghiasi's body, and so we will pay you half of your fee."*

I made myself a few centimeters taller. "You're going to pay me *all* of it, or we're going to have a serious problem."

The Quinix skittered back along their cables. The one with the shell-gun chambered a cartridge. His arms weren't steady, though. Depending on what kind of shell he had slotted, it might not matter much. *"You have to kill Hito Ghiasi! This was the agreement! He is not dead! Go and kill him for once and always, and we will pay!"*

"So, what, you need more proof? Like what? A death certificate? More body parts? You know what I went through to bag that scum? You know the *risks* I took?" I grew a bit bigger—my "full height," if you like. A bit over two meters.

This line of questioning seemed to upset them, and they *really* didn't like it when I changed size again. The two didn't answer. They just scurried away, swinging from cable to cable and climbing up stone outcroppings as fast as their eight arms could pull them.

I stood there watching, feeling like the world's biggest chump. "Shit."

I sank into a more natural shape for me—that of a dense little blob of fleshy glop—and glommed on to the side of the canyon. I spread out pseudopods to nab handholds and began to pull myself up, toward civilization.

Ada was going to be pissed.

* * *

It's a four-kilometer vertical climb from the depths to the lower regions of Krakoth City. Easy enough to manage in a crawler, but I was on my own. Took me over an hour.

Krakoth, biggest city on the planet, is where modern tech meets Sadura's unique vertical environment. Mammoth arches of concrete and organic steel formed a floor for the foundations of large buildings that hung over the abyss; the walls of the canyon were hollowed out, made into a warren of interlocking tunnels and caverns. A main tramway spiraled up from the lowest settlements all the way up to the landing pads for intra-atmospheric flyers and grav-skiffs a full twenty kilometers up, and each of its stops formed a new locus of tunnels and cliff-hanging structures. Stretched among all this—the glowing spires of Lhassa casinos, the industrial efficiency of Dryth trams and crawlers and floodlights—were the glittering cables of the native Quinix, across which fleets of private cars and traditional, spider-spun gondolas slid, threading past oblong arachnid nesting places and spherical temples.

I found Ada at a dirty Thraad hotel and bar in the laborer slums of the Krakoth neighborhood called the Middle Tunnels. The whole building was a centrifuge, spun up to create the high-gravity environment of the Thraad homeworld—more than double Sadura's pretty standard g-force. I hated it. You think high g is bad for the average biped? Try dealing without any bones.

I chose for my form a compact male Dryth—one of those squarish, squat guys you see working excavation crews. I even mocked up a little hard hat for myself. My membranes are very good at this—I've trained intensively, and smooth, hairless Dryth skin is a pretty easy task. Well, it would be but for the inertial forces that began to pound on me as the antechamber spun up to match the speed of the bar. Keeping my assumed shape from sagging took even more of my strength than the vertical climb. I plodded inside.

The air was humid and heavy as a chain-mail blanket. Big, snail-like Thraad slid around on a floor that was inch-deep in some kind of muck that tasted like cigar ash and mucus. The doorman—also a Thraad—stretched out a chin-tentacle to hand me a cane. I took it, using all of my effort to not let the thing sink into me like a pin into a pillow.

Ada was reclining in a trapezoidal chair at a table with two Thraads wearing decorated synthetic shells that marked them as members of some merchant Consortium. They were all using two-pronged forks to spear eel-like fish from a big bowl that comprised the majority of the table's surface area.

I smiled at her and flashed my eye color from gold to blue and back—our little signal. She grunted at her two companions. "Pardon me, friends. Got biz to chuckle—drinks on me."

I pulled Ada to a private booth. It was grotto-like and it closed like a clam as we squeezed in. I let myself sag a bit once we were hidden from view. "Why do you always hang out in this horrible place?"

Ada scowled. "Because it's the only slagging place in this shithole of a planet that isn't full of giant spiders."

"I feel like I can't breathe."

"Suck it up. If I gotta hang around this stupid city and talk to Thraad about commodities futures, you can handle some heavy *g* for a few minutes." Ada pulled a cigar from her jacket and lit it. It smelled like dead moss—earthy and, like everything else in here, moist. "Tell me they paid us the whole bit?"

"They didn't."

Ada puffed, frowning. "Half?"

"They said we hadn't killed him."

"You explained it wasn't a clone?"

"Shit, Ada—do you think I'm an idiot? They don't think the bastard is dead enough, okay? We need additional proof."

Ada snorted. "Faceless, we dropped that cable car, like, seven kilometers! It's all over the freaking heralds! What else do they want?"

"See if you can lift the death records from the central database." I let my outer membrane ripple—effectively a stretch for me, though it did nothing to alleviate my discomfort in the doubled gravity.

Ada put her cigar down. It made a thump on her chair's little drink platform. "Shit." She shook her head. Her smooth Dryth features seemed to wrinkle in the heavy air. "We should never have come to this nasty little rock, Faceless—business is terrible and the clients are worse. Blasted spiders."

"Hito Ghiasi was a big contract, Ada. This is just what I promised." I tried to make my face smile, but the gravity was too much and the mouth just drooped.

Ada grunted. "You promised me glory, Faceless. You said we were going to make history." Ada hefted her cigar with an audible grunt. "This ain't that."

She was right. Though you couldn't go anywhere without some herald transceiver blabbering all about Hito Ghiasi, Sadura's favorite mega-industrialist, falling into the abyss in a screaming fireball; we'd made it look like an accident, and an accident it currently stayed.

There were two kinds of assassination contracts in our business. One of them was the public job—"murder by proxy"—you killed somebody for someone else and they claimed responsibility for the act. If anyone was mad about it, they would go after the ones that hired you and not yourself. This was accepted practice in the Union and how most assassins' careers were made. It was also only really available to those organizations powerful enough to defend themselves from easy reprisal. In other words, the big guys could murder the little guys and claim responsibility, and nothing would happen. As a bottom-dweller myself, this whole business rubbed me the wrong way.

The other way—the way I had recently convinced Ada to go—was riskier. You worked what was called a "covert job." You did the deed anonymously, no shielding from any organization taking responsibility. Murder off the books entirely. This broadened your client base a lot. This raised the fees you could ask for. This also let you stick it to the powerful once in a while. That was why I wanted it this way: if I was going to kill people, I might as well kill the *right* people. The people who had it coming, like Hito Ghiasi.

But, while I might be here for a cause, Ada was here for the publicity. Like the rest of the Dryth, her primary concern was her own fragile ego. She wanted to be a legend, and hiding in the shadows wasn't her thing.

I tried to be diplomatic. "Plan was we'd keep a low profile, and eventually the reputation piles up. But in the right corners. House Ghiasi can't know about us. Not yet. It'll work."

She took a long drag on the cigar and let the smoke drop out of her nostrils. The smoke floated there in a cloud in front of her face, flaunting the inertia that pulled the rest of us into the floor. "We should get the hell outta here. Find somewhere they pay. Somewhere we can get a rep worth a damn. Screw this charity work."

"Ada, we had to outlay a lot of trade credit to rig that cable-car malfunction. One thing to break even, but I'm not taking a loss because some giant spiders can't get their heads wrapped around death." I was sinking out of my Dryth disguise, the false gravity pulling me down into a puddle in the fat, trapezoid chair.

"Well, you better figure it out," she said. "My patience ain't infinite, Faceless. Don't think I can't work without you. A glorious death beats the hell outta this shithole, and no mistake."

I couldn't take the weight anymore—I could scarcely breathe. "Just get those records. I need some air."

"Yeah," she said, trying to blow a smoke ring, only to watch it collapse a few centimeters from her mouth. "Don't we all."

Ada's anger ate at me. A Tohrroid like me needed every friend it could get, especially if I hoped to avoid a life being locked in the compost sink of some starliner, eating rotten algae and recycling sour air. My long, slow climb from the gutters of the galaxy was thanks, in large part, to Ada's status as an Unhoused Dryth mercenary. And, as it happened, her status as a mercenary was, in large part, due to the subtle talents of her partner—me. We needed each other, as much as that grated sometimes. It was hard for me to trust a member of a species that had enslaved mine so long ago there was no record of our home planet, and it was no doubt hard for a Dryth to owe so much to a creature most commonly found living in sewers and eating shit.

But hey, things're tough all over, right?

For the next few hours, I tried to think like a Quinix. I tried out a Quinix form, shaping myself into a tight little abdomen and thorax and eight spindly legs. It was a terrible disguise. I had trouble keeping all the legs coordinated as I tried to crawl along, and I couldn't get the frenetic movement of their palps right. I didn't learn much. Damned spiders.

But they were what drew me here, right?

I got a ping from Ada over the Q-link—it was going to take a few hours to get the documents, which left me with plenty of time to get back down to the wreck and get some more parts of Hito Ghiasi as proof. Another long climb.

On the streets of Krakoth, nobody much noticed the occasional Tohrroid oozing along the gutter. To them—to the Great Races, the species that had mastered the stars first—I was invisible. A nothing. A Lhassa or a Dryth or a Thraad could cut me up and serve me for dinner, and nobody would have anything to say about it, except maybe "yuck." The anonymity had its uses—kept me alive all these cycles, after all—but another part of me hated what it meant about me in the grand scheme of things.

I fed on that hatred.

I glommed on to a cable car—it was full of tourists, taking them on a scenic ride around the outskirts of town. A pack full of Lhassa mares with their innumerable fuzzy children clinging to them, a couple Dryth in House Ghiasi colors, two or three Thraad with some drone assistants, taking furious notes with their chin-tentacles. The tour guide was a Dryth male, young and skinny. As I clung to the outside of the car, I listened as he listed off interesting trivia on Sadura's endless canyon system, its seismic instability, its bizarre biome.

Somebody asked, "Aren't the earthquakes dangerous? Couldn't the city…you know…fall?"

The young Dryth showed his blunt white teeth in a restrained smile. "Thanks to House Ghiasi, seismic stabilizers and flexible organic building materials have made the city very safe. Only the strongest of quakes could threaten Krakoth, and our early-warning tech would give everybody ample time to evacuate."

This mollified them somewhat. The tour guide pointed over the railing. "Pretty soon, we'll be passing the place where authorities believe Hito Ghiasi's cable car suffered its fatal accident. A moment of silence, if you all wouldn't mind, for the great architect of this beautiful city."

It occurred to me that the tour guide never—not once—made even passing mention of the Quinix, or the fact that it was their cables, made from *their* bodies, that made their stupid tour possible. Or that those "seismic stabilizers" made the *rest* of the spiders' planet even *more* unstable.

This was my stop. I leapt to a nearby ledge and clung. One of the Lhassa pups saw me go. "Gross! There was a smack glomming on to our tour car!"

Laughter and shouts of disgust echoed through the endless caverns as the cable car's mechanical hands deftly transferred it from one Quinix cable to another. The old one shuddered from the release while the new one bowed with the new weight. I watched it go, holding still.

Once it was gone, I began my descent. The view was beautiful, no doubt. From here, on the far side of the near-bottomless Krakoth Canyon, the city could be seen in its full splendor. It looked like a colony of seaborne parasites, all clinging to the maroon rocks of Sadura's middle strata, glowing to shame the bioluminescent fungus that grew naturally along the walls in striated patterns. With my wide-angle vision, I could see it all at once, a riot of light and motion. I could make out arenas and hotels from amid the webs of the Quinix. House Ghiasi's towers sat at the center of it all, cable cars and crawlers buzzing around it like insects. I oozed down my sheer rock face and considered the metaphor—House Ghiasi as insect hive, the Quinix as spiders. Predators become prey.

About four cycles back—fifty years—the Quinix were alone on Sadura. They lived here, deep in the canyons and caverns of their planet, far from the radiation-soaked hell that is the surface, and did their spidery thing. I have no real idea what that was, mind you—they spun webs and cables, built their little cocoon-like houses, and ate whatever local wildlife seemed appetizing. From what I've seen, their technology never got out of the ironworking stage.

Kaskar Indomitable, a Dryth Solon of House Ghiasi, scouted this planet around then and landed with a series of retainers. They made contact. Probably killed sufficient arachnids to make it clear they were not to be messed with. Next thing you know, there were Dryth living here. Where the Dryth go, the Lhassa follow. Then the Thraad. The Lorca and the Voosk. Everybody. Sadura wasn't alone anymore; it was part of the Union of Stars, whether the Quinix liked it or not.

Enter Hito Ghiasi, Dryth architect and administrator. Past two cycles that guy did more to build Krakoth up than anybody. Put in arenas. Built up the tourism industry. Slapped his name on anything made of glass or concrete or organic steel. The whole foundational floor of the skyline I was looking at right now was his plan, his baby. Kaskar Indomitable himself supposedly paid a visit to the guy, and let me tell you, Dryth Solons do not come to visit *you* unless you are a really big deal.

Along the way, the Quinix got shoved aside. Hito's projects displaced tens of thousands of kilometers of cables, and the seismic "overflow" from the stabilized city destroyed hundreds of Quinix settlements in the surrounding region, killing thousands. Sure, the arachnids were welcome to rent apartments and live in the city like everybody else—most of them did—and some others managed to string their weird, sack-like little homes amid the new architecture. Some, though, just got mad. Hence why they offered to pay me twenty thousand trade credits to kill Hito Ghiasi.

Which I did.

I made it to the scene of the crime after a four-hour climb. The cable car was a field of charred debris with pieces strewn down a forty-five-degree slope. Far above me, I could see search teams of House Ghiasi dragoons in AG harnesses sweeping the area with spotlights and EM scans—they were getting close.

That didn't seem possible to me, them being this close already. The problem with a search party in Sadura is that there's wreckage all over the place if you look for it—it's pretty hard to build lasting structures onto vertical surfaces when the whole planet

suffers category-five earthquakes on a regular basis, seismic stabilizers or not.

Whether I thought it was possible or not didn't make a difference. They were closing in. I didn't have much time.

I drew a knife and crawled to where I had found Hito Ghiasi's body last time. I was thinking maybe the Quinix would
believe he was dead if I brought them his gonads or his hands
or something. Stupid fucking spiders—how was the *head* not
good enough? I wondered if maybe they didn't really know
how important heads were, since they had none of their own.
My job then was to cut off a piece that the ignorant morons
knew he couldn't live without. Maybe his heart. The Quinix
had hearts. Well, I was pretty sure, anyway.

The air hummed with the sound of a big, fat AG engine of
Lhassa make. A patrol skimmer, coming close. Shit. I sucked
the knife back into my body and darted into the nearest crevice in the rock. It was narrow—no more than five centimeters
across at most—but I managed to squeeze enough of me inside
that I doubted I'd show up on any casual scans. They weren't
here for me, anyway.

Floodlights bathed the scree slope in a kind of blue-white
brilliance totally alien to the depths of Sadura. An abyssal crab,
albino white and a meter across, raised its claws in challenge
and scuttled away from the hovering vehicle. I saw a laser flash
across the ground in an unbroken band, cataloguing the nature
of the wreckage. The floodlight narrowed and slid over to high-
light the headless, half-eaten corpse of Hito Ghiasi.

So much for getting more physical evidence.

I had to wait in that crack for a few hours while a bunch
of purple-clad Ghiasi dragoons did a sweep of the area. One
of them peeked in at me but moved on—to him I was just
another smack, glomming for garbage like the rest of my species. They didn't care—they were looking for the cable car's

maintenance recorder. The recorder that would tell them that Hito's death was anything but an accident. I did a lot of cursing to myself.

They shouldn't be here. Not this soon. The only way they would have found the wreckage this quick was if they knew where it had landed, and there were only two people who knew exactly where that was.

Finally, I started back up the vertical cliff face. Another couple kilometers of climb with nothing to show for it. This time, though, I was pissed at Ada.

At the Thraad bar, Ada and I slumped in couches inside a little clam-shaped alcove and listened to the herald channel chatter about Hito Ghiasi's nefarious murder. They were offering a reward of twelve thousand trade credits for the capture of the assassins—us, in other words.

She was drinking something opaque and yellow that smelled like fungus. Neither of us had talked much since we sat down.

"You tipped them off," I said.

Ada smiled. "So what?"

"This isn't funny, Ada. We're in breach of contract now."

Ada chuckled and took a sip of her weird, slimy drink. "Oh, you mean the contract our clients weren't paying us for anyway? *That* contract?"

"Don't give me that shit. You didn't do what I told you to."

Ada rolled her eyes. "I'm not your employee, Faceless, I'm your partner. It wouldn't have even mattered if the slagging spiders had paid up in the first place."

"You deliberately put a target on our heads."

"We were careful," Ada countered, hefting her glass and drinking again. "I did us a favor. Our cachet just improved. Stop whining."

"And if our clients don't pay?"

"Then I just showed this dirty little frontier planet that it has a freelance assassin worth hiring. One who can be effective, discreet…"

"Not if the Ghiasi dragoons find us first."

Ada placed her drink heavily on the little table so that some of the yellow stuff spilled. "Faceless, I get it—you want revenge on the Dryth and you want the spiders to pay you for it, but get some perspective, will you? This whole thing was messed up from the start, anyway. Twenty K for Hito Ghiasi? Robbery is what that is, even if they *had* paid us. Our clients are stupid little bug aliens, so who gives a shit what they think? I care more about what our next employer thinks we're worth. And the next after that. Preferably on a planet with real money changing hands. Forget the spiders— they're done, Faceless. You're just fooling yourself."

I didn't say anything. This was all beneath her now—what had first sounded like an adventure had now become a slog. The endless twilight of the Saduran abyss, the vertical land-scape, the thick, humid air—all of that seemed hostile to her. She felt buried alive, forgotten in some dark little crack. I sympathized. This place was never meant for bipeds.

And yet here they are anyway, I thought.

"Give me the death records."

Ada hefted a small chip from her pocket and set it carefully into my "hand." It almost pushed through my palm, it was so heavy in the amplified gravity. "I should go with you this time," Ada said. "If they pull their shit, we can kill them together."

"No," I said. "They could ID you if they're caught."

Ada rolled her eyes. "You think Ghiasi dragoons are going to take those spiders *alive*? Please."

I firmed up my Dryth disguise and ducked out of the clam-shell. "I'll be back in a few hours, tops. Meet me here."

Ada tried to shrug, but her shoulders could scarcely lift. "Where am I gonna go, anyway?"

* * *

Back down into the abyssal depths and the eternal twilight of the Quinixi habitat. There was a lot more activity this time around. Scores of little arachnids, not much more than ten centimeters across, were scurrying all over the cliff face. An egg must have hatched. The Quinix gave birth to whole clans at once—one big egg contained a couple hundred of the little things, all of which would grow up together, form a society together, work as a team. A few hundred brothers and sisters in arms.

Many died, as I understood it. Predators, earthquakes, violence with other Quinixi clans, common accidents, starvation—all of them took their toll. Eventually, those who reached full maturity would mate, lay eggs of their own, and new clans would be born. New communities that would strive to do better than their parents had—a new beginning for a whole bloodline.

But was that the case anymore? How had the coming of Krakoth City changed that life cycle? Hito Ghiasi hadn't built a foundation atop which the arachnids could reach the stars—he had paved a ceiling over them, keeping them forever in place.

The same two arachnids met me as last time. I wondered if they were the last two survivors of their own brood. Maybe I was talking to the end of a bloodline—two males, relegated to old age and death with no chance for redemption. Maybe that was why they hired me.

The death records did not impress them. I played a few minutes of the House Ghiasi herald channel, let them listen to the preparations for Hito's funeral, the state of his body when it was found, and the loss he represented to the community. "He's dead. Surely you see that."

"No." The one with the knives rubbed his palps together. *"You do not understand. He still lives."*

"How? Explain it to me."

They stared at me with their palps twitching, their rear legs rubbing over the draglines that held them aloft. Finally, the other one spoke. *"What about the rest of Hito Ghiasi? When will you destroy that?"*

"Rest? What rest?" I tried to think like a spider. "Like, his children? His family?"

"No!" The one with the knives spread his legs wide. *"Leave his children be!"*

"His weave!" The second one sounded ... plaintive? It was hard to tell—the translator worked murder on their intonation, their nonverbal cues. *"What about his weave? It must go!"*

His weave. What in all the stars...

His weave. Like, what he had woven. Like the cables with Quinix created. "You mean ... you mean everything he *built?*"

The translator fuzzed a bit as they tried to say the word "built" and failed. *"Yes. Yes, that is the word for it. It is part of him. It must be destroyed."*

I held still for a moment, not sure how to respond. I felt... stupid. Miserable. Sad. "You're talking about Krakoth. What Hito Ghiasi built—the whole entire city, held up by his designs, by his life's work."

They rubbed their forearms together in excitement. *"Yes! Destroy it, and your reward will be great!"*

"You want me to destroy a whole city. For twenty thousand."

"This was our arrangement."

I sagged out of my bipedal form and reverted to a blob. I felt sick with pity. They wanted the Great Races gone; they wanted their world back. They thought I could give it to them. The two of them—giant, shadow-dwelling monsters but naïve as children.

And why wouldn't they think it possible? Hito Ghiasi had built something beyond their wildest dreams. Something loud and bright and *permanent*. Something that connected the deepest regions of Sadura with the farthest stars of the Union. Compared to their little oblong houses of webbing and their delicate cables, it was an act of a god. And if it could be built by a god from beyond the heavens, why couldn't it be torn down by another one just as easily?

I don't remember what I told them, but I remember them being satisfied. I climbed back up and out of the depths, feeling heavier than I did in doubled gravity.

Above me, lining the walls of the massive Krakoth Canyon, the city stretched up as far as I could see, gleaming like starlight. Part of me wanted to do like they asked—to tear it all down. To kick the Great Races in the teeth so hard, their grip on this world would falter and slip. More than anything else, that was why I had come here. Why I had brought Ada here. Why I had reached out to the arachnids to see if I could work for them. Because I knew what House Ghiasi meant for the Quinix. It was the same thing some other Dryth House had probably meant for my people.

In a few centuries, I could see a Sadura transformed into a playground for the Dryth Houses and the Lhassa Cartels. The earthquakes tamed. The predators made extinct or kept in zoos. And the Quinix living in the gutter, eating trash.

Just like me.

But throwing it all down was beyond my power. So far beyond it, in fact, that it made me want to laugh. It had taken almost three hundred hours of work to get Hito Ghiasi, and he was only one powerful Dryth among thousands. Even now, the Ghiasi herald was reporting his replacement in the House hierarchy. How many buildings would she build before somebody like me pitched her down a pit for short money? Ada was right. I'd been fooling myself.

The futility of it all made me sick.

I went back to the Thraad bar. Back into the weight of the artificial *g*-force. At that moment, it felt right, being squeezed like that. Felt like I deserved it somehow.

I sat across from Ada in our alcove again. This time I had a drink—something strong and slimy and orange. It tasted tangy and burned me from the inside out.

She was laughing. "They said *what?*"

"It isn't funny."

Ada slapped her knee. "No. It is. It *definitely* is."

I slurped some of my drink up through my "hand." I wished I could get drunk, but I've never had that advantage. Another thing the Great Races hold over the rest of us—their booze only really works for them. For some stupid reason I drink it anyway. "At any rate, I know how we can get paid."

Ada's laughter faded as she realized what I meant. She looked at me with a half-grin, as though wondering if I was serious. "You want to make the call, or should I?"

"Me," I said. "It has to be me. No one knows my face."

Ada nodded, chuckling again. She was a little drunk. "Because you don't have one."

A few hours later, the Ghiasi herald reported that their dragoons, acting on an anonymous tip, had confronted and killed a pair of Quinixi separatist radicals in the regions below Abyssal Point. It was believed that they were the ones who murdered Hito Ghiasi, and Hito Ghiasi's head was found in their possession.

The twelve thousand was transferred into my dummy account that hour. With my share, I rented a little place in Abyssal Point with an overlook into the depths—somewhere Ada and I could sit and drink and not have to feel twice our weight. One night, about a week later, we were sharing a bottle of Lhassa spirits, reclining in frame chairs on the narrow little balcony. Ada leaned back, looking up at the city that spread above us. "Maybe we shoulda done it. Just tore it all down."

"Really?" I watched her face, waiting for the joke. "All those people?"

"Sure." She shrugged. "Screw them all, anyway."

She didn't really mean it, though. She'd never mean it. I chewed that over, looking up with her as I also looked down, watching the little arachnids try and climb their way out of the shadows and into the light.

They didn't usually make it.

Infection Vector

The death of any single organism is something of no consequence to the universe at large. Nowhere is this more obvious than during a plague. Thousands, maybe even millions die, and yet the world still goes on—planets turn, stars drag them along in their courses, and even life continues its infinite cycles without pause or care for those left behind in the evolutionary dust.

This particular plague I was enduring was the first I could recall, though it maybe wasn't the first I'd experienced, given my poor memory. As I understood it, plagues of this fashion were rare in the Union of Stars. This was not only because of the advanced medical technology available to a loose confederation of interstellar civilizations but also because diseases just don't *jump* across species from totally different planets very easily. Sure, a whole bunch of Lhassa might come down with something, but the odds of it affecting their Dryth or Thraad or Voosk neighbors just wasn't very good.

But this plague *did*. It was killing thousands in the deep canyons of Sadura, and it seemed to be leaping easily between the various Great Races. The wails of the ill and the bereaved echoed through the twilit abyss. The smell of ash and cooked flesh was thick in the air, thanks to the portable incinerators posted at most major shelves or tunnel intersections—a ready means to dispose of the dead. When House Ghiasi had deployed them, some of the more-sentimental cultures with more-elaborate funeral rites had resisted using them. This, of course, had made the plague worse, since the dead bodies spread the plague as easily as the living ones, if not more so, and inviting extended family or clones or egg clutches or what-have-you to a funeral was a great way to kill off a solid percentage of a population group.

Anyway, life went on, just worse and less pleasant than usual. The locals—the inhabitants of dim, dark Sadura—were having a pretty good time of it, actually. The Quinix are a species of intelligent arachnids, and they seemed immune to the mystery illness. They were making a lot of money collecting bodies, which they spun up in sacs of their webbing and attached to their abdomens in bundles like so much dirty laundry. I wouldn't say the mood was celebratory, necessarily—Quinix body language was hard to read—but given how many of the spiders probably would have preferred that their planet had never been invaded by aliens from beyond the sky, I couldn't imagine they were all that broken up about their numbers being thinned. Their keening, shrieking music—made by them rubbing their various legs together—joined the chorus of miserable sounds filling the usually placid and quiet dark of the endless canyons.

I, myself, was also immune to the disease. Like the Quinix, my physiology is wildly different from that of the more ordinary intelligent species of the galaxy. Unlike the Quinix, I was very much not enjoying myself. Off-world trade was down, a lot of off-planet people were hitching rides up the gravity well and enduring quarantine long enough to abandon this remote outpost of a world, and, most importantly, people were staying home. People who stayed home didn't make a lot of enemies. They didn't make a lot of money. And they didn't meet with assassins very much to spend that money on the removal of their enemies, especially not when this damned plague might do it for them for free. For a professional assassin, that combination was bad news.

The good news is that I had, at long last, gotten a lead on a contract. My stash of trade credits was running low, such that I had been considering reverting to my species' primary source of food—garbage—instead of buying actual meals from actual eating establishments. I'd come a long way from the gutter, and I was very much *not* looking forward to destitution forcing me back into it.

I always insisted on meeting clients in public—no professional killer should feel at ease walking into somebody's apartment, and no private individual should feel at ease inviting one in—but public venues that hadn't been closed down by quarantine were few and far between. The meeting place was a fungal garden on a shelf near the Middle Tunnels, a good three kilometers above my own neighborhood, way down at the bottom edge of Krakoth City.

I took a Quinix gondola to get there, since at that moment they were the most plentiful and also the cheapest method of transport that didn't involve long and precarious vertical climbs. The gondola was woven from Quinix web fiber and stiffened by some biological process they could manage, making it very lightweight but also strong as steel. This particular gondolier had been thoughtful enough to pack the insides with a fluffy carpet of purple moss, making it practically cozy. The whole thing hung from one of the thick Quinix cables that crisscrossed the vast canyon that comprised the subterranean city of Krakoth. The gondolier had some kind of ratchet system devised such that, as they swung back and forth from a dragline beneath the gondola, the whole contraption sort of *wound* its way up the gentle incline of the cable at a smooth and steady rate. It wasn't fast, but it was direct—any other method of travel involved a complex combination of funiculars and ground cars and winding tunnels that would take just about as long and cost five times as much to charter.

Besides, I was enjoying the fresh air and the view. We were halfway across the canyon, far from the stench of the incinerators and the putrid sick filling the gutters. Around us, the city bloomed in its full glory. Here, far away from the claustrophobic hustle of the tunnels, Krakoth was luminous—a many-hued pattern of buildings clinging the canyon sides like mollusks, the glow of bioluminescent fungus and plants and animals speckling the titanic rock faces, and the silvery sheen of Quinix cables and spherical homes knitting them all together. It was, in many ways, a hostile environment—dark, hot, intensely vertical—but it was beautiful, plague or no plague.

For my form today, I'd chosen a sober and sedate Lhassa bull in his late middle age—a fine set of antlers, a thinning coat of fur, and long robes. A real bull in this position would probably have his whole heredity embroidered into his robes—all the mares he'd impregnated, all the children they'd borne, and so on—but while I'm an able shapeshifter, I can't really do *that* and also walk around and talk convincingly. A couple of Lhassa wearing microbe-repellant shrouds on their heads—sort of like large lampshades—watched me as I stepped off the gondola and flipped the gondolier some credit chits, probably wondering who this mysterious fellow was who wasn't bragging about his sexual prowess. I ignored them.

The fungal garden was a short walk from the edge. It was dominated by tall trunks of some kind of bright orange mushroom-type thing that, according to little tags written in Dryth Basic at their foot, was actually native to much higher strata in Sadura and had been transported here "to beautify the Middle Tunnels and delight the occupants." The occupants—primarily homeless Quinix and hapless indigents of a half dozen species—didn't seem particularly delighted. Some of them were coughing and puking on the beds of delicate fungal lace that lined the footpaths. Others were sleeping on beds of many-hued moss. A couple of them were dead. I moved past them, not giving anyone a second look.

My meeting was at the far edge of the park. She was standing right where she'd said she'd be, wearing just what she'd said she'd wear—so far, so good. She was an elderly Lhassa mare, tall and graceful, clad in a flowing gown that was tattered at the edges. She, also, had one of those lampshade things on, so that I could only get a basic translucent outline of her face and head. She did not look armed, but I wasn't stupid enough to assume so. I kept my own weapon—a compact laser with a thirty-second burn time—hidden away in a fleshy vacuole inside myself, close to the surface of my body.

I stopped a respectful and safe distance. "Mother Candoor, I presume."

She turned slowly and looked me over for a moment before replying. "Are you the representative?"

"I am."

"How do I know the Faceless Assassin will hear my entreaty?"

"You do not. No one knows their identity, not even myself." This was a lie, of course—I *am* the Faceless Assassin. The thing about being literally faceless, though, is that nobody ever knows who you are. This is an advantage for infiltration and stealth, but it creates problems from a business standpoint. For that reason, I'd devised a few "intermediary" personas that I used to talk to people. It added to the mystery, to my mystique. It also meant no one could say they'd actually met me.

"I don't like this arrangement." She laid her ears back against her slender skull. "This *place* is filthy."

"If you are interested in remaining clean, then perhaps contracting a deadly assassin is not a wise course of action," I said. I turned as though to withdraw.

"No! Wait!" She held up one hand. She was missing two of her fingers—an odd detail, especially when limb regrowth was a pretty common technology. "I have asked every other assassin in this wretched hole of a city, and everyone has turned me down. You are my last hope."

This didn't bode well. I wasn't exactly keen on taking a job literally *everyone* else wasn't willing to do. "The Faceless Assassin asks a high price, Mother. Can you pay?"

"I am the owner of the *Enlightened Dawn* interstellar cargo freighter. We supply this city with its entire store of Gurindio tabac and Juriolian Distillation. I have trade credits, I assure you."

I wasn't sure about Juriolian Distillation—I never had a taste for that particular kind of Lhassa booze—but Gurindio tabac was a chewing narcotic that I found delicious, though everyone else used it to get high. Every lounge in Krakoth bought it in bulk. They had it in little trays on every table, especially in the Perfume Houses in the lower strata. "Assuming you tell the truth," I said, "I think we can assume your credit is good. Who is it that you wish the Faceless Assassin to remove?"

"This is covert, yes? This contract was not posted and I do not wish it posted," Candoor said, glancing around.

"The Faceless Assassin specializes in covert assassinations, Mother. The target will die. No one will take responsibility. No one will ever know." This was only partially true. I was good at covert jobs, but I didn't particularly like them. They always came with baggage a public job didn't. When somebody posted a public contract on someone's life, everybody knew how it was supposed to work—the assassin takes out the target, the hiring entity claims responsibility. It was neat, clean, uncomplicated. Covert jobs were often muddy.

"Who is the target?" I asked.

Mother Candoor clasped her hands and rubbed at the stumps

where her two missing fingers had been. "That is the complicated part—I...I don't know their name."

"Do you have a picture? A holo? Some other identifying information?"

"No."

I bowed. "I'm sorry to have wasted your time, Mother. Good day."

"I want you to kill the person or persons responsible for this plague!" she shouted, maybe too loudly for someone contracting murder. None of the diseased indigents around us seemed to care.

She had my attention, though. "What makes you think it is any one person who is responsible?"

"I know it is," she said. "I have proof." She fished something out of a pocket and held it out to me—a small, crystalline cube. A data archive.

I took it from her. "How much are you offering, assuming the Faceless Assassin wants the job?"

"Everything. I will give them *everything* I have."

The data archive contained a bunch of scientific data I had no prayer of interpreting, not only because I actually don't know very much about science but also because it was written in Voosk nomenclature, with their bizarre mathematical symbols and weird parallel informational narratives intended to be read simultaneously in order to be understood. I can see all over the place, yeah, but I needed to concentrate to read, and I couldn't do it in multiple places at once without getting dizzy. I finally broke down and purchased a cut-rate Voosk textual translation device with most of what was left of my dwindling trade credits. Even then, it was hard to parse it all.

The important part was that there was some kind of Voosk scientific facility in orbit around Sadura that did biomedical research, and from context I was forced to assume that Mother Candoor believed they were responsible for the plague. As far as the Great Races went, the Voosk were a distant fourth in terms of population density on Sadura and probably fifth or even sixth in terms of overall power in the Union at large. It wasn't impossible to imagine a scenario where they manufactured a bioweapon to weaken the other species' hold over Sadura. The only problem was that it was the Peace period of the Cycle—attacks like this were forbidden. If the Powers That Be got wind of this…

It was around that time that the Powers That Be knocked on my apartment door. I could see clearly on the security vid that I'd set up that it was a Node Vassal—a mutated Dryth of some kind, his-now-its head sporting asymmetrical outgrowths that featured a variety of additional eyes. It was wearing a long black robe, as Vassals often did, which doubtlessly concealed a variety of other unsightly and possibly recent additions to its physiology. That the Vassal was knocking on my door at all was a courtesy that didn't go unnoticed—it probably could have broken it down without trouble. It wanted to talk, not kill me.

The Node was an elaborate sensory organ deposited here by the void-dwelling macro-organisms known as Marshals. The Node created Vassals by infecting normal bipeds with a suite of parasites that overrode their original identity and slaved them to the directives the Node set out. There were two ways this happened, to my knowledge. First, it took volunteers—crazed apocalyptic lunatics or selfless believers in the Holy Law who walked into the Node and had their brains and bodies rewired. The second kind of conversion was much less voluntary, and it involved breathing in the spores that a dead Vassal released in big, thick clouds. This was the central problem with Vassals: kill one, and you just made a lot more. Conversion happened fast, as I understood it. Within seconds.

The Vassals served the Node and the Node was part of a Marshal. The Marshals were the arbiters and enforcers of the Law that bound the Union of Stars together. They enforced the Cycles—periods of War, Recovery, and Peace, all sacrosanct. And the punishment for violating these cycles? For waging War during Peace? There was only one: the Marshal ate the planet in question, the innocent and guilty alike. I wasn't sure exactly how that worked, but my understanding was they would strip every viable resource from the planetary crust, people included, thin the atmosphere of useful gasses, and leave a barren rock behind.

For these reasons, my initial instinct at seeing a Vassal—a person who had been "recruited" by the Node to act as its eyes and ears—was to run for it. Nothing good came from talking to, dealing with, or confronting Vassals. Then again, if it had managed to track me here, kilometers away—and I *knew* I hadn't been followed—there was very little chance I could lose it by bugging out now. All it would mean was I'd have to abandon this apartment, and I liked this apartment—the balcony gave me a good view of the city.

So, against my better judgement, I took the form of the selfsame Lhassa bull I'd used to meet with Candoor and opened the door, my laser and the data archive still hidden on my person. "Ah, Node—how can I be of service? Nothing amiss, I hope."

The Dryth—the *thing*—looked me over with its half dozen asymmetrically arranged eyeballs and pushed past me into the apartment. "You met with a Lhassa mare earlier in the Middle Tunnels. One Candoor, matriarch of *Enlightened Dawn*. Of what did you speak?"

This was a tricky proposition. I knew perfectly well that my shapeshifting abilities had pretty hard limits when it came to fooling a Vassal—those extra eyes saw into all kinds of electromagnetic spectrums of light. There was a nonzero chance it could literally see the laser and the data archive inside me right then. I decided to tell the truth. Or most of it, anyway. "She shared with me her belief that this plague was artificially created."

"To what end did she share this belief?" the Vassal asked. It was looking around my apartment now—peering at the thin gel-pad I never slept on, taking a look at the kitchen which I never cooked in. Observing my lack of art, lack of spare clothing, lack of really *anything* that might indicate some old Lhassa bull lived here. If it were to talk to my landlord, she would tell it that this apartment was rented by a stocky Unhoused Dryth laborer.

"I believe she is distraught. She just needed somebody to listen to, I guess."

"Why you?" it asked. "How is it that you know her?"

"We're related, indirectly." This was a safe bet—Lhassa familial networks were vast and complex. The odds that any given Lhassa was a cousin to any other were surprisingly good, given their reproduction rate and their polygamous mating habits.

The Vassal wasn't buying it. "You are not a Lhassa. You are a Tohrroid."

Shit. My species was widely considered to be non-sentient, so not a lot of people would make a guess that a Tohrroid was walking around, talking and renting property and whatnot. Figured the Node would be enlightened like that. "Is there some kind of problem with me talking with this lady?"

"She has been seeking to hire an assassin for a covert job. It is my suspicion, therefore, that you are an assassin."

Assassination was not technically illegal—the Law only covered very, very broad things—but it *was* frowned upon. The Marshals thought of it—to the extent a being that vast has understandable "thoughts"—as a means to circumvent the Recovery and Peace aspects of the Cycle. To be fair, they were exactly right—that's why we existed.

Vassals acted like investigators, but their duty wasn't necessarily to the truth. Their duty was to find their master some planetary lunch. This thing was asking all these questions so it could send a report up the chain that would, somehow, wind up informing a vast, planet-eating, sentient cloud that Sadura had been very naughty and, therefore, was good for a solid meal. I wanted, very much, to keep this thing from sending any such report.

I considered my surroundings, my options. Killing this Vassal would not pose a problem, but killing Vassals usually *created* more problems than it solved (the aforementioned "cloud of infectious spores"). It seemed unlikely *I* could be infected by those spores, given that I was just a talking blob, but I very much doubted breathing that shit in was healthy.

Another, more mundane problem was this—there was no telling who else knew this Vassal was here. Every Vassal in Krakoth might be fully briefed, for all I knew. I kill this thing, and then all of its friends are looking for me minutes later, and probably *all* of them could track as well as this thing could. How to manage this?

I got an idea. "I don't want any trouble." I put up my simulated hands and backed away, toward the back of the apartment.

"Then tell me what I want to know." The Vassal kept pace with me as I retreated. I couldn't see *its* hands at all, and I generally assumed that was because beneath that cloak was at least three arms, one of which probably ended in a very sharp, crab-like claw. Vassals almost always carried weapons, too. It could be anything—laser, multipistol, plasma thrower, even a primitive shell-gun or slugger.

"I've told you the truth," I said. I backed out of my sleeping area and onto the balcony. The smell of the incinerator ash from lower strata tainted the air. The void—the sense of a vast empty space that was the canyon—made me shudder a little.

"You are plotting an escape. Do not attempt it," the Vassal said. "We will only find you again."

"How can you be so sure?" I asked, moving so I was pressing against the railing that separated me from the yawning abyss.

The Vassal reached out with one of its mostly Dryth-looking hands and grabbed me by the wrist, tight. If I'd had bones, there was no way I'd escape that grip.

I do not have bones.

Rather than slip out of the grip, I reinforced it—I dropped my form completely, grabbing the Vassal by the head, the neck, the waist, the legs, and, yes, even those three arms and two tentacles it had hidden beneath that cloak. It was bound to me—no escaping.

Then I threw myself and it off the balcony by just tilting our weight backward so that we would tumble over the edge together. As we fell into open space, I grabbed the railing with a part of me that had, until pretty recently, been playing the role of "foot." As for the Vassal, I let it go. It reached out with its tentacles, but gravity was in control now. For all the thing's various mutations, not even Vassals could fly.

I oozed back up onto the balcony, a little winded but none the worse for wear. I wondered how long it would take that Vassal to hit the ground, wherever that was, far, far below. Probably a minute but not much more. I wasn't sure how long before it would be it was noticed missing. The Node was sort of a collective intelligence, but they didn't communicate via any kind of mystical telepathy or anything. They had to call each other on their Q-links like everybody else. As for the spore bloom, that was somebody else's problem now—someone far, far below me, beyond the city limits.

It looked like I'd have to abandon this apartment after all. I snagged whatever food I had left in the cold-storage unit, ate it. I took one last look off that porch, soaking in that view, and then left with no plans to ever return. With the money I'd get off this job, I told myself I'd upgrade to a much nicer place, anyway.

Getting to an orbital station from a deep, dark hole in the ground was a complicated affair. For one thing, this research station wasn't accepting tourists as visitors. For another thing, the planet was in the midst of a nasty pandemic, and that made off-world travel difficult. Any attempt to ascend the orbital strand to the spaceport would find me being put through quarantine, and in quarantine they would find out I was a Tohrroid, not whatever it was I was pretending to be, and then they would not only refuse to let me off the planet but probably stuff me in a jar and poke me with electrodes for the rest of my natural life. That was assuming they didn't just kill me immediately.

I asked Krakoth's skennite core—an intelligent crystalline being that worked as a sort of city database—a bunch of probing questions about this Voosk orbital lab. It gave me a bunch of vague answers—the best info that it had—and I, in turn, told it a few things in return by way of payment. Namely, I told it my apartment was now available for rent. I wasn't ripping off the skennite, either—it, being some kind of talking rock, had no particular investment in the progress or lack of progress of the plague, so all of this information was more or less equivalent from its perspective, which is, yes, deeply weird but very handy in a living database when you are short of funds.

What I learned was this: the Voosk were actively studying the progress of the disease and had several Quinix on their payroll who were collecting biological samples from the deceased and shipping them up-well somehow. I knew "diseased tissue" was very much *not* the kind of thing you would walk through quarantine to have shipped up to the spaceport, and their little orbital lab very obviously did not have the power reserves to do direct matter-to-energy translation of biologicals, so that meant they were doing their own pickups with a transorbital shuttle of some kind. All I needed to do was find it and stow away.

To do this, I tracked down the Quinix in question and followed the spiders as they went door to door in the West Shelf, rubbing their legs together to make a screeching sound announcing their intention to clear out the dead. This was a Lhassa neighborhood and the disease had a particularly high mortality rate among juveniles, so they did a brisk business in poor little lumps of fur and big ears, wrapped in blankets and still. In a Lhassa neighborhood, everyone was related, so everyone came out, all wearing their lampshade-hats, to watch as the little bundles were stacked on the cart the Quinix had tracked down somewhere. There was wailing and moaning and the occasional angry trumpet from a young bull, hoping there was somebody he could punch that would make the pain go away. I watched, hidden in a gutter, and wondered how many more people would get sick as a result of this emotional send-off.

And this was a species that conquered the stars?

I trailed the Quinix as they towed their cart full of a half dozen dead Lhassa pups until they were deep in a tunnel with nobody around. Then—and only then—they took off the blankets and started wrapping the corpses up in their webbing. I wondered how their relatives would have reacted to this. Probably violently. The Lhassa had so much sentiment around their progeny that I found it frequently baffling and often counterproductive. Of course, they have a population of untold trillions spread around the galaxy, and *my* asexual, antisocial species eats their trash, so maybe there was something to it.

The Quinix had an easier time with the bundles adhered to their abdomens and walking than they did pulling the cart, which handily enough folded up and was adhered to an abdomen as well with a little spot of webbing. Following them got difficult when they came out of a tunnel and crawled vertically up the canyon wall, but I'm an able climber myself, so I was able to keep them in sight long enough to figure out where they went—a tunnel just beneath the Upper Shelf, where the orbital terminal was.

The tunnel led to another tunnel to another tunnel—a warren of natural limestone caves hollowed out by the flow of ancient rivers sometime in Sadura's prehistory. I would have gotten lost had these spiders not been talkers, but as it was, all I had to do was listen for their scraping, chittering language. We went a long way—two hours in the tunnels, and I had the gradual realization that if this plan didn't work, I had no idea how to get *out* again.

Eventually, they stopped at a kind of storehouse—piled in a cave were cylinders and crates, all of Voosk design, meaning they were lightweight and had a lot of handles for group lifting. Payment for services was left in a little package on a crate at the center of the room, and no Voosk flocks in sight. This was just as I'd hoped—the Voosk weren't eager to rub feathers with the guys who went around collecting plague-ridden bodies all day. The Quinix carefully softened the web sacs containing the dead pups with their venom and, once it was soft enough, ate it again. The process had been described to me as disgusting, but I thought it looked fairly practical.

After that, they slid each of the pups into a little polymer bag, sealed it, and laid them in crates. They did so gently, almost tenderly. These Quinix weren't heartless mercenaries— they saw themselves as doing a service, and a solemn one. I wondered if they had any suspicion the scientists they worked for were connected to the creation of the plague in the first place. I guessed they didn't.

I found myself getting angry. Something about the way in

which the Union always managed to make the arachnids into fools filled me with the desire for fiery vengeance. I felt the same way, but to a lesser extent, for the Lhassa pups. They were children—innocents who had no idea about how the world worked or why. They likely died confused, afraid, and all because some species of avians wanted a new perch. It was always the innocents who got it worst. The guilty just got to cruise past. They barely needed to notice the carnage they left behind.

But they didn't account for me. *I'd* make them notice. They wouldn't soon forget me.

As I was crouched there, swearing vengeance in the dark, I recognized I had another problem. A Node Vassal—a different one from the one I'd tossed off my balcony—*also* sneaking up on this little science experiment. This one had been a Thraad, but its shell was cracked into pieces, and from these cracks emerged five spindly legs that it used to propel itself along the tunnel, gripping the rock in sharp claws that dug into the floor, walls, and ceiling. It was possibly the most grotesque Vassal I'd ever seen. It was carrying some kind of weapon in its chin-tentacles, though what it was, I couldn't make out in the very dim light of the patches of bioluminescent fungus scattered around.

The Node, it seemed, had been doing its own investigation—probably with dozens of Vassals spread throughout Krakoth, probably asking the skennite core their own sets of probing questions. I should have known that shaking them wouldn't be that easy.

If the Node found out that the Voosk had violated the Peace by engineering a bioweapon, the whole planet was as good as dead. Despite being between apartments, the wholesale consumption of an entire world was not something I wanted on my conscience. This Vassal would need to die and I'd need to figure out how to hide the evidence of this whole affair, or they would just keep coming and coming until one of them saw what they needed to see and then got word to the Node, which would then send a message across the void to the Marshal, which would then make its way along the solar winds until, at last, maybe years from now, it arrived, enveloped the planet, and killed it.

I didn't want the Quinix caught in the crossfire, so after I drew my laser, I shouted at them in a deep, gruff voice, "This is the Node! Surrender or die!"

This is not something that Node Vassals say, mind you, but it didn't really matter. The Quinix might be a planet-bound Lesser Race, but they weren't idiots—when the Node shows up to ask you questions, you *run*. All the spiders dropped what they were doing and scattered, each leaving by a different tunnel. When they were clear, that was when I started shooting.

The Vassal, who had heard my yell just like everyone else, spotted me almost immediately, despite my blending in perfectly with the cave wall. Fortunately for me, the weapon it was carrying was not a laser or a multipistol or even a slugger—it was a bulkhead cutter. A mutant Thraad with spindly claw-legs was skittering straight at me with a *giant motorized sawblade*.

Two swipes of the laser and I'd cut off half its legs. The thing hit the ground but was still coming—barely a meter or two away now. I crawled up on the ceiling as it swung the heavy piece of industrial demolition equipment at me with more strength than I'd ever seen in a set of Thraad chin-tentacles. The whirring blade buried itself in the cave wall, kicking out a dust cloud that fouled my aim on my next laser burn.

I made myself into a ball and bounced clear of its next wild blow, which also cut a huge gouge out of the cave wall. I rolled into a tripod position for my laser, trying to get a good shot at its head or its heart or whatever kept it alive.

I didn't shoot. Instead, that end of the cave collapsed on top of the Vassal with a concussive *thump*. Goop—Thraad blood, the ichor of its various mutations—spurted everywhere. Its legs quivered for a moment, then lay still. It was dead.

A second later, the cave was filled with a cloud of dusty particles that were distinct from the rock dust that already choked the air. Node spores—very dangerous. I didn't think I was susceptible to them, but I crawled inside one of the Voosk storage cannisters and screwed the lid shut. I stayed inside until I couldn't hold my breath any longer and then unscrewed the lid and surveyed the damage.

I was no geologist, but I knew the Voosk would probably want to pick a new cave to do business in for the future—this one was going to collapse, though probably not right now. Fortunately for the Voosk, I was about to make all their long-term plans irrelevant. I opened one of the cannisters and removed the dead pup. Then I formed my body into an exact simulation of that cannister, with the pup inside me. With any luck, the Voosk would take me up to their station without a second glance. I waited, cradling the little body, and thought about the kind of person it would take to callously murder thousands.

Maybe it was hypocritical of me, a professional killer, to judge these scientists for releasing their tailored pathogen. But, for all the lives I'd ended over…however long I've been alive—I don't remember—I have never, to my knowledge, killed *indiscriminately*. I was a tool. A scalpel, not a bludgeon. I removed individuals from society the same way I understood an immune system might remove hostile microbes—one at a time, and for the overall benefit of the host organism. I was, I told myself, one of the good guys.

The Voosk came after five or six hours of my sitting there, stroking my own ego, which is never a healthy enterprise. The Voosk are a collectively intelligent species of avians—they group themselves in flocks of anywhere from five to as many as thirty, and those flocks basically behave and act as one intelligent being. They do this through their incredibly complex and rapid language—a blistering series of beeps, chirps, squawks, and screeches that transmit information to one another every bit as fast as your regular, average alien thinks.

The flock that came to collect me was ten members strong, each standing only just over a meter in height, and wearing vests plated with some kind of reactive armor that sprayed a fine mist of what I presumed to be disinfectant all around themselves, making them look like they were wearing little clouds of fog. They had similar plumage—a rust brown with white markings—and short, blunt beaks that were constantly twittering to each other. They moved as a perfect team. A few of them took up guard positions with high-grade, lightweight lasers that put my own to shame, a few others checked the cannisters, and a few others inspected the damage to the cavern, shining wing-mounted flashlights all over the place while they hopped around on their clawlike feet.

I don't know if there was a discussion about whether I was an authentic cannister or not, but I do know that more than one of them tapped at my simulated control pad and wondered why I didn't spit out diagnostics. I guess it was decided that, as I was clearly *full* of something, they may as well take me along. It took three of them to carry me to a grav-skiff, where I was stacked with the others, and then they pushed us along another series of tunnels until we came close to the surface. This I knew because the temperature rose and I heard the little radiation detectors on their ankles beeping ominously. There, hidden in a large cave with actual crimson sunlight pouring in from a distant entrance, was their transorbital shuttle, just as I'd guessed. I was loaded aboard and up we went.

The shuttle was speedy and the trip was quite short—an hour, no more. I heard the docking clamps engage and the cargo bay doors open. Even more Voosk with the rust-and-white plumage, though these were unarmed, came along and carried the storage cannisters and myself into the station, which was full of curious Voosk wearing various kinds of headsets and vision enhancers. The corridors were a cacophony of birdsong, so much so that I wondered how they could keep it all straight. It was clear I was in the right place because, as someone who was once a prisoner in a laboratory, this whole place was giving me a certain very familiar feel—glass-enclosed chambers where Voosk in thick environmental suits were manipulating secure containers, banks of holodisplays involving suites of data that flashed by so rapidly, I couldn't resolve it, cold storage rooms full of cadavers on ice, and so on.

They took me to this last one—each container was placed in a slot on the wall in this chilled room and slid in, a vault door closed behind. The cold was bad enough—I could feel my membranes stiffening—but the prospect of being trapped in here was enough that I decided to make my move.

I primed my laser and struck. I cut down five of the six Voosk before they could react. I was feeling pretty good about myself, ready to ice the sixth, when I found out what a "collective intelligence" was all about. The room went into lockdown immediately—heavy-duty shielders, the kind of thing meant to keep out the hard vacuum of deep space—clapped down over the exits, the air vents, everything. I was trapped, along with the sixth member of the flock that had carried me in here.

I couldn't figure out how they'd done it. I was fast—really, *really* fast. They didn't have time to raise an alarm, didn't have time to hit any emergency switches, and I knew with near certainty that little menial laborers like this wouldn't be walking around with kill switches on their hearts or anything.

That's when I noticed that the noise—the birdsong, their language—was still chirping over the intercom and the last

Voosk was chattering too, even as she was cowering in a corner with her wings spread over her face. The intercom wasn't *just* an intercom—it was two-way. Every Voosk on this station was chattering with every other one *simultaneously*. I had expected having to deal with flocks of ten or even fifteen birds—however many could reasonably fit within earshot of one another—but this? This was a mind some three hundred Voosk strong. A mega-intellect.

To say I hadn't planned for this was a severe understatement.

"Don't hurt me!" the cowering Voosk said, and by that I could assume it was also being said by all the hundreds of other birds on this station sharing an endless torrent of data over the intercoms.

I scoped out the intercoms—there were five of them in the cold-storage room alone, and each of them was pretty sturdy. I could destroy them, sure, but then I was definitely trapped in here until I froze or suffocated, whichever came first. No, if I was ever getting out of here, I was talking my way out. I pointed my laser at the Voosk still with me. "Better let me out, or she gets a lot shorter very fast!"

"What do you want?" the Voosk asked.

Tricky question. Saying "to kill you all, you biowarfare-waging raptors!" seemed unwise. I also couldn't reasonably say I meant them no harm, given all the bifurcated dead bodies in smoking heaps around me. "I know what you did!" I said, instead. "You created the plague!"

The Voosk in the room poked her beak over her wings and tilted her head so one big eye was blinking at me. "Why do you think that?" she/they asked.

"Oh, come on—a trans-species plague with a high fatality rate, one that doesn't pattern off of anything Dryth medical nanobots can react to, just *happens* to show up right when you bunch start doing 'medical research' in orbit? What are the odds?" I had taken a form now. Clearly, the Voosk all knew what I was—the one I was looking at had transmitted it to the others instantly—but there was something uncomfortable about being *seen* at all. I was in the shape of another Voosk now—taller, bigger, more brightly colored than this flock, but still a Voosk. I didn't talk like one, though. My disguise was literally only skin-deep.

"We didn't bring the plague here," the Voosk said, calmly now. Much too calmly for my liking. "We followed it here. It originates from off-world. We are not the *cause* of the disease. We are its cure."

"I don't believe you."

"Your belief is not essential for our mission to be true," the Voosk said.

"My belief is essential to keep me from killing this one," I said, pointing the laser again.

The Voosk didn't flinch from the weapon. "We have discussed it with our member," she said. "If it means safeguarding our mission, she is willing to accept death."

So, an impasse, and me without much leverage. I tried a different approach. "The Node is on to you, you know. Even if you eliminate me, the Vassals are tracking your operation. You're going to get found out."

The Voosk trapped with me was standing up now, her claw-like hands clutched near her pointed chest, her wings folded back along her flanks—pretty standard Voosk posture. She seemed completely unafraid. "That sounds like a problem for us to solve on our own—your participation is neither needed nor warranted." She sounded smug. She opened her beak a bit to indicate how funny I was, some mere Tohrroid trying to threaten her whole flock with just one laser.

Me? I was tired of being outnumbered. I fired the laser, cutting through each of the intercoms in turn. *This* got the Voosk's attention. She hopped toward me, claws outstretched, screeching in protest, but she wasn't suicidal enough to throw herself on me. Instead, a quick flash of my laser beam and she kept her distance, shrieking but little else. When I was done, the birdsong ceased. At last, some *quiet*.

"Now, let's see how tough you are without the rest of your buddies cheering you on," I said, pointing my weapon at the now *actually* alone Voosk.

She was back to cowering. When she spoke, her Dryth Basic was broken, hard to understand. "No no shoot shooting. Please and please?" A lot of her language skills belonged to others in the flock. She had been coached, a moment earlier. Whereas before she had seemed confident, assured, now she was terrified and off-balance. Which was perfect for me.

"Tell me what they do up here," I said, hopping closer on my poorly simulated Voosk feet.

She shivered at my approach—an effect I have on bipeds sometimes, when they realize that I don't *quite* match the thing they think they're seeing. I'm...eerie, I guess. Out of place. "Doctors!" she trilled. "Doctors heal!"

I slapped my other wing against the little coffins full of dead Lhassa. "These people don't look like they're healing, do they? What about them?"

"No lie! I no lie! Doctors! We...we...fix sick! Believe!"

Even still, she was keeping to the flock's story. I felt sick to my stomach, and all I *am* is stomach. I raised my weapon. "I've heard just about enough of this."

The chamber shuddered as the lockdown was retracted. They were coming for their flock member after all. I moved quickly, leaping across the room and pulling the Voosk in front of me like a shield, my laser pointed at the middle of her back.

The Voosk threw a smoke grenade and then came in with their trademark precision teamwork—five members, all armed, moving in all directions—right, left, two leaping above me. If I weren't me—if I couldn't see everything, all at once—I would have been dead. As it stood, I shrank myself to a heavy blob clinging to the back of my hostage and fired around her shoulders and waist. My aim wasn't perfect, but I got two of them. Their aim wasn't perfect either—they missed, aiming largely by dead reckoning. They were assuming where I'd have to stand in the smoke cloud to make the shots I did, but they were wrong.

By the time the smoke cleared, sucked out by the ventilation system, I was in a corner, the Voosk—now once again calm and in control—between me and my assailants. There were six Voosk in the room, all with lasers pointed at me. The hostage wasn't going to work much longer.

"Let me go," she said, one eye looking over her shoulder. "We promise not to hurt you if you let me go."

"Why would you promise that?" I looked for a possible escape route. The vents were too far away or too high up the wall for me to get to in time. I couldn't fight my way out, either. Even if I got this group, my enemy was hundreds strong. I should have brought a bomb, a bigger gun, *anything*. What had I been thinking?

I hadn't been, that was all. I was dining out on my own reputation. A death sentence for any assassin, but especially me. No wonder all those others had turned Mother Candoor down for this asinine mission. What made me think I was so special? My anger? My loneliness?

There was no way to fight it out. I dropped the laser. "Fine," I said. "Let's see how well you keep your word."

The Voosk surrounded me from a safe distance, their weapons still leveled at me. "Come with me," my former hostage said. They hopped out the door, surrounding me in a little circle.

They took me down a corridor and down another, past glass-enclosed laboratories and packs of Voosk manipulating three-dimensional molecular models in holodisplays. "We are telling you the truth, assassin," my hostage said. "We have been working nonstop for years, trying to cure this terrible disease. We have tracked it across three systems. Sadura is its latest victim."

It was very possible they were still lying. Even if they weren't, it was still my duty to kill them all. That was the job. Incredible wealth awaited me, once the deed was done—the contents of a huge interstellar freighter, enough to keep me out of the gutter for cycles to come. I stayed alert, looking for my chance to escape. "Where do you think the disease comes from?"

The Voosk stopped outside of a heavy, reinforced door marked with all kinds of hazard warnings. "That's just it, assassin. We believe we now know." They honked and twittered to one another for a moment—the whole station did—as though having some kind of internal debate. Finally, my hostage fluffed up her feathers and said, "We believe it was engineered by the Marshals."

"What? That makes no sense—the Marshals don't conduct biowarfare; they *end* it. They wouldn't..." I trailed off. The words sounded stupid as I spoke them.

The Voosk seemed to understand how I felt. "We, too, felt as you do. It was why we could not crack the disease—we were blind. But once we did, well..."

One of my guards hit the release panel for the big armored door. It slid open quickly, silently. There, inside a furnished bedroom in the style of its species, was a Lhassa pup. A living, breathing, totally healthy Lhassa pup, its eyes big and bright, happily eating a bowl of some kind of worms and porridge at a little table. What the...

"The cure," the Voosk said, "has been discovered."

The Lhassa pup spotted me and waved. I waved back. It hopped off its chair and scampered closer to me, its little nose twitching, its ears tall and tufted. "New birdies!" it squealed.

It ran to me and wrapped its arms around me and *squeezed*.

A "hug," I believe, is the term. I'd never been hugged before, or at least not outside the context of a desperate wrestling struggle for life and death. My membranes, dense thanks to how tightly I'd packed myself into a Voosk form, compressed painfully in the little Lhassa's grip. It licked me on the side of my head, and then it realized what it was feeling, what it was smelling, what it just *tasted* wasn't what it expected. It bounced away from me, its head cocked to one side. "Whatizit?" it asked in one word.

I opened my fake beak to answer, though I wasn't sure what to say. This pup—this had to mean the Voosk told the truth, right? Nobody kept a Lhassa pup in a bedroom on their science station to hedge against this very rare, very *unusual* circumstance. Mother Candoor was wrong. These people—this *person*—wasn't the cause, they were the cure.

And I couldn't kill them.

It was then that my former hostage shrieked in pain and dropped to the floor. The Voosk squawked and chirped as they hopped to her and helped her up. When she lifted her head, however, there was blood running from her beak and, from this beak, a long, fleshy tendril that ended in a single, lidless eye. A Node infestation. The Voosk had become a Vassal or would be very soon. It screamed incoherently from its beak, in what I was certain was not any part of the Voosk language.

"Vassal!" one of the flock yelled. "Isolate! Isolate!"

But it was too late. Other Voosk in the little circle, probably infected around the same time they got in close proximity to her or maybe to *me*, were also falling down, clutching their faces, their beaks, their bodies. They contorted themselves in pain, mumbling in hysteria.

It had to have been contamination from the crates they'd brought aboard. Their quarantine system had been insufficient to keep out Vassal spores—something they hadn't anticipated. A fatal mistake for a supposed super-intellect.

I—and everyone in this compartment—was moments away from incineration or worse, as the Voosk collective sought to contain the spread. I grabbed the Lhassa pup and threw it over my fake shoulder, my membranes bowing under the weight, and then I ran as fast as my simulated legs could carry me.

Laser beams traced through the corridor behind us—the Vassals fighting back, cutting their way through the uninfected. Some of the Voosk returned fire, which served only to spread the infection further. It was probably in the air vents now. Maybe their containment system would hold, maybe it wouldn't. It wasn't my problem anymore. I simply ran.

By the time I made it to the shuttle bay, the birdsong coming over the intercom had degenerated to something closer to noise—Vassals, using their new vocal cords to add disinformation to the system. A Vassalized Voosk leapt at me, but I shot it with a laser I'd picked up on the way and didn't hang around to see the spores bloom. I made it onto the shuttle and slammed the door closed.

The Lhassa pup on my shoulder was howling in terror. I placed it in the copilot seat and, not sure what else to do or say, worked on getting the onboard AI to take us back to the planet.

I met Candoor again as the same Lhassa elder bull a few days later. The herald channels of House Ghiasi had reported the station's fiery descent to the surface with some befuddlement but also the sadistic glee of someone looking for bad news to happen to others for a change. She knew I'd succeeded, though she had no idea how or even if I'd intended to do it.

This time, I met her aboard *Enlightened Dawn*. A long-haul trans-stellar freighter, the ship was several kilometers long and massed in the millions of tons. It was, or had been, an industry unto itself. As I walked through its empty corridors, the steel gratings biting cold beneath my simulated feet, I got a sense that I was about to be underpaid. She said she would pay me everything she had, but an empty freighter with no freight and no crew was of no use to me. Out here in Sadura, on the edge of the Union, I couldn't even sell it.

She was on the bridge, sitting in a command chair, looking out a long bank of narrow windows that showed the ugly, radiation-scarred face of Sadura. She was wrapped in a shawl made of some kind of fuzzy material. She was alone.

"They did it," she said when I arrived. "The assassin was true to their word. They're dead—all of them."

"They were not responsible for the plague," I said. "They were doctors. They were trying to help."

"I don't believe it," she said, still not looking at me. "I know what I know."

"The Node did it," I said. "The Marshals also created this plague in an attempt to create a pretense for devouring planets."

"Are you telling me the Faceless Assassin won't accept payment?" She swiveled her chair to look at me. She looked just as disheveled as she had when we met, maybe more so. "Are you telling me your employer killed *innocent people* for nothing?"

"Didn't you hear what I just said?"

Candoor's eyes were pure venom. "You have your story. Why should I care what it is? What do I care what's *true* when I know how I *feel?*"

"And how is that?"

"When the plague took what was most valuable to me, I swore an oath. The oath is fulfilled. You want me to hunt the Node next? A *Marshal?* No. It can't be." She turned away from me in her chair. "This must be true, because it is the only way I can go on. *You* wouldn't understand."

I wasn't sure what she meant by that—whether she meant me, as a Lhassa bull, or me as the representative of an assassin, or me as someone who hadn't lost everything to the plague. It hardly mattered. "I've seen what you're offering to pay with." I gestured to the ship. "And my employer has little need for an empty ship without any crew. *You* misrepresented your resources. That has consequences." I produced a Voosk laser pistol, charged and ready.

Candoor didn't move a muscle. "Go ahead. Do it. Kill another innocent."

"You're not innocent. The blood of those doctors is on your hands."

"Everyone is innocent," Candoor said, her voice cracking and her body shuddering. "It…it never makes any difference. Don't you see? It doesn't matter. Just…just kill me. Please? Don't leave me like this! End it!"

She kept raving, never rising from the command chair, her legs tucked under her. She shouted threats, she begged, she wept. I put the laser away, spun on a heel, and left.

On the way back to the shuttle pad, I got turned around and found myself in the personnel quarters. They were a riot of color and design—each door a different collage of images and shapes. Paintings of little Lhassa pups playing on the shuttle deck. Of Lhassa juveniles necking with their beloveds. This had been Candoor's family—she was a mother in truth, though that was hardly surprising for a Lhassa. I could imagine the place bright and happy and noisy with the chaos of the Lhassa—fighting and laughing and singing together, way out in the void.

The deck beneath my feet was as cold as the rest of the ship. The doors remained shut, the silence telling me everything. For a moment, I got a taste of her grief. Of a home, hollowed out by invisible violence by an unseen hand. A world drained away for no knowable reason.

I went back down the well, back into the plague zone. I

thought about the Voosk doctors, their collective intelligence in shambles thanks to the Vassals in their midst. I thought of them isolated from one another as the station plummeted through a thin atmosphere to certain death. When you came down to it, everyone went like that in the end—holding on and barely understanding the reasons. That was no excuse to spread the misery around, though. The Voosk, at least, had understood that.

Once back, I made another stop. To that Lhassa neighborhood in the West Shelf, in the shape of an Unhoused Dryth with a fuzzy bundle across my chest. The pup had fallen asleep during the gondola ride, its little heartbeat a steady rhythm on my membranes. I unwrapped him—it was a male—and placed him on a doorstep, still asleep. When he awoke, he would be surrounded by his own kind, cared for, even loved. Immune as he was to the plague, he would grow to become an adult and hopefully not a stupid one.

Before I had caught a gondola back to the depths, I could hear a cheer rise up from that sad Lhassa street. I could hear the trumpeting of bulls in triumph and happiness. For a second there, I thought of myself as something special, maybe even heroic.

But I'm not. There were hundreds of me everywhere, in every gutter and trash basin in the city. The only difference was I had stood up, looked around, and done something about it. Small steps, but life maybe was all about the moments and less about the grand arc of history.

That, at least, was what I'd keep telling myself.

Acknowledgments

These stories span about seven or eight years of my life, and so there are a great many people to thank for their creation and their long journey from an odd idea I had to the collection you are holding in your hands. First, I'd like to thank the JABberwocky team—Lisa Rodgers, Christina Zobel, Susan Velazquez, my agent, Joshua Bilmes, and everyone else who took these stories and helped bring them together for a story collection. Thanks also to Dirk Berger, who managed the impossible by drawing a cover that depicted a formless alien being in a way that both blew me away and captured the essence of the character perfectly.

Of course, these stories wouldn't have made it this far if not for the editors and publications which saw fit to give them a home their first time around. Many thanks, then, to Trevor Quachri and the team at *Analog Science Fiction and Fact*; Mur Lafferty and Valerie Valdes over at *Escape Pod*, and Lezli Robyn at *Galaxy's Edge* for all of their support and faith in this strange little blob and its violent little problems.

Finally, I'd like to thank my team of faithful beta readers: John Perich, John Fraley, Rich Pellegrino, Brandon Rahhal, Ariel Jaffee, and Zac Topping. Without their help, I would have had significantly more trouble forging this thing into a coherent whole. Also, of course, I have to thank my family, and particularly my wife Deirdre for her tireless support and tolerance of my odd habit of barricading myself inside my office and plotting the gruesome demises of intergalactic despots and oligarchs.

Oh, and of course thank you, the reader, for reading this far and for choosing my little book. I hope very much to bring you more Faceless in the future, if I could only find the sneaky little jerk and get him to commit more quasi-justifiable crimes on paper for me.

About the Author

Auston Habershaw is the author of over thirty short stories published in a number of venues, including *Analog Science Fiction and Fact*, *Beneath Ceaseless Skies*, and *The Magazine of Fantasy and Science Fiction*, among others. He writes both science fiction and fantasy and sometimes even a mix of the two. He lives and works in Boston, Massachusetts, and he is not, so far as any of you know, a shape-shifting alien. You can find him online at aahabershaw.com.

Don't Miss
Auston Habershaw's Novels!

What happens when an ambitious teen and a centuries-old genie become business partners?

"Irresistibly fun and funny, with a ton of heart and depth! This is the kind of book that sneaks up on you and sticks with you!"
—Sarah Beth Durst,
New York Times bestselling author

"A cozy, comical confection."
—*Publishers Weekly*

Saga of the Redeemed
Books I–IV

Rogue, duelist, criminal, and very reluctant hero Tyvian Reldamar wrestles with the magic ring on his finger that prevents him from doing evil and pushes him to do good in this epic fantasy series.

FOR NEWS ABOUT JABBERWOCKY BOOKS AND AUTHORS

Sign up for our newsletter*: http://eepurl.com/b84tDz
visit our website: awfulagent.com/ebooks
or follow us on twitter: @awfulagent

THANKS FOR READING!

*We will never sell or give away your email address, nor use it for nefarious purposes.